MEET YOUR MATCHA

COMMON THREADS BOOK #7

NANXI WEN

COPYRIGHT

PROLOGUE
~PIPPA~

Boston, February

"It's my life to ruin!"

Heads turned to gawk at me. The loud music from the club pounded like angry ghosts inside my ears. It followed me as I stumbled out into the night. I glared at the people waiting in line outside of Icon Nightclub until they dropped their gazes.

Lowering my voice, I protested, my words tumbling out before I lost courage, "Mom, I know what I'm doing. It's just a break."

I didn't know if I was trying to convince her or myself. Over the video chat, my protest was met with skepticism. Even though it was ten o'clock in Boston and nine in Dallas where she and my dad had traveled for a work trip, my mom still wore one of her custom blazers, with a full face of makeup and blown-out hair.

"You're throwing your dream away." Her words cut through the boisterous conversation and music from the revelry.

"Is being a lawyer *my* dream? I'm not sure anymore."

"Pippa."

That single word, with the sharp emphasis on the first syllable, conveyed more than I was equipped to handle at the moment. At least let me get out of my short dress that did nothing to shield my bare legs against the winter chill. How come going-out wear for men consisted of jeans, comfortable shoes, and a great jacket, while women were pressured into tight dresses and wobbly heels?

"Mom, let's talk about it another time." *Like never.* "Oh, *bzzzz*… I think I'm losing you. *Bzzz*… what? Bye, Mom. Say hi to Dad. *Bzzzzz. Bzzzz.*"

As if I weren't a twenty-nine-year-old adult avoiding my parents, I hung up. There were only so many buzzes I could fake without losing my dignity. And only so much disapproval that I could stand radiating from my mom over Face-Time before I acquiesced and crawled back to work.

With my phone still in hand, I stared at the nightclub door. I had come here with the express purpose of partying with my friends until I forgot I quit my job. Technically, I was on an official six-month sabbatical from my law firm. In reality, I faced months of nothing on my calendar.

Half a year to buy myself time to think about what I wanted to do with my life. Six puny months to get rid of this restless feeling within me and get back on track.

Work hard. Party hard. That was the motto I had lived by.

For the past few years, I acted the serious overachiever for seventy hours a week, all my hours tracked and allocated at fifteen-minute increments to each client. As of yesterday, I had the coveted recognition as the youngest partner at my firm, and only the second female partner.

Squeezed in between work had been precious hours to let loose with my friends—nights out at clubs, Boozy Tea Parties with my best friend, and date after disastrous date that went nowhere. Because time outside of work had been so limited, I had thrown myself into everything, as if parties were going out of stock in the immediate future.

Without the seventy hours of work each week, what would I become?

Suddenly, with my mind in a doubting muddle after the call with my mom, the neon interiors and crowded dance floor of Icon repelled me. I wasn't ready to tell my friends inside the club that I had only lasted one day as partner. The thought of pretending I had no cares in the world wearied me.

My parents had a house nearby, where I stayed when I visited Boston. The idea of cozy blankets and maybe a couple episodes of *The Great British Baking Show* tempted me. Texting a quick message to my friends that I had a headache, I wobbled up Charles Street in my four-inch, feet-numbing heels.

Even though the winter holidays were past us, the revelers didn't seem to remember. Drunken laughter spun around me. Leftover lights twinkled outside from every tree lining the street.

A rotating display in a nearby store window caught my eye. A graceful doll in an elaborate velvet dress held a tiny lace umbrella as she spun around and around on a pedestal.

I hated the doll on sight.

Somewhere in an unused room in my parents' mansion in Beacon Hill lay dozens of porcelain dolls just like this one. Each one exquisitely handcrafted, each one meant to be displayed, not played with.

After every one of my parents' longer business trips during my childhood, when I would be left with the nanny du jour, a doll would show up on my desk. Once upon a time, I must have exclaimed with delight over the novelty of the initial doll. Over time, they had become unwanted symbols, stacked next to each other in display cabinets, like soldiers. Or spies.

Each and every last one of them a bribe.

Not a literal bribe, but unspoken tokens from my parents to me. An implicit agreement. My parents provided the funds for my private schools, designer clothes, birthday parties with the next rising singer to serenade me, while I acted as the poster child, the crown jewel of their investments.

"What do you mean, you're second in your grade? There's still time to catch up. Only the valedictorian matters."

"You can't quit ballet. We already paid for the year. Where do you think money grows?"

"Smile, Pippa, and go talk to the guests. Nobody wants to hang around a sad cat."

"If you take the foot off the pedal, everyone else will catch up. Everything you do needs to be intentional toward the ultimate goal."

In revulsion, I staggered out of my memories, my steps quickening on the uneven ground. In the coldness of the February night, I made my way on the sidewalks that edged along the Public Garden.

Never had I felt more alone.

What an oxymoron—to be alone in the midst of a crowd. Yet, at that moment, loneliness seized me. So heavy that air caught in my throat, struggling to fill my body. The loneliness, heighted by the darkness of the winter night, opened the door for doubt to creep in and root in my brain.

Did I do the right thing to leave my job? What the hell was I doing with my life? What the fucking fudgesticks did I want with my life?

Without my brain firing off the command, I yanked out my phone. Forget Netflix and a chill night. That way led to too much time with myself.

Instead, I called for an Uber. Twenty minutes later, I stood outside my best friend Tia's apartment in Inman Square. When she buzzed me in, I rushed inside, sinking into her hug. Relief chased away the anxious thoughts.

Shaking myself to pull away from the dark edge, I proclaimed, "Hi, surprise! I'm in Boston for a few days."

"It's ten o'clock, Pippa, on a Tuesday night." Even so, Tia waved me in and threw a kettle on the stove.

Heels off by the front door, I put on the fuzzy pink slippers with pompons that Tia kept especially for me and plopped down on the only couch in her studio apartment. A half-finished cup of tea and an empty glass of water stood on the coffee table, along with two bowls. A pang of longing pierced me.

"Where's lover boy?" I asked.

Pink crept along Tia's cheeks. "He went out to get more ice cream. These pints are so small. Why can't they be bigger?"

"Because then they wouldn't be pints."

"Shush you and your lawyer-y logic." Pulling the kettle off the stove, Tia poured the hot water into a cup filled with loose leaf tea and placed it on a coaster in front of me. "Where have you been lately? I've missed you and our boozy tea parties."

"I made partner yesterday."

"What? That's amazing, Pippa!" Her cheer of joy almost matched her enthusiasm for snacks. "Let me text Andrew to get some champagne while he's out."

"I quit this morning and drove to Boston."

"What?" Her shout of surprise was equally loud.

"Not quit. Technically, I'm on a sabbatical."

"You said making partner was your dream." Tia offered a shortbread cookie to me.

Before making partner, I would have declared via a full-page ad in the *New York Times* that this was my dream. I might even have believed it. But I had known Tia since I was a kid, and after the call with my mom, I was too… frayed. "I might be in a midlife crisis. I should be ecstatic about this, right, and tell my managing partner that I was sleep-deprived when I asked for the sabbatical?"

"*Aiyaya.* Wait, slow down. You're doing that auctioneer-rapid-fire-talking thing when you get riled up." Her hands pressed down on my knees in a soothing touch. Her words measured, she said, "You've been acting restless for the past few months. Maybe a sabbatical or even full-stop quitting will help you figure out why you panicked, and whether this is what you want. Have you told your parents?"

"Unfortunately." I grimaced. "I thought about hiding it. Or at least, party my brains out for a couple days, see you, and then write my parents a letter that hopefully gets eaten by a pigeon over the Atlantic."

"I thought your parents were in Dallas right now?"

"Flying over land doesn't sound as dramatic as over thunder-tossed waves, does it?"

"Hm, you have a point. Do pigeons eat paper?"

"Have you seen those monsters in the Common? Can't put anything past them."

"Knowing your mom, she'd have trained the pigeon to deliver the letter to her. Better they heard from you than from someone else." Tia magically procured me another shortbread cookie, even though I saw no cookie tin or box in sight. One of these days, I would learn where she stored her endless supply of snacks.

"Yeah, that's what I feared. I texted them when I got to Boston." My brain replayed the way my mom had overly enunciated my name, backed by a wealth of motherly disapproval. "My mom FaceTimed me while I was out. I was a coward and pretended my phone had poor signal."

Tia's laugh surrounded me, light and warm like the best kind of hug. "Oh, Pippa. What are you going to do with all your free time?"

Endless time and boredom loomed before me. If I didn't have my job, what did I have? I took a third cookie from Tia's palm. "I don't know. Make a bucket list of adventures and travel for a few months?"

"You'll still make it to China for my wedding reception in June?" she asked.

"I wouldn't miss it. I'll plan my adventures around it," I promised.

With a nervous twirl of her fingers through her straight, black hair, Tia winced. "I have another idea. It's kind of wild."

"Tia, your idea of *wild* is eating chips and salsa on a white couch."

"Don't forget ending my engagement to get back together with my ex-not-so-ex-husband." Her dark-brown eyes glowed with joy.

"How is it going with Andrew? You're confident you made the right decision to go back to him?" I probed her for any sign of regret.

Her sly giggle told me all I needed to know. For hell's sake, she taught computer science, the driest subject you could ever teach. Now, Andrew caused her to giggle like an infatuated fan seeing Harry Styles at Nobu.

While I had *The Great British Bake Off* or partying with giant crowds, she was all sexed up, loved up. I was happy for my best friend.

Truly.

Happiness for Tia didn't negate the tiny part of my heart that twinged with envious longing. Or maybe it was just my arteries protesting all the shortbread I had gobbled up tonight.

"Speaking of love," Tia said, shaking herself from daydreaming about Andrew, "what do you think about applying for *The Journey of Love*? I think you'd be perfect for it. You're so vivacious and funny, guys would fight over you."

The room fell silent. I waited for her to laugh and say it was a joke.

When she only beamed at me, I asked, "What the hell is a journey to love? If it's anything like what you and Andrew experienced, I'm out. I'd rather stick to my dating apps."

"No, this is a dating show called *The Journey of Love*," she insisted. "They have twenty to thirty contestants stay at a resort in St. Lucia for two and a half weeks. Unlike *The Bachelor*, where everyone fights over one person, you can pair up with any of the other contestants. It's like *Survivor*, except you fight for love and you can shave."

"So not *Survivor*?"

"Hm, like *Temptation Island*, except you don't go in as a couple."

"Way to rub it in that I'm single."

"*Too Hot to Handle*, except no robot telling you to keep your hands off each other and no money prize."

"I understand *nothing*. So you fight as a single, hairless person without incentives?"

"*Aiyaya*." Tia threw up her hands. "It's a group of men and women who hang out on the beach, with the express purpose of trying to date each other. You have fun competitions to see who goes on dates. At the very end, if you get engaged, the show pays for your engagement ring and sends you on this amazing trip."

"Who would get engaged after two weeks?"

"If you are forced together on the beach, with no technology or other distractions, I think it's reasonable. It's like summer sleepaway camp."

"I've never been."

"Trust me then—forced proximity is an aphrodisiac like none other." Tia's eyes glazed over. "Just ask my fifteen-year-old self who pined over my fellow math campers as if they were the next coming of twinkly *Twilight* vampires."

"No, that's not forced proximity." I grinned back. "That's you getting the life sucked out of you because you willingly chose to do math in the summer."

"You missed out. Math jokes are the best. Which king loved fractions? Okay, fine… one couple from the first season just got married." Tia's eyes lit up. "What if you found your person on the show?"

My heart sped up. Immediately, my brain reprimanded my heart to stop acting like a fool. "I'm more likely to get sunburned than find a long-term partner on a TV show."

"What's the worst that can come out of it? I'll have aloe ready for you if you get sunburned."

"Hell, no." I stood up, pacing the tiny studio. Did I give off that desperate of an energy? "I can't take the time off—"

"No job, remember? The show's taking applications now. If they like you, they'll interview you in LA and let you know by the end of the month. Since filming doesn't start until July, even if you got picked, you still have half a year to travel."

"Technically, I'm on a sabbatical. I haven't *quit*. But I get it, I have time to kill." I sighed. Trying a different path, I argued, "No one finds love on TV."

"How're the dating apps?"

That was the problem with having best friends. They knew too much about you, and they knew just which buttons to push. Now, I regretted every last one of our late-night calls of me complaining about another date gone awry.

The dates almost never resembled their photos. When they did, they knew they were hot shit. I was lucky if the guy didn't scroll through an app surreptitiously during the date, looking for more *options*. Or worse, assume I'd sleep with him because he paid for Italian. I should write on my dating app profiles: bruschetta and risotto are not enough to show me your dick.

At least wait until after tiramisu.

Tia arched an eyebrow even though both eyebrows lifted. "Think of it as an efficient way to meet guys. Instead of scrolling, texting, and all that jazz, you get a beach full of guys to choose from."

As decent as Tia's points were, I couldn't imagine myself floating around a beach, pining for a guy, or throwing drinks in mock horror at some drama. Where did a reality TV show fall on my road map?

All the more reason to do it.

Here was a golden opportunity to shake myself out of this sense of *offness*. A different environment, a break from life. Maybe that was what I needed.

I stomped out that rebellious thought. "I don't know if I'm ready for a serious relationship. Just because you're googly-eyed over Andrew doesn't mean I'm looking for someone serious."

"I'm not dickmatized," protested Tia as the door opened.

Her ex-husband-turned-real-husband, slash my former law classmate, sauntered in, a bag filled with Ben & Jerry's ice cream in one hand. To undercut her protest, Tia's face lit up as she flew toward him.

Him, the guy, not the ice cream.

What did it say about me that I would have grabbed the ice cream first?

Instead of Andrew's usual scowl, he lifted a hand to wave at me before his lips were claimed by Tia. One hand on her ass, he whispered in her ear, drawing out fierce blushes.

Giggling, Tia whispered, "Andrew, stop, that's not a challenge for another round."

A smirk spread over Andrew's face as he gazed at Tia in wonder as if she invented ice cream. *Fuck my life*. I escaped the streets of happy families and couples to enter the den of the most loved-up couple I knew.

I was *not* jealous.

Really.

Maybe a little?

It was the truth that I couldn't pinpoint what I wanted for a relationship. Finding a serious relationship hadn't been a priority in the past. Short-term flings or distractions had been enough. Sort of.

What would it be like to be so comfortable with someone, to be unabashedly yourself, the way Tia was with Andrew? What would it be like to love someone enough to throw away an engagement, a high-flying lifestyle with a seemingly perfect man, for the one who created a home for your heart? Or even as simple as finding someone to hold your hand on a cold February night or bring you ice cream, for no other reason than to see you happy?

I questioned my previously ironclad priorities. Somewhere, deep within my heart—the part that cried over Hallmark movies even though they never made any logical sense—I wondered if I should have put myself out there more.

"Sorry." Tia giggled again, lifting her head. "Where was I?"

"You're right. What's there to lose? I have all the time in the world and am single as a dollar bill. I'll apply for the show, but you better have aloe prepared when I come back with nothing more than sunburn."

PART 1

ST. LUCIA, JULY

CHAPTER ONE

~PIPPA~

In the moment (ITM) filming, Day 1, 2 p.m.:

Greta: *Pippa, let's start the ITMs. We'll pull you out of filming a few times each day to get your thoughts on what's happening, give the viewers some behind-the-scenes information. I'll ask questions to give you some prompts. Don't look at me. Speak directly to the camera. Ready?*

Pippa: *Okay, sure.*

Greta: *First, why don't you introduce yourself?*

Pippa: *Hi, I'm Pippa Fleming, and I'm twenty-nine years old. I'm a patent lawyer based in New York.*

Greta: *Where did you grow up?*

Pippa: *I was born in Chicago, but I moved around a lot for my parents' jobs. They're serial entrepreneurs. I've lived in Beijing, San Francisco, London, Boston, New York, and San Jose.*

Greta: *Your parents have founded or co-founded a string of incredibly successful companies, including one that IPOed this spring. Tell me what it's like to be their only daughter. Is there pressure?*

Pippa: *I'd rather not.*

Greta: *Do they know you're on this show?*

Pippa: *I told them I'm taking an intensive French immersion course to help land a large French client, with no outside contact allowed.*

Greta: *At least the no outside contact part is true. Of course, we'll give back* *your phone and laptop at the end of the experience. Okay. Let's switch topics. Why did you decide to come on the show?*

__Pippa__: I was at a crossroads. I had just decided to take a break from my job, had lots of time on my hands, and no luck with dating. Why not?

__Greta__: Do you think you'll find love?

__Pippa__: Is Henry Cavill on the show? No? Then, can I get back to you after I've met the others?

"Are you ready, Pippa, for your life to change?"

Uneasiness trickled through my body at the question. The man in front of me smiled in expectation. His long, black hair was braided and twisted up in a bun. His loud flamingo Hawaiian shirt clashed with his green swim trunks covered with crocodiles, their mouths open in an unintentional warning. Beyond him was an archway that opened to stairs going down to the beach.

I was the first contestant to arrive.

With a nervous chuckle, I glanced behind me at the crew carrying cameras. One of the producers, Greta, made a circle motion with her hand, a silent request for me to turn around. A not-so-subtle command to pretend that I wasn't surrounded by dozens of crew members, with hidden cameras likely everywhere except, I hoped, the bathroom.

When I didn't speak, dozens of identical frowns appeared on the wall of crew members. Even the host, Mark Wellington, tapped his feet in impatience.

Before I left for the show, Tia had given me a giant list of information based on her very extensive reality TV watching experience. Getting the coveted first-to-arrive-spot meant the producers had high hopes to wring drama from me either as the heroine or villainess.

For the first time since I clicked submit on the application, I realized the precarious position I was in. The show touted itself as a vehicle to find love for unlucky singles—something I had grasped onto in a weak moment of loneliness when I signed up.

However, at the end of the day, the key word was "show." Every show had heroes and villains whose narratives were crafted by producers. It was just that in scripted shows, the actors knew the story line. On this supposedly fun lark of a show, my story line was still undecided, and at the whim of these strangers frowning at me.

Greta reached up to adjust her headset, pressing a button on the earpiece.

Before she could report to whoever was on the other end of the line, I flashed a wide smile.

Burying my trepidations under the sand, I drummed up enthusiasm to smooth over the awkward moment. "Mark, I've never been more ready to find love. Let's do the damn thing!"

Tension seeped out from the crew wall behind me. With renewed energy, Mark gestured to the beach. "Head on down to the beach! This will be your home for the next two and a half weeks. Your luggage is already in one of the cottages. I'll see you later at tonight's welcome party."

Dismissed.

Down the steps, colorful cabanas and daybeds greeted me on the sand. Unlike the main part of the resort, which consisted of a single large building a hundred feet away, this part was spread out over the beach. Half a dozen thatched-roof bungalows, palapas, and gazebos of different sizes fanned out, sprinkled with three pools, and connected via winding paths. To the left of the steps stretched out a row of cottages.

Outside of the lone bartender at the large outdoor bar, it was just me and a handful of camera crew. Most stood by the tree line in the distance, with one walking backward in front of me, camera zoomed in on my face. I waved at the bartender, who returned my greeting before returning to his prep.

With nothing to do, I stood around awkwardly. Was Mark going to give me further instructions? When would the other contestants show up?

Tia had sung about falling in love and happily ever afters. Prince Charming or Prince Fling, here I am, come sweep me off my feet.

"Hey, Pippa," called out Greta, jogging down the steps onto the beach. She must be the producer assigned to me. "Why don't you go run along the water?"

"Now?" I asked. Had Tia accidentally signed me up for a fitness slash survivor show? Did she not remember that my idea of exercising was exercising moderation in front of a cheese plate?

"Yes, run along the edge of the beach. We'll do some B-roll." Greta lifted her hand to indicate the ocean waves.

With a sigh, I shuffled toward the water. For the next twenty minutes, I ran along the same stretch of beach. A camerawoman followed me, along with Greta, yelling at me to speed up or slow down my pace. I hoped this effort was worth a decent edit.

Careful not to get the microphone around my back wet, Greta splashed some water on my front. "Okay, Pippa, I want you to walk slowly toward the stairs…

slowly, hold on. Okay, now. Wait, let's start over again. I want you to look as if you just came out of the ocean. Okay, go."

It was a good thing I hadn't ever dreamed of becoming a model. If I had, that dream evaporated with every command Greta barked out. My speed, walk, and how my hair moved in the wind all required retakes.

Annoyed, sweaty, and wet—not the good kind—I was standing in the center of the sand when another contestant walked down the beach. He froze at the sight of me.

For nothing else than he looked fresh, and I was simultaneously hot from running and cold from the water that Greta splashed on me, I despised him on sight. Grumbling, I barked, "What are you staring at?"

The stranger's steps slowed until he stood only two feet away. Never glancing past my neck, he stared at me. The narrowed eyes and frown told me all I needed to know about his impression of me. This stranger found me wanting.

Part of me felt mean and guilty for taking out my heat-induced frustration on him. The other part, the part that was still sweating from Greta's commands, was too surly to take back my words.

He paused, his gaze making me squirm. "I'm August," he said, his voice chilly.

"Pippa." Automatically, my hand extended.

He glared at my hand as if I were covered in lava instead of sand and water. *What a douche canoe.* Embarrassed by his slight, I tried to recover and raised my hand to brush back my tangled hair, as if that had been the original intention.

"Pippa," he tested my name. His whiskey voice pulled me a step forward. That voice… something about it seeped into me, held me to attention, soothing away my earlier annoyance.

Warmth, completely separate from the Caribbean sun, traveled through my body. In shock, I tilted my head up. Since sunglasses were banned—covered too much of your face, as Greta told me when she tossed mine away—we squinted at each other, sizing each other up. Or maybe he had already moved on to tacos while I checked him out.

Medium-length brown hair. Brown eyes. Right at six foot. A plain white tee covered his chest. He wasn't the brash sort that I was used to. Instead, he exuded quiet confidence.

There was nothing remarkable about him at first sight. Yet, I couldn't tear my gaze away.

Mentally, I slapped my head to get it straight. August was not the usual type of guy who piqued my interest. I liked cocky guys who were the center of the party, who were willing to take a midnight flight to anywhere just for the hell of it or mutually ghost each other to avoid any deeper entanglements. With them, I knew what they wanted from me: fun, no strings attached.

However, wasn't this partly why I had decided to apply? To put myself out there and explore? Maybe there was a reason my past "types" hadn't worked out.

"Hiiiiiiii!"

In unison, we turned toward the scream, watching as two almost identical women teetered down the stairs in platform heels. They seemed to have also split a single bikini, given the precariously little material painted on them. Behind them followed a tall guy with tattoos covering his chest. Judging by the way his eyes were glued to the twins in front of him, he thanked his lucky stars for the bikini shortage.

With a quirk of his mouth, August said, "Let the chaos start."

As if he couldn't wait to get away from me, August abandoned me to head to the bar. Left by myself with the bikini-shortage twins and their number one fan, I glared daggers at August's back. Imaginary daggers that he ignored, unfortunately.

Within what seemed like minutes, the once-empty beach filled up with contestants. Hot, confident men who had never met a shirt or skipped a day at the gym. Attractive women with full-on makeup. All single. All eager to mingle.

People were my jam. Parties and entertaining people energized me. They squashed the nervousness that I had felt earlier. I danced. I pretended to twerk. Maybe I overexaggerated with my hands and my expressions to get my point across, but people laughed.

Why hang out with a stuck-up guy who escaped at the first chance, when there was an entire beach of potential prospects who tried to draw my attention? Except, I couldn't help but seek him out in the crowd. Only to find August assessing me as if I were a weird alien creature that he didn't understand.

As a mental middle finger to him, I drummed up my charm, moving around the small groups forming on the beach, flirting with the men, chatting with the women. At some point, a DJ showed up and the official welcome party started. When the DJ amped up the music, I led a group of tipsy contestants to dance near the ocean waves.

Every single male contestant, minus August, screamed twenty- or thirty-something-year-old trying to recover their college days. Still… it was hard not to feel flattered when men actively sought me out to flirt.

Like Bobby, who was a pilot and promised he could take me on private flights. Or Garrett, who brought out his guitar to serenade me. There was Juan, the salsa dance teacher from Argentina, with magical hips and expressive hands. Or Timmy, who did push-ups with me on his back.

This was the purpose of being on this show—to find a temporary distraction, to feel wanted for a short while, right?

Unlike August, who carried a permanent frown whenever our eyes met, the other men jostled for my attention. If I noticed that August took the opposite approach from my mingling and seemed to be in deep conversation with only one woman the entire afternoon at the periphery of the rowdy crowd, well, it wasn't my business.

If a small—tiny, *infinitesimally* miniscule—part of me was hurt that he didn't seem interested in me, that was just my ego talking. Plus, my ego wasn't *hurt*, per se. I was only slightly miffed… marginally peeved.

I was making too big a deal out of his whiskey-smooth voice. With another non-glance at August and his chosen partner sitting under a cabana, I mentally dragged him into a box of not-a-prospect.

Grinning so wide that my cheeks hurt, I let an overly muscular guy flexing his biceps pull me to the bar to do a round of tequila shots. Followed by another round of shots, which made me forget the cameras.

Followed by… I wasn't sure how many shots we did, just that my mouth tasted of salt and lime, while my throat burned from the acidity.

"Babe," slurred a tall, dark-haired man who resembled Michael B. Jordan. He shouldered his way between Bobby and Juan to wrap an arm around my shoulder. I was pretty sure his name was Aidan. Maybe Jayden…

"I'm Kaiden. You are so hot. Have I told you how sexy red hair is? I love your blue eyes. They're so… blue. Wait, babe, stop moving. Do you have a twin standing next to you? Whoa, she's sexy too."

My vision blurred. I squinted next to me, eighty percent sure I had no twin. I'd know if I had a twin, right?

"Babe, do you want to come skinny-dipping in the ocean? You or your twin, or both? That would be hot," said Kaiden, his eyes twitching between me and the empty space next to me.

Despite the who-was-counting-number of shots and Kaiden's attempt at flattery, skinny-dipping in the ocean with a guy who was indifferent to whom he skinny-dipped with didn't appeal to me as much as… well, lying down somewhere cool while eating chocolate chip cookies.

Affecting a casual laugh, I extracted myself from his arm and liquored breath. "How about you go with my twin? You go first, she'll follow."

I gave him a gentle push toward an empty cabana. Beaming at my nonexistent twin, Kaiden zigzagged backward. As soon as he sat down, he lost all bones in his body. His lovely muscles collapsed like Jenga pieces into the cushions. Making sure he was safely snoozing on his side, I waved away another contestant to wobble back up a set of stairs toward a row of cottages lining the beach.

"Do you know where my suitcases are?" I slurred to the cameraman following me.

He pointed to the nearest cottage. "That's where all the women will sleep. We've put your luggage up there."

I stumbled before catching myself. Those shots roiled around my stomach, quickening my steps as I stumble-ran toward the cottage. At some point, I had lost my sandals, and that likely saved me from pitching over the stairs.

After battling the doorknob, acutely aware the camera recorded my clumsy efforts while my mic pack captured my cursing, I hurled around the cottage until I found the bathroom. Against the surprised expression of the cameraman, I shut the door. In relief, I sank down, hugging the toilet for dear life.

A few minutes later, a knock sounded on the door. "Pippa?"

"Go away," I croaked, my throat still burning from tequila and the aftermath of too many shots. I hated that even in my drunkenness, I recognized his whiskey-deep voice.

Before I could rein my thoughts in, I complained, "Why are you even here? You haaate me."

"Just because I didn't throw myself at you like the other guys doesn't mean I hate you." August paused. "You were stumbling around and needed help."

With a groan of embarrassment, I willed him to turn around and leave. Of all the times today to notice me, it was at my worst. First day of filming and I made best friends with tequila. Not the glamorous start I'd envisioned when I woke up this morning.

Just my luck. All I wanted was to melt into the floor in peace and quiet. Instead of reading my mind and leaving, August paced outside the bathroom door with the world's loudest shoes. Each footstep clanged as if he wore metal hammers on his shoes.

Was it possible to be drunk and hungover at the same time?

Ignoring him, I clung to the toilet, even as my body had nothing left, taking deep breaths to repel the dry heaves. I was not ready to face anyone, especially someone who sounded annoyingly sober.

Plus, August already thought I was rude. He didn't need to add "messy" to the con side of his mental list of me. With me looking as miserable as I felt, I didn't need company in the small bathroom with me.

"I have Advil and ice chips," he added.

Cursing under my breath at his offer, I flushed the toilet, washed my hands, and found some mouthwash to rinse. There was nothing I could do about my rat's nest of red hair, but at least my face had regained some of its color. Instead of appearing like a ghostly mess on national TV, I'd upgraded to a regular mess.

Or was it downgraded? On the mess scale, was ghost better than regular?

I cracked open the bathroom door and froze.

With the light from a nearby lamp behind him, August's brown hair turned into a halo around his head. *Angel of the night.* The shadows across his face elevated his guy-next-door appearance into an enigma. A frisson of awareness broke through my alcohol daze to course through me.

"Pippa, are you okay?" August stepped in front of me, careful to block me from the waiting camera, before closing the door behind him.

His deep, even voice soothed my fraying edges. Even his movements were calm, unhurried. If I focused on him, the chaos within me slowed to a bearable degree.

Inside the fluorescent light of the bathroom, he transitioned from mysterious angel back to the guy next door again. Outside of some sand on his shirt, he looked as if he had taken a stroll around a park in seventy-degree weather. Damn August for appearing so clean and put together, whereas I… At least my breath smelled minty.

"I'm feeling better now," I lied, flicking some hair behind me. On a normal day, my long red hair would swish behind me, cascading down my shoulders in gentle waves all the way to the middle of my back. Tonight, my messy hair flopped around as I tried to untangle my fingers out of it.

"You look awful," August said, his gentle voice belying the words.

"You're supposed to not notice and tell me I'm sexy," I retorted as I sank down to the tiled floor. Too weak to sit up, I let my body droop until I lay sprawled.

"You are sexy… even now," he mumbled under his breath, red flags rising on his cheeks.

Pleasure bloomed over me at his unexpected confession, even if he hadn't meant for me to hear. With one hand behind my back, he brought me to a sitting position. Behind me, his hands worked briskly to yank off my mic pack before reaching under his shirt to turn off his.

When he faced me again, the redness in his cheeks had faded. "I don't think you want the mics to catch this moment. You're in for a major hangover. Here, take the Advil, it'll help with tomorrow."

I took the tablet and bottle of water from him, chugging before he yanked the bottle back. "Hey, I'm thirsty."

"Don't drink so fast. I don't want you to get sick again. Suck on these ice cubes instead."

With a glare at August, I grabbed an ice cube. The coldness was such a relief that I moaned in happiness as I sucked on the frigid delight.

Fixated on the ice, August backed away. His mouth opened and closed before he cleared his throat. "Um, I—do you—um…"

"Stay, please," I asked, one hand holding on to my piece of ice like a life jacket. I had already embarrassed myself in front of him. What would a few more minutes of his soothing presence hurt?

CHAPTER TWO

~PIPPA~

ITM filming, Day 1, 10 p.m., aka five tequila shots ago:

__Greta__: You've had a chance to meet everyone, Miss Popular. Has anyone caught your eye yet?

__Pippa__: Lots of them, except August.

__Greta__: Why "except August"? You don't think August is handsome?

__Pippa__: What, no! He's... he's... fine... if you're into that clean-cut, guy-next-door look.

__Greta__: Right, because no one is into the Chris Evans-type.

__Pippa__: It's a moot point. We didn't get off on a good foot. He's not interested. Did you see how into that other woman he was? Why chase him when there are so many others chasing me?

__Greta__: I did see him. What's interesting is that you noticed too, even though you claimed he didn't catch your eye.

__Pippa__: It's not my fault he stood out.

__Greta__: Stood out, even though he was just sitting for most of the night?

"Stay, please. I don't like being alone." The confession should have never tumbled out. Yet, in that moment, I needed August to stay with me more than I needed to pretend.

A flush spread over me when August hesitated. The warmth had nothing to do with alcohol and all too much to do with the way he stared at the ice cube melting in my hand.

A wild image of me licking the water from my fingers while he watched flooded me with desire. I crossed my arms to hide my hardened nipples and tried to joke my way out of lust. "Who would fetch me more ice cubes if I ran out?"

"Do you want me to help you off the floor?"

I shook my head, slumping back down until I lay on my stomach, with my head resting on my hands. The floor was clean and cold. It wasn't as if I could make any worse of an impression. "Let me lie here for a bit. Talk. Pat my back, as if I'm a cat. Please."

August sat down on the floor, crossing his legs. Hesitation shadowed his face as he stared at my back. Sucking a deep breath in, he reached out and let his hand rest against the bare skin of my back.

Even in my drunken stupor, electricity radiated from his hand across my body. His fingers played with my bikini straps, strumming the ties in a nervous gesture. There was no one and nothing as vivid as his touch at this moment. All my senses stood at attention, craving more.

Over the sound of my stilted breathing, August sucked in air, letting it out slowly. So steady, so careful, a wild contrast to my erratic breaths.

At this moment, I no longer remembered that I was on this show for a diversion before I went back to my law firm, or that I was confused about what I wanted in life. It was just me and August, and his hand on my bare skin. I wanted to ask—nay, demand—that he explore me. Hell, untie my bikini top.

Then his hand moved. To my utter mortification, it wasn't to strip me or to slip his strong hands under to cup my breast. Instead, he pulled away.

August didn't seem like the normal, cocky guys that I interacted with. The guys I knew wouldn't bring me ice cubes and water. They would have been lying on the floor next to me, blacked out, talking to my nonexistent twin. Or still on the beach doing kegs upside down or trying to get laid. Or comparing social media followers… anything, besides *not* touching me after I invited him to pet me like I was a kitten.

I bit my tongue to stifle my need, to prevent me from pleading. Only pride kept my mouth shut. If August didn't make a move while I lay here in offering, then he was absolutely, one hundred percent, not interested in me.

Embarrassment welled up. In my drunken fog, I had confused his unexpected kindness for something that wasn't there. If there was any time for the floor to swallow me, now would be the time.

Clearing his throat, August said, his voice deliciously low, "What do you want me to talk about? I'm, um, pretty boring. I have an older sister who is married to one of my best friends, and they have twins. My parents have been married for thirty-five years. I've taught high school history for a few years. Last year, I moved back to my hometown to teach and coach our boys soccer team. I like backyard barbecues and campfires. Not as glamorous as your life, I bet."

He shrugged, laughing in an uncomfortable, self-conscious way. In my world, people puffed themselves up, never down. If someone said they owned a yacht, it meant that they sailed in a dinghy once. If they called themselves an international sports star, they barely made the practice squad in Svalbard, Norway.

Rolling my eyes as best as I could with the room still spinning, I pushed down my embarrassment. No better way to recover than pretend I hadn't been made a fool by his earlier rejection. "If you say it like that, then everybody sounds pretty boring. I could say the same thing about myself. I'm a single child. My parents have been married for almost forty years. I'm a patent lawyer. I like matcha lattes."

Another genuine smile flashed across August's face. Stupefied, I watched as the corners of his eyes crinkled. When did crinkles become sexy?

He's not interested, remember that.

"What made a supposedly normal guy sign up for a reality show like this?" I asked.

Tilting back his head, August stared at the ceiling for so long that I thought he had forgotten my question. Finally, he responded, "Mark asked me that when I arrived at the beach. I told him I wanted to find love, and where's a better place than a tropical island like St. Lucia? But it's not the full truth. Who finds love on a reality TV show? I don't have any real expectations for that to happen to me."

"If you're not expecting happily ever after, then why come on a dating show?" I probed.

"I teach high school history. In some ways, I feel stuck in the past," said August. "My sister and I grew up in the same house our entire childhood, outside of Boston. I went to college and grad school in Massachusetts and still teach in the state. I've had the same group of core friends since kindergarten T-ball. My last long-term relationship was almost a decade ago, and it didn't end well. I've dated since, but nothing serious. I love my life, but what if there's something else out there? When my sister nominated me for this show, I realized this was my chance to step outside of my comfort zone."

August was so, so wrong. As I knew too well, jaunting around the world for the past six months after pausing my job didn't mean I'd found something better. Sometimes, people traveled all over, did wild things, because they were still frantically searching for themselves.

Hiding my errant thoughts, I joked, "You couldn't have just dyed your hair purple if you needed to rebel, like the rest of us, huh?"

There—the twinkle in his eyes was back. "What about you? I find it hard to believe you have trouble finding a date. So, what diversion did you need from your life?"

"Dates are easy." I shrugged. Or rather, as much as being slumped on the floor would let my shoulders move. "Would you believe me if I said I was a hopeless romantic buried under this drunken mess?"

"Is it true?"

The gentleness with which he asked made me *almost* wish I could tell him the truth: I had spent too much time chasing a career and living a supposedly perfect life that along the way, I got lost. The desire to confess to August was due to tequila. Right?

With the earlier dizziness and churning stomach gone, I became more aware of the absurdity of having a conversation while I lay like a dead body. On the bathroom floor. If only my regular party crew could see how much I'd fallen, literally.

Though, did it matter if August saw me like this? It wasn't as if I was trying to impress him.

But it wasn't as if I *wasn't* trying to impress him. That made sense.

Sort of?

I sucked in a breath to rein in any foolish confession and straightened my elbows to sit up. "Nah, I'm more of a jaded grump than romantic. My best friend, Tia, encouraged me to sign up. She's a hopeless romantic who's living in a world of soul mates and orgasms. I don't believe in soul mates. However, I do have a lot of free time nowadays. I left my law firm in February and have been traveling around, trying to figure out what to do."

"Have you found your answers?"

"No. The only thing that I feel sure about is that I haven't found *it*—whatever *it* is. Minus not working, it hasn't been all that different, hopping from place to place. Unlike you, I have no deep roots. I've never belonged anywhere." I bit my tongue, wishing I could claw back the words. What was it about August that made me spill as if I were chugging truth serums?

"Maybe the answer is me moving to a cabin in the woods and eating pizza all day." Playing off my previous confession as a joke, I tried to find my way back to safer ground. "I'm open to whatever comes my way. I don't think I'll find my happily ever after on a TV show where people signed up for social media followers. But I'll take a fun summer."

"Not everyone is here for social media," August countered. "I don't have any."

"Yeah, you're completely different," I responded, with full honesty.

"In a good way," I amended, feeling shy when his eyes lit up with surprise.

The sudden shortage of air was definitely the reason for the word vomit that came next. "You don't have any social media? Not Twitter, Instagram, Facebook, TikTok, LinkedIn, Pinterest, Clubhouse, Snapchat, Reddit, WeChat, BeReal, WhatsApp, Hive, YouTube, Telegram, Triller, Periscope, Academia… no? Dating apps? Bumble, Coffee Meets Bagel, Tinder, eHarmony, OkCupid, The League, Plenty of Fish, Raya, Zoosk?"

"I can't tell if you're tossing in random words with real apps." August shook his head, as he leaned closer, as if I fascinated him. "I live in a small town, not under a rock. Even us high school teachers know what Facebook or TikTok is. Zoosk, Raya, Triller—no clue."

"What do you do with your time? How do you get in contact with people?" I asked, horrified and impressed.

Shrugging, August said, "I read books; I like historical fiction and mysteries. I call or text my friends if I want to hang out or check in on them. If I'm bored, I fish by the pond."

Forgetting that I'd had so many shots that I lost count, I scootched closer to August until his face was all I could see. In mock horror, I quizzed, "Hold up, your words do not compute for me. One, you call people instead of just checking in on their social media. What if they answer you, and you have to have a real conversation?"

Two fingers out, I waggled them in front of his smiling face. "Two, you willingly choose to read books about dead people rather than spend hours watching random people dance to the same sound? Three, you fish to get *rid* of boredom? Isn't fishing the epitome of boring? Who are you and what century did you come from? Next thing I know, you'll tell me that your hobby is to traipse through the countryside like a Jane Austen character."

Laughing, he reached a hand to brush an unruly curl away from my face. The light touch didn't feel like a throwaway gesture to help tame my hair. Not when his hand slid down to cup my face, tilting me toward him with a subtle pressure.

I forgot all about fishing and Jane Austen.

Just as I gathered myself to lean closer, he dropped his hand, planting it firmly on the floor. He stared at his hand for long enough that my heartbeat calmed from a sprint to a gallop.

His voice raspy, he said, "It helps that almost everyone I know lives in the same town of five thousand, with only one coffee shop, church, grocery store, and The Diner. I see everybody at The Diner, my school, or at soccer games. Those are the hip places to be in Beach Falls."

His hands fisted against the white tiles of the floor. "See, that's why I need to get out more. I can't believe I called high school 'hip.' If I don't do this, I'll become the stereotypical old man who complains about hedges."

My heart twisted at the sight of red flagging his cheeks once again. I reached out to pat his cheeks. It was meant to be a lighthearted, joking pat to get him to cheer up.

Instead, my hand lingered against his skin the way I wished his hand had stayed on mine. In my mind, I stroked his face, the beginnings of a beard, and feathered over his cheekbones, traveling down to explore his full lips.

Would he suck my fingers in? How would his lips feel on my palm? Up my arm, teasing out the sensitive spots on my neck, up to my lips?

Would he be gentle, coaxing me to open? Or reveal a darker side, plundering, pulling us under an inescapable wave of lust?

My breath caught at the images of August exploring me, of his whiskey voice muttering commands…

My eyelids heavy, I lifted them to look at him. Desire blazed across his face. At this moment, he wasn't the nice boy next door. He was danger and fire, darkness and stark hunger threatening to overwhelm me.

His whole body tensed, as if he barely kept himself in check. What would it feel like to have that intensity unleashed?

Up close, his eyes weren't a monotone of brown, but flecked with shades of amber. Instead of a two-dimensional color, they were warm, the colors changing depending on the angle of the light from above, like oak trees on a stormy day.

As my gaze faltered and dropped, I followed the labored up and down of his chest, our breathing aligned. He wasn't as skinny as I had originally thought. True, his muscles didn't bulge the same way as others on the beach. Yet, I couldn't help but notice the way his shoulders stretched his shirt, pulling the material tight across his chest. Lean, toned, and strong, he had the body of a soccer player.

Impulse control had never been my strong suit. Because I couldn't help it, I caressed his cheek, covered with the beginnings of a stubble. My hand drifted lower, down to his shoulders, and squeezed.

August sucked in a breath.

My eyes fluttered down, staring at his fisted hands on the floor, willing them to move. Aching for them to touch me. With no active thought other than undiluted desire, I wriggled even closer until my knees touched his crossed legs.

And waited.

I had no qualms about kissing a guy or suggesting something more. But it was different when I knew the guy would reciprocate, that me making a move *first* was a matter of timing, not a matter of willingness.

In August, I had a mystery. Despite the desire flickering across his face, he made no move.

Flustered and intrigued, I held back. Kissing him didn't feel like a casual action, easily compartmentalized. August was good and kind, someone you spent weekends barbecuing with or cuddling in bed. He wasn't for someone like me, with an unrelenting need to find distractions, who couldn't stay still in a single place.

Though, for the last half an hour, I hadn't felt that itch to search for something new… something different.

In a low, growly voice, August murmured, "Why don't I take you to your bed?"

CHAPTER THREE

~AUGUST~

ITM filming, Day 1, 11:37 p.m.:

Greta: Hi, August. Let's get started. Tell us how you heard about this show.

August: *I got a call right after school ended from a casting agent. I had planned to spend the summer building my deck, painting my kitchen cabinets—*

Greta: *Got it. We don't need to get into details on home renovations. Did you apply for the show?*

August: *No, I hadn't heard of this show until the call. She told me she had received an application from my sister, June. Then, I went to LA for interviews and received the invite.*

Greta: *Two and a half weeks to meet new people, without distractions, in a beautiful location, with fantastic, romantic dates. What an amazing way to meet someone. I think you'll find someone here.*

August: *I'm open to it.*

Greta: *Has anyone caught your eye, like Annie? You spent a lot of time talking with her tonight.*

August: *She's nice.*

Greta: *"Nice" is rather bland. How about Pippa?*

August: *What about her?*

Greta: *You keep frowning at the men Pippa's talking to. Even now, you're stealing glances at her.*

August*: I am not. Hold on, she's heading up to the cottages. I don't think she's steady. Is someone going to help her?*

When Pippa whispered yes, it took everything in me to force out the clarification. "To your bed. Alone. For you to sleep it off."

Even drunk, smelling of tequila, sitting on a bathroom floor, Pippa remained the most beautiful person that I had met. In the intimacy of the small space, away from the cameras and other people, she seemed approachable.

Not like the woman who'd barked at me on the beach earlier this afternoon.

While my steps had faltered at the sight of her on the beach, she had looked at me as if I were a gnat invading her personal space. She was a walking red flag —too beautiful, too glamorous for me.

I had been burned before by women who were out of my league. Chasing Pippa would lead to nothing but frustration. No, I made the right decision to walk away on the beach, instead of fighting for her attention.

There were thirty contestants on the beach, plus dozens of crew members and staff from the resort. There was no need for Pippa and me to be around each other.

So then, how do I explain why I sprinted after her with Advil and ice cubes to make sure she was okay? I could have asked one of the other contestants, who had been hanging all over her, to check in on her. Or one of the handlers, like Greta, with her eagle eyes.

Yet, when I saw Pippa stumbling up the steps by herself, and the cameraman did nothing except tilt his equipment to catch the almost-fall, I felt an inexplicable urge to protect her. No one deserved to have their drunken antics captured on camera for the world to see.

Here I was. Instead of trying to explore possible connections on the beach, I chased after someone who had flirted with every guy on the beach except me. Make that make sense.

Except she didn't seem repulsed by me tonight. To my surprise, Pippa had been funny, self-deprecating, and vulnerable. Tonight's version of Pippa didn't fit the grumpy or the life-of-the-party versions from earlier. Which Pippa was the real one?

In silence, I carried her from the bathroom to an empty room and deposited her on the bottom bunk. Before I could pull up the blankets to tuck her in, Pippa fell asleep. With her hands clasped and resting under her cheek, she curled up on her side.

I watched her breathing even out. I stayed, only to make sure she was okay. If my hands ached to touch her cheeks, it was out of curiosity to see if they felt as soft as they appeared.

"August? What are you doing here?"

Guilty, I spun around to see Annie at the entrance of the room. Admitting that large gatherings made her nervous, Annie and I had spent most of the evening hanging on the periphery of the party.

I stumbled, stepping away from Pippa. "She wasn't feeling well. I'm sorry for leaving you by yourself at the party earlier."

"I wasn't alone," Annie said, her voice gentle. "There was a beach full of people. It gave me the push to talk to others. Though, I'm not sure I understood what I signed up for until today. It's certainly different from small-town Arkansas."

"We'll be the odd ducks out then," I assured her. "I'm going to go. Can you check in on Pippa to make sure she's okay?"

"Sure, it was getting too rowdy on the beach for me." Annie nodded. "I'll take the top bunk. Don't worry. I'll take care of her for you."

"Not for *me*. Take care of her, for *her*," I corrected.

"Whatever you say."

Ignoring Annie's smirk, I backed out of the room into the empty living room. The cameraman had left already. Judging by the shouts and laughter on the beach, I suspected he had left to film something more exciting.

I should have rejoined the party. After all, wasn't this my big gesture to try something different?

But all I could think about was Pippa. As pitiful as she was drunk, she still fascinated me. Poor first impression aside, I couldn't shake the idea that she might have a different side—a side that mixed brash confidence, honesty, and hints of vulnerability. As risky and as different as she was from me, she pulled me to her.

Inside the men's cottage, one of the producers directed me to a small room with bunk beds and reprimanded me for taking off my necklace mic. After unpacking my suitcase and getting ready for bed, I climbed up to the top bunk. With my arms crossed behind my head, I stared out of the large windows into the darkness.

Who would have thought Mr. Small-Town Guy would be on a national reality TV show? I hoped that come September, when the school year started again, my students wouldn't roast me for making an ass of myself. Even if my principal had approved my request to go on this show, I didn't want to ruin my chances of getting tenure.

Although I had taught for several years at another school in Massachusetts, I had only completed one year at Beach Falls. Back home, I needed three years in the same district before achieving some stability.

It was one thing for some of the other contestants who wanted to use this opportunity to be in the entertainment industry. They could play up their personality and engage in drama. For me, my small-town world was my reality that I needed to get back to. One wrong move, and I would need to look for a new job.

Lulled by the distant music, ocean waves, and occasional laughter, I drifted off to uneasy sleep. In my dreams, a red-haired beauty teased me with beguiling smiles. Her attention focused on me as she danced and laughed… but always out of reach.

By the time I woke up, I was exhausted from chasing after Pippa in my dreams and unsettled by her appearance in the first place. Shaking off the last vestiges of sleep, I hopped down from the top bunk, surprised to find that my roommate had come in sometime during the night.

Flip-flops still on, he was sprawled on the bottom bunk. One hand clutched a guitar even in sleep. I recognized him as Garrett—the guy who played songs for Pippa on the beach last night.

Annoyance swept through me. Stepping over his discarded clothes, I rushed through getting changed and left the still-quiet cottage. A sleepy camerawoman followed me outside for a few feet before realizing that I intended to run, not stir drama.

Thirty minutes later, exhausted from running on the sand, I headed back. Though it was only seven thirty in the morning, the island sun blazed across the sky. I took off my shoes and socks and walked through the gentle waves to cool off.

Red flashed in the distance. Pippa strolled down the steps from the cottages onto the beach. This morning, she had no makeup on and no jewelry. In jean shorts and a plain white tank, she created an illusion of approachability, like the girl next door who might say yes if you asked her on a date. I was transfixed.

Then, as if to laugh at my momentary lapse, she tossed her long red hair behind her, breaking that illusion. I might be good for Advil and ice. However, in the brightness of the day, Pippa was still the glamorous woman who had the world at her feet, while I was plain old me.

My heart twisted with pleasure at seeing her and frustration at knowing that she was never going to be for a guy like me. I had made the mistake once when I was younger. In the process of daring to reach for the impossible, I had been tossed back, pride wounded. When my ex, Zara, left, she had made it clear that I wasn't enough.

"Good morning," she called out, raising her hand to wave.

"Hi, Pippa." My racing heart belied my attempt to be casual.

"I, um, wanted to thank you for taking care of me last night," she started, redness brushing her cheeks. "Thanks to you and a good night's sleep, I don't feel like shit this morning."

"Yeah, no problem," I said, digging my toes into the sand to keep myself from walking closer to her.

Pippa opened her mouth and closed it. She raised her hands, stuffed them back in her shorts pockets, and pulled them out again to play with her hair. Her nervousness surprised me. The fact that she was letting me see this part of her… was it possible that last night wasn't an illusion?

Taking a deep breath to gather myself, I asked, "Pippa, would you like to go—"

"August, I wasn't myself last night," she said at the same time, her words tumbling out. "If I've insinuated anything… anyways, thanks for helping me. I'm glad I have you on this show with me… as a fr-friend."

One of her hands stopped playing with her glorious mass of hair to extend toward me. I shook it as if she were nothing more than one of my student's parents, even though all I wanted was to pull her against me.

Wasn't that grand? How much more of a reminder did I need that she wasn't the girl next door? That she was so far out of my league that I couldn't even see what league she was in? Interest in her would only lead to pain.

Not that I had been interested in pursuing her. She wasn't my type.

Liar.

Telling my inner self to quiet down, I said, "You were drunk and needed help. It's the least I could do. I didn't want you to get hurt. Or have the show capture anything embarrassing of you."

Pippa's eyes widened. Instead of the open, clear blue of the morning sky, they flattened to a dull blue.

"Did I say something wrong?" I asked, walking toward her.

Jutting her chin up, she recoiled and took a step away from me. "I don't need your pity. If they caught something embarrassing, that's on me. It's not like anyone would expect anything different. Haven't you heard what others are saying? I spent the past few months flitting from party to party. While you've been teaching students, I've been an eager student of the best clubs."

I stared at her as her words tumbled out cold and fast. Despite her admission, despite what everyone else said, and even my own first impression, I couldn't reconcile the shallow socialite she projected with the genuine warmth that I had experienced last night.

"I didn't help because I pitied you. Why are you playing into the gossip about you?"

"Because it's true! Just because you're a goody-two-shoes Boy Scout, doesn't mean I am." Her mouth pulled into a tight, unhappy line. Her breathing sped up. "Anyways, glad that's all cleared up. Let's forget about last night. I'm going to head back to the cottage to get changed for filming."

With a quick flick of her hands, she dismissed me. This time, her stride back to the cottages was quick, almost businesslike.

Just like I thought, we were too different. Sober Pippa had no use for me.

A quick shower later, I stood in the living room of the guys' cottage. With a basket of mics, one of the producers, Nate, handed me a roped necklace with a large bead. "Test the microphone."

"Hello, hello," I spoke into the bead with the microphone built in.

"Good, you're all set. Next," called out Nate, pulling another necklace from the basket.

My roommate, Garrett, walked by, guitar in hand. "Yo, August, right? Dude, I wouldn't have expected it from someone like you. Damn, you move fast!"

Puzzled by his Cheshire cat grin, I asked, "What are you talking about?"

"Pippa!" he shouted, chortling. "The hottest girl on this show, and you stole her away last night. All this time, we were fighting over her, while you played it cool. Wow, who knew she'd go for the guy who ignored her."

"She *did* ignore me. I'm not pursui—"

"You're talking about Pippa?" One of the other contestants, Troy, popped his head out of a room.

Garrett nodded.

"Did you check out the private room?" asked Troy, letting out a whoop. He thrust his hips in the air, then shook his face, motorboating the air.

Was motorboating boobs still a thing to joke about? I stared at Troy as he mimicked various sex positions while Garrett doubled over in laughter.

Choking back words, I fisted my hands to keep from shutting them up for spreading rumors about Pippa. Even if she leaned into the gossip, I didn't want to be part of the rumor mill.

Remember, need to have a drama-free summer.

Cutting through Troy's one-man act, which now included sounds, I raised my voice, "She wasn't feeling well, so I brought her water. Nothing happened."

"Oh?" Troy stopped in mid… I don't know, mid-lick of whipped cream? He got points—crude points—for his tenacity, I had to admit. "You're not calling dibs? She's still single?"

I crossed my arms to keep from smacking the smirk from his face. "You can't call dibs on a person."

My words went into a black hole. With a whoop of glee, Troy ran through the cottage, knocking on doors, yelling, "I get dibs on Pippa!"

Anger, frustration, and defense of Pippa boiled up within me. I started to go after Troy, but Nate stepped in front of me. "Let him go. He's a jerk at best."

When I hesitated, Nate continued, "Go on, head over to the main gazebo. Word of advice for you, just because I like you, man. There are two paths you could pick. Pick someone low-key, like Annie. You two are compatible. The editors will give you a great edit if you two stay together. Or fight with everyone over Pippa, but it'll be messy. Your choice."

CHAPTER FOUR

~PIPPA~

ITM filming, Day 2, 9:15 a.m.:

__Greta__: Tell us why you joined The Journey of Love.

__Pippa__: My current ways of meeting guys don't work. I've tried dating apps, blind dates, meeting people at parties. Why not a reality show about love?

__Greta__: It's hard to believe that someone who looks like you has a hard time finding a date.

__Pippa__: Looks like me? Pfft, maybe that's the problem. People assume I'm nothing more than my looks. I date plenty. But they all turn out to be jerks. For example, I dated this hockey player—

__Greta__: Rumors are that you dated The *Alex Turgenev, who led the Bruins to a Stanley Cup Championship.*

__Pippa__: Yeah, him. Though, I'm pretty sure his first name is 'Alex,' not 'The.' He asked for my number through a friend and sent me flowers for weeks before I agreed to a date. Then, he rented out the whole Rockefeller ice rink that was strewn with roses—

__Greta__: Sorry, this is an example of a bad date?

__Pippa__: That part was fine. It's the after. *He took me to his hotel room and dropped his pants. He yanked out his dick—am I allowed to say dick on national TV?*

__Greta__: We can edit. Please continue.

__Pippa__: Okay, he yanked out his dick and said, 'Blow it.' Then he had the gall *to get mad at me when I dared to suggest, 'Eat me first.' I don't understand boys. That's what they are—every single one of the guys that I've dated or who has expressed interest—boys. Not men. They throw some pretty words and flowers at you and expect your panties to drop. They equate liking to have fun as having low expectations. The hotter they are, the quicker they expect panties to fall and the less effort they put. In fact, Alex had the nerve to tell me he could get twenty women to show up at his place before I left the building, with a single Tweet. Maybe I'm tired of guys like Alex who only want sex.*

"Ladies and gentlemen. I hope you've enjoyed your first day. I saw some flirting, some connections being made… even a couple sneaking off during the party last night." The host, Mark, winked at me, while a few contestants hollered.

With the amount of elbow jabbing coming my way, I was surprised my arms weren't black and blue. My face heated as I forced myself to stare straight ahead at the ocean.

Bright triangle flags fluttered in the wind, strung across the beams of the colorful gazebo. A dozen chairs formed a U underneath the wooden, cone-shaped roof. The producers had placed some of us on the spindly chairs, and others standing behind us.

If I twisted a few degrees in my chair, I could catch a glimpse of August behind me. It was already mortifying to know he had helped me because I was trashed last night. Now, to throw salt on my pride, I'd have to listen to my fellow contestants giggle about a hookup that never happened.

Not able to resist any longer, I glanced back at August to check his reaction. He shrugged in a what-can-you-do way. So calm.

So unaffected.

Maddeningly *unaffected* by the other contestants' teasing, by my maybe-alcohol-but-maybe-not flirting last night, and by me today. Maybe it was that he was one of the few people on this beach who wouldn't overlook my faults. Or that August seemed innately good, so if he saw positives in me, that must mean something…

Talking with August last night, even while sprawled across the bathroom floor, had been a rare moment of connection for me in a sea of interactions that never touched beyond the surface. Unfortunately, last night had been one-sided. The entire conversation was a charity gesture.

Oh, he denied the reason he checked on me last night, but what other explanation could it be? He had only bad impression of me after bad impression. The rudeness when we first met. The embarrassing drunkenness last night. The prickliness this morning.

For reasons that I couldn't articulate, I wanted this man to feel *something* about me that wasn't pity. A raw part of me twisted so sharply that I could feel it even through the self-erected walls. I wanted his good opinion, even knowing that his opinion of me was likely in the pits.

When I flipped my hair to catch another peek at August, he frowned. My cheeks flamed up more. I was surprised no one remarked on how my cheeks matched my hair color at this point.

At least August had reacted. I winked at him, just to see what he would do.

His frown deepened in surprise. Just as I was about to sink into my chair in embarrassment, his lips quirked to one side. All of a sudden, my day became brighter, I felt lighter, and all that cheesy jazz. Second day on the show, and already I sounded like a Hallmark movie commercial.

Yet, despite my self-cringe, I couldn't hide my answering smile. It was a start.

A start of what, I didn't know. Did I even want a start with him? August didn't seem like the type of guy who started *something* with an eye on the next "prize."

Cutting into my thoughts, Mark tapped a knife against a champagne glass. "Welcome officially to *The Journey of Love*! Here's how it will work. There are thirty of you here looking to make meaningful connections, away from the distractions of the outside world. This is a life-changing opportunity to meet your forever someone. For those lucky couples who fall in love and decide to get engaged, you will get a dream vacation and a paid engagement ring from Tiffany's that is worth more than a quarter of a million dollars."

Palpable excitement flittered through the group. The contestants scanned each other, mentally calculating their chances of coupling up.

With a dramatic sweep over the gazebo, Mark continued, "To help you explore those connections, we will be giving out date cards at various times throughout this journey. In fact, I have your first date cards now."

On cue, one of the crew members carried over a wooden podium with three large, white cards on top. One of Mark's brows arched up so high that I dropped my head to stifle my giggles.

Staring at the sand underneath my flip-flops, I heard Mark announce, "I have three cards with names. When I call your name, you will ask someone to be your date. The three lucky couples will go on an incredible adventure where they can deepen their love connections. Remember, this is a journey to find your soul mate. Good luck."

For inexplicable reasons, I looked back at August to check his reaction to Mark's announcement, only to find him staring at me again. He was calmness personified, in the midst of all of the loud personalities jostling for attention. For inexplicable reasons, I wanted to rile him up, see what was under his unperturbed surface. Like the mature person I was, I stuck my tongue out at him.

This time, without hesitation, he grinned back at me, shaking his head.

I waggled my eyebrows as his shoulders shook with silent laughter.

Not that I noticed, but if I was the noticing type, I might have seen that August had broad shoulders. While I was *not* noticing his shoulders, he had toned arms too.

And while I *definitely* did *not* check out his shoulders and arms, he was probably thinking what a weirdo I was.

At least he thought I was amusing. I was moving up in the world, from stumbling mess to a *slightly* amusing, *slightly* weird toy you'd find on sale. Grinning, I faced the front again, just in time for Mark to hold up the first card.

"Ladies and gentlemen, here we go. The first person with a date card is Pietr. The second is Kaiden. Last, we have—" Mark paused for dramatic effect.

In unison, the group leaned forward to catch the last name. Damn, Mark and his single arching eyebrow were well versed in creating dramatic effects.

My heart skipped half a beat faster. If August's name was on the card, who would he pick? I had to force myself to not turn around again. Hell, if I turned around for the third time, I should probably get my neck checked out.

"August!"

With no subtlety or self-control at all, I swirled around on my defective neck. If I was shocked, August was double that. Not that he should be. After all, there were only thirty of us. There was a twenty percent chance of either getting a date card or being asked on a date.

Still… August with a date card. The same August who couldn't meet my gaze anymore, whose cheeks flagged pink.

Was there an outside chance that—no, *not my type*. Even worse, he had rejected all my clumsy advances last night and confirmed today that he helped me out of pity.

From the center of the gazebo, Mark called out, "Pietr, you have the first date card. Who will you pick?"

A tall, muscular, blond guy with no shirt walked up to the front. I had a vague recollection of him introducing himself as a retired football tight end. He had been very confident, bordering on cocky.

Pietr resembled and acted too much like all the guys I had dated in the past. I felt rather sorry for the woman he would take on a date and prematurely drop his pants on.

With no hesitation, Pietr grabbed the date card and strutted across the gazebo like a model on a Milan catwalk. "Pippa, will you please go on a date with me today?"

Oh no, I was the poor woman who would be on the receiving end of premature pants-dropping.

Stopping my oh-fuck eye roll, I stared at Pietr. He stood mere inches away from me, holding out the date card. I wanted to step back, but I could see the camera crew moving around to get better reaction shots.

It was a not-so-subtle reminder that this was a show. My every reaction and word could be spliced and twisted to amplify drama.

Smiling at Pietr to buy more time, I wracked my head, trying to come up with ways to turn him down without sounding like a bitch on TV. It wasn't that he wouldn't be a fun date. It was that I was sun addled, with a broken neck that kept trying to turn back to look at someone who was decidedly not my type.

The sun had frazzled my brain so much that an unpretentious conversation in the bathroom sounded more thrilling than flirting with a hot athlete. Old me would have laughed in my face.

Pietr darted his gaze from me to the cameras before landing back on me. "We didn't have a chance to talk much yesterday. From the quick interactions, I'm interested in learning more about *you* and seeing if we can form a true connection."

His statement surprised me. Maybe I had judged him wrongly, too quickly.

Giving in to temptation, I twisted to check August's reaction. His face showed nothing, not even a frown. Instead, he stared straight ahead, past me, past the colorful rainbow gazebo, at the ocean. He was the picture of utter boredom.

Changing my mind on the spot, I nodded at Pietr and took the date card. In a chivalrous gesture that made me hope for a date with no premature cock showing, Pietr kissed the back of my hand.

Amidst the clapping, Mark waved Kaiden to the front. For all I knew, Kaiden still thought I had a twin that he skinny-dipped with last night. With eyes still glassy from last night's tequila, Kaiden stared at me and then at the empty space next to me. His face scrunched up in concentration. In horror, I shook my head, hoping he wouldn't pick Blippa or Tippa, my nonexistent, mysterious red-haired twin.

With an extra scrunch of his nose, he yanked his gaze from me to my far left. "Vidhya."

A curly-haired woman with golden brown skin leaped up from the crowd. Too many decibels too high, Vidhya shouted with excitement, before jumping into Kaiden's arms.

With only the slightest wince, Mark waved the couple aside before calling out the last name, "August."

My vision blurred. The only person who I could see clearly was August walking up in that unhurried, even way of his. He scanned the gazebo, skipping over me, before landing on a woman a few seats to my left.

Damn my swiveling neck. I needed to make an appointment with my doctor to get it checked out. *Doctor, doctor, I've lost control of my neck.*

The woman at the center of August's focus was the same person he had spent all of yesterday chatting with before he played white knight to make sure I didn't melt onto the bathroom floor. Damn, she was beautiful: golden curly hair, large green eyes, and dimples. Sweetness oozed out of her. *She* would never be caught drunk on the floor.

"Annie," August called out. There were no frowns for her as Annie walked up to take the date card. No tension in his broad shoulders as he bent to hug her.

What did I expect? For August to mope?

Not my type.

Clear as the St. Lucian water, I wasn't his type if he was interested in Annie, never mind his multiple rejections. She seemed sweet, and I felt anything but that at this moment. She was petite and voluptuous, whereas I was tall and skinny. She wore a simple white T-shirt with loose jeans, and no makeup or jewelry. Her simplicity stood out in sharp contrast to everyone else, including me, who dressed as if we were on a photo shoot, rather than in the hot sun with sand everywhere.

I didn't know why I was sad. I had no right to be sad. *Zero* right. If my logical brain could start working again, it would tell me that this feeling of loss was irrational. After all, was it even a loss if August was never mine to start with?

Broad shoulders and a decent conversation did not equate to any sort of commitment. Yet, I stewed as Mark dismissed us to get ready for the dates.

Annie approached me, her eyes sparkling. "Oh, isn't this so exciting? Gosh, I can't believe I'm on this island, with all of these amazing people, and to be able to go on dates."

When I didn't respond, because my mind was still trying to remember the last time that I had heard "gosh," she stammered, "I'm sorry, I didn't even introduce myself. I'm Annie. I'm your roommate. You were… um, asleep when I came into the room last night. I'm an early bird and went for a walk before you woke up today."

If my jaw tensed any further at the prospect of hearing my *roommate* sing August's praises after their date, I might never open my mouth again. Before I could scare off the poor woman, I grimace-smiled. "I'm Pippa."

"I'm so glad to meet you. Yesterday, I was too nervous to approach you. You were surrounded by so many people," she continued, looking so earnest with her large, round eyes. "Gosh, you're beautiful, by the way. I'm sure you know that and hear that so often. I hope we get to know each other more. Are you so excited to go on a date with Pietr? He's so handsome, almost unreal, like he stepped out of some photo. You must feel so lucky that he picked you."

Studying this strange, chatty woman in front of me, I said in a deadpan voice, with a hint of sarcasm, "Yes, so excited. I've never been more excited."

My sarcasm flew over her head. Annie glowed in happiness for me.

Hoping she'd be half as chatty about other topics, I probed, "What about you and August? Are you excited to go on a date?"

She glowed even brighter at the mention of August, despite my forced words. If she lit up anymore, I'd swear I was still drunk-sleeping, dreaming of Disney princesses.

"August is so kind. I was so surprised that he picked me and so honored. He could have picked anyone, except you and Vidhya," she started.

With a self-deprecating wince, the first sign that she felt anything but cartoon-like happiness, she stared at her utilitarian, brown sandals. "The other guys intimidate me. I mean, it's probably me. I'm not used to being around all these guys. None of them seem to own shirts. I don't know where to look."

I barked out a surprised laugh. "What's the point of shirts when you have muscles that need to be displayed? The travesty!"

"Exactly." She nodded with enthusiasm. "Anyways. August isn't like those other guys in the best possible way. He noticed that I was sitting by myself in a cabana yesterday, so he came over. He made me feel comfortable."

Jealousy pinched me at the notion that August might have interacted with Annie in the same calm, friendly manner as with me. Did he give her ice cubes and rub her back? That awful, *awful* guy, going around making women comfortable.

Whispering—irrational since I was still wearing a mic pack that picked up everything—I admitted, "I have dated a lot of guys, and guys like August are not the norm."

Gritting my teeth, I lied, "I hope you enjoy the date."

CHAPTER FIVE

~AUGUST~

ITM filming, Day 2, 11:30 a.m.:

Greta*: Wow, you got one of the first dates. A hike up the Gros Piton and a picnic. We managed to convince the tourist board to block off the entire trail for you and Annie today, so you can have privacy. Are you excited to go on the date with Annie?*

August*: Sure, she seems nice.*

Greta*: Nice is the kiss of death. How do you feel about Pietr taking Pippa on a date?*

August*: What does that have to do with my date? I don't care what Pippa does on the beach.*

Greta*: So you wouldn't have picked her if you had gone first?*

"Should I call for help?"

To my right, Annie shook her head. One hand clutched at her heart. Sweat trickled down her face and the back of her plain white shirt.

Worried about her erratic breathing, I turned toward Nate, the producer chaperoning us today. He had his hands over his knees, bent over, to catch his breath. Two crew members were half collapsed on the rocks, cameras forgotten by their sides. Another handler, Ben, stretched out his calves.

"Remind me to never go on another date you've planned," muttered Nate to Ben.

"Gros Piton was on a list of romantic things to do. See, the view." Ben flapped an arm toward the scene in front of us.

True to his words, the view in front of us was spectacular. I had researched St. Lucia before arriving on the island, but reading descriptions online was no match for experiencing it in person. The twin peak of Petit Piton lay to one side, the lush green of the mountain and the forest juxtaposed against the azure blue of the waters. Tiny white dots floated in the Jalousie Bay.

Almost half a mile up on the mountain, the clouds looked close enough to touch. Did exhilaration and wonder at being on top of the world propel Icarus to fly too close to the sun?

Ignoring the slight soreness in my legs, I grabbed a bottle of water from my backpack and handed it to Annie. She chugged half the bottle before letting out a sigh of relief.

A few feet from the edge, we stood in companionable silence. With her pale face rosy from the sun and the three-hour hike, and green eyes that glowed from happiness, Annie was beautiful. She was also sweet and kind. Any other time, any other place, I would have been eager to explore a relationship with her.

Yet, I felt nothing beyond platonic comfort around her. No matter how much I tried to muster interest on this date, my efforts failed.

Instead, my curiosity zeroed in on a red-haired, prickly firecracker. It didn't matter if Pippa had defined us as friends. It didn't matter if I *shouldn't* be interested in her. My thoughts flew to her, like the sailboats below returning to their harbor.

I could try to convince myself that my fascination with Pippa was due to her natural charisma or her beauty, but that shortchanged her. I could tell myself it was because she was a puzzle that I hadn't solved. Yet, that didn't explain why I was drawn to this particular puzzle.

No, there was something fundamental about her that triggered an Icarus-need to get closer. A wild fascination to see what would happen.

To tempt fate.

Just my luck, my siren was on a date with someone else.

"Did you imagine this is what could happen when you signed up for the show?" Annie's arms stretched out to indicate the postcard beauty.

When she beamed up at me, a prickle of unease floated through my brain. "Not this."

"I had two firsts today." She raised one finger. "One, hiking in a foreign country. I'm glad Pippa lent me this pair of shorts. It's much more comfortable than hiking in jeans or a skirt."

Before I could ask why she would ever hike in a skirt, Annie raised another finger. "Two, going on a date."

Her sentence ended with a giggle. The feeling of unease intensified. While my head wrapped around what to do, I tried to buy some time. "This is my first time out of the country. Look at us, two small-town people, like fish out of water on a dating show in the Caribbean."

"August, Annie." Recovered from the hike, Nate interrupted us. Behind him, the crew had picked up their cameras once again, the lenses pointed toward us. A few feet away, Ben spread out a picnic blanket on a patch of flat rock.

Even though we wore mics for the entire hike, the renewed activities of the production crew gave a visual reminder that we were on a show. Guessing from Nate's frown, small talk was not the type of entertainment the show was hoping to get from this date.

As suspected, Nate prodded, "Talk about something else. Why don't you ask each other about past relationships? Here, come with me. Sit on the picnic blanket."

A few minutes later, Nate had positioned us in a V shape on the blanket, facing more toward the camera than each other. In front of us lay a charcuterie board big enough to feed us in case we got stranded for a week.

That is, once we picked off the glue that held the food to the wooden board. To prevent things from falling over on the hike, Nate had explained. He had also warned us not to eat anything to avoid catching chewing sounds on the mic.

Next to me, Annie shifted, stealing glances at the cameras. Nate spun his fingers in the air. "Don't look at the cameras. Pretend we're not here. It's a romantic date. Act natural."

Turning, Annie stared at me and opened her mouth to talk.

"Turn your face more this way," directed Nate from behind the cameras. He pointed to a distant rock. "We want to see you on film. Okay, okay, now, pretend we're not here."

In front of glued food that we couldn't eat, turned in such a way that I couldn't see Annie's full expression, I choked down laughter at the absurdity of it all. From the side, Nate gestured toward us, mouthing, "C'mon. Past rela-tionships."

Shaking my head, I ignored Nate's gestures and said, "Annie, we don't have to talk about anything you're not comfortable with. I'm sure the others can stir up enough drama that they don't need footage of us."

"August!"

After a quick glance toward Nate's horrified expression before settling back on me, Annie shrugged. "No one that I know will watch this show. I-I think we should listen to Nate. Talking about past relationships seems like something normal people do on dates, right?"

Dates.

I was on unsteady ground if Annie perceived this as a real date. Why shouldn't she? I did ask her, and despite the audience, a picnic on top of a mountain was romantic. The idea of leading someone on while my thoughts were elsewhere didn't sit right.

"Annie—"

"I divorced my husband after he cheated on me with multiple women, sometimes multiple at a time."

As soon as the words left her mouth, Annie clamped both hands to shut herself up. Off to the side, Nate waved the cameras to zoom in closer.

"Are you sure you're comfortable talking about this on camera? Even if no one you know from *before* will see this, people you meet *after* this show will know." Shifting, I turned my body to shield her from view, a futile attempt to protect her since we still wore mics.

In slow motion, she dropped her hands away from her mouth. With a determined nod, she moved a few inches away from me, putting herself in full view of the cameras again. "I didn't plan on saying anything, but why not? I'm tired of feeling ashamed for something he did."

"I'm sorry. You don't deserve to be cheated on or made to feel ashamed," I said, unsure what to do. "How do you feel?"

"Amazing! As if two hundred pounds were literally lifted away. Is it petty that I enjoyed airing his dirty laundry on camera?" Giggles escaped from her before she stared at me, her expression somber again.

Forgetting Nate's rules about being in a V shape, she faced me. "I married at eighteen to someone who was well established in our community. In many ways, I was privileged. We had a nice house, and he gave me enough budget to run the house, buy nice clothes for myself, and give my parents extra to help them out. He was a good provider, but he wasn't kind, especially when others weren't watching."

"Did he ever hurt you?" I asked, anger rising.

Annie held out a hand to stop my thoughts. "No, not the way you're thinking. He said mean things but mostly left me alone. When the scandal came out, I felt sadness for the women he had tricked and relief for myself. I'm happy that I left and that I can meet people like you. I'm excited to get to know you more."

I was an ass for not clarifying before this date, or even sometime in the car ride over, or the three-hour hike, that my interests lay elsewhere. That this was a *friend*-date, not a real date.

"I—I… Annie, I don't think I'm the right person." I didn't want to be another piece of proof that assholes existed, especially not after her confession. But the alternative of pretending didn't sit right with me. "Here's a funny story. To my own surprise, I keep thinking about—"

"Pippa?"

"You know?"

"Of course." She beamed at me in approval. "It makes sense."

"It does? Because it makes no sense to me. You're not mad?" With relief, I let out a deep breath.

"Why should I—" She burst out in laughter. "You think I want to date you? Oh no! I don't mean to hurt your ego. I like you as a person, and I would love for us to be friends. You see, I don't have many friends. You'd be my first male friend whom I'm not related to."

Her eyes dimmed. "My ex-husband thought men and women couldn't be platonic friends. Now, looking back, I think he was projecting his inability to be friends with a woman without cheating with her. I would like to prove him wrong."

If I ever met this asshole ex-husband of hers, as her *friend*, I wanted to shove him up a tree. Instead, I promised, "Let's prove him wrong then."

Her lips trembled, before pursing them to steady herself. With determined optimism, she bounced up in her seat. "Enough about me! When are you going to make a move on Pippa?"

"Never." I picked up the champagne glass in front of me. It was the only item not glued to the picnic blanket. Chugging down the bubbly liquid, I squashed my disappointment. "It's best Pippa and I avoid each other on this show."

"Okay then, if you're not interested, I guess I shouldn't tell you." Her own champagne glass in hand, Annie tilted her head to examine it before sipping it. She winced at the taste and put the glass down again.

"What did she say?" Despite my earlier statement about avoiding Pippa, the question tumbled out before I could stop it.

"I thought you weren't pursuing her?"

"I don't know. I'm curious about her," I admitted. "Others are saying she's a spoiled socialite who breaks hearts." *Or they were all wrong, and the real Pippa was funny, intelligent, and feisty. And hadn't met the right man. Which was not me.*

"That's not true," Annie protested, shaking her head so her curls bounced. "We had some time before the dates started to hang out and get ready in our cottage. She got into the tabloids after dating an athlete. The rest is simply mean-spirited rumors. Don't let the other contestants' gossip get to you. Besides, Pippa's interested in you."

"What?" I tapped one ear to clear out any word-distortion syndrome caused by the altitude.

"When Mark was explaining the rules of the show, Pippa kept looking back at you," Annie shared.

"Maybe I had food on my face."

"She asked what you and I talked about last night at the welcome party."

"So? She could be nosy." That wasn't a sign to get more invested, either, despite the pleasure spreading through me.

"I talked with Beckett too. She didn't ask about our conversation."

So what if the thought of Pippa asking about me, just me, made me want to run down the Gros Piton? "Nosiness about each other doesn't mean that we'd work."

"Why not?" asked Annie.

The part that wanted to yank Pippa away from her date with Pietr repeated that question. *Why not? Why not try?*

The other part of me, the part that still remembered the past, kept me rooted. Even though it had been several years, Zara's breakup speech echoed in my head: *Your ideal world is too small for me. I don't want to try anymore. I want something more exciting.*

I thought of diverting this conversation. However, Annie had trusted me enough to share something serious about herself. Plus, I was ninety-seven percent sure that everything I said would end up on the cutting room floor, in favor of more dramatic moments from the other contestants. What was the harm?

On the plus side, speaking my reservations out loud might hold me to them. Or at least, that's what everyone said about New Year's resolutions.

"My last serious relationship was in college," I started, letting my mind drift back. "We dated my junior and senior year. We made plans. I'd go to graduate school for teaching, she'd work for a couple years in finance in New York, and then we'd get married. Settle down in a small town, start a family."

"What happened?" Annie asked.

"We graduated." I laughed, the sound bitter to my ears. "I didn't realize how much of a bubble college was. All the students lived on campus out in western Massachusetts, away from big cities. There, it didn't matter what your family did or your plans afterward. You still had to live in a small dorm with roommates, eat cafeteria food, and go to classes.

"After college, Zara moved to Manhattan while I stayed for grad school. She wanted to fit in with her new friends, who got bottle service at clubs on weekends. Meanwhile, I lived in semi-rural Massachusetts, working a construction job on the side to help pay for school for a future job that still wouldn't pay millions. She decided she didn't want me any longer."

Before Annie could chime in, I added, "She wasn't the only one. I've had others tell me that civilization ended where the T ends—that's the subway system in Boston. Or complain about how it's weird for an unmarried guy to choose to live in a small town instead of the city."

The pain of losing Zara had faded a long time ago, but the fear of it happening again lingered. How could it not, especially when it had been reinforced by a crappy dating history? I was still the same person, craving the close-knit fabric of my hometown, choosing to invest in my little corner of the world, instead of seeking something *bigger*.

Shaking her head again, Annie argued, "Pippa is not your ex or any of those women you've dated in the past, just as whoever I date in the future is not my ex. Knock on wood."

"Agreed. Pippa is her own person," I said.

Her own complex person. Too bright, too charismatic to be happy with a small piece of the world. I felt as if I were a kid again, on the precipice of releasing a rare butterfly that I had sheltered as a caterpillar. The same impending sense of sadness and loss taunted me.

"However, whatever the tabloids say about Pippa, she has admitted to a jet-setting life," I said. "She might find my life interesting or tolerable at first, but outside of this bubble, she would be bored. Or resent me for wasting her time. You see, a relationship with Pippa would be a complete nonstarter."

"You need a way to test your attraction so you don't have regrets." Annie wrinkled her nose, before a sly smile spread over her face. "Maybe you should remove the idea of a relationship from your head. What about a fling?"

CHAPTER SIX

~PIPPA~

ITM filming, Day 2, 12:15 p.m.:

Greta*: Let me grab you for an ITM before your date. How do you feel about Pietr asking you on one of the coveted dates?*

Pippa*: I guess, excited.*

Greta*: You guess… hm, what do you think of your fellow contestants?*

Pippa*: They seem fun. I don't know them well yet, except Aug—um, Annie. She seems nice. Peppy. Kind of like a Disney princess… but not. I can't put my fingers on it. I think the peppiness is just on the outside.*

Greta*: She seems to have caught the attention of August.*

Pippa*: Really? I hadn't noticed.*

In the lobby of the main resort building, Pietr waited in the middle of the cavernous room. He was undeniably conventionally handsome. I could understand why he had been so popular in the NFL despite his lack of plays.

Yet, I couldn't help but compare his brown eyes to… no one. *No one else.*

Wishing I had ignored Greta's directions and brought a cover-up for my two-piece, barely there, red bikini, I glided gingerly across the room in my heels. Pietr reached out to twirl me around. "Wow, Pippa, you look amazing!"

"Hi—"

"Let's do the entrance again," Greta called out, catching up behind me.

"Pippa, go back around the corner. This time, why don't you run and jump into Pietr's arms?"

"In my heels?" I asked, arching a brow.

In her comfortable sneakers, Greta nodded. "Yes, run enough that you can get some lift when Pietr picks you up. This is not the same as going to the dentist. This is your first date. Act excited!"

With a sigh, I strode out of the lobby. Turning around, I plastered a smile on my face as I walked back. On the periphery of the lobby, Greta made a sweeping motion. Hoping my bikini stayed in place, I picked up my feet to jog toward Pietr.

He waited until I was at arm's length before picking me up to spin me around. "Wow, Pippa, you look amazing!"

I stared in confusion at his repeated words. "Hi—"

"Wait, hold on," interrupted Greta again. "Let's try this one more time. Pippa, this time, try to jump into Pietr's arms. Hug and jump. Straddle him. Okay?"

Saying nothing, Pietr kept his hands in his pockets as he nodded along to Greta's instructions. Miffed, I strode out of the lobby.

Smile stuck on, I jogged back. If Greta wanted a hug and jump, then an epic hug and jump she would get. Damn if I had to redo this again.

At the sight of Pietr, I waved both hands in amped-up enthusiasm. I gathered speed close to him and leaped up into his arms, wrapping my legs around his waist.

"Wow, Pippa, you look amazing!" said Pietr, as he twirled me around.

Was he for real? Did he prepare one generic line for the date he was determined to get on camera? Glancing quickly at Greta to make sure she allowed me to continue, I said, "Thanks. I'm excited to see what we're doing today."

"Greta told me we're taking a limo to Jalousie Dock to go on a boat ride," said Pietr with more genuine enthusiasm than I had expected.

Wonder what August and Annie are going to do?

Hard nope. I shoved that thought away, in the same place as all the previous walks and jumps.

Maybe Pietr was just nervous earlier, I thought, focusing my attention on him. Or maybe he repeated the same phrase because Greta had instructed him. Catching on to his excitement about the boat ride, I let him hold my hand as we headed outside to the waiting limo.

"Pippa, Pietr," said Greta, who had followed us outside. "We'll go ahead in the van and meet you at the dock. You'll still be wired up for sound, but save any serious conversations until we get on the boat and get cameras on you again."

With a wave, she closed the limo door on us. Left in the silence of the car with just Pietr, I giggled awkwardly. He dragged his eyes from the deep vee of my swimsuit and smiled back.

"So," I started, "that was weird, right?"

"What was?" Pietr peeped at my chest again.

"You know, having to record a silly greeting three times." To annoy him since his inability to stare beyond my tits annoyed *me*, I swung my hair forward as a makeshift cover for my chest.

He stared at me, as if I had asked him to solve a calculus equation on the fly. "Why is that weird? It's important to get the right footage."

"It's supposed to be a *reality* show," I insisted.

"*A show*. The crew's just trying to make it entertaining. Don't you want the audience to be invested in our romance?" Pietr brushed some of his blond locks to the side, hiding a small bald spot that I hadn't noticed before. "We could be *the* power couple on this show. With our looks—whew, the world is our oyster. Think about the sponsorships we could get. What should our couple name be? I'm partial to Pietppa. Pipptr? Hm, maybe P and P?"

My earlier, so-brief-that-I-almost-forgot, moment of excitement about going on a date with Pietr plummeted. Like a gut punch, I knew the answer. Yet, I still heard myself asking, my words tumbling over each other in a rush to get out, "Why did you pick me? I thought you asked me on this date so we could get to know each other and see if there's a spark to explore further. Why me?"

Understanding dawned on him. He took my hands in his sweaty ones. "I see. You're wondering why I chose you when I could have chosen anyone on the beach? Have some confidence in yourself, Pippa."

"No." I tugged my hands free. "I'm not questioning *my* worth. I'm asking why you picked me for your grand scheme when we hadn't spoken more than a few words before today. The truth. Not the lies from earlier."

"Can't you just be excited about the boat ride? I've never been on a boat before." Pietr squirmed in his seat.

I shook my head. "No. I want to know."

"You're the hottest chick here, and you seemed like you enjoy a good time, if you know what I mean. Why not?"

Fuming on the inside at his sullen confession, I removed any emotion from my face or voice. "I don't know what you mean. You picked me because you wanted to fuck me?"

"Not just that. We'll get way more followers on social media as a couple. Plus, you get a vacation and free ring if you get engaged."

"You're thinking of getting engaged after two weeks?"

His eyebrows raised at my question, as if I were the ridiculous one. "It's not a real engagement. You just have to hang out, make some appearances, post a few photos online, and bam! You get to keep that ring and sell it. You heard Mark. The engagement rings are worth over a quarter mil."

"You'd get engaged for sex, a ring, and social media followers?" I clasped my hand under my chin to keep my jaw from falling off.

Sneering at me, Pietr said, "Not everyone has your money, princess. Unless you're the best or last a long time, even retired NFL players have to get jobs. Isn't that what the show is about anyways? It's hot people stuck on a beach, where the goal is to hookup and build a following. What else are we supposed to do?"

"We're supposed to find real connections," I argued.

Call me a contrarian. Sure, I realistically knew that hookups were more likely than love matches, but the more Pietr talked, the more I wanted to argue. If he thought this show was for hookups and money only, then I'd defend the show as the greatest matchmaker in TV history.

Shaking his head in disappointment, Pietr muttered, "I can't believe you believe in that shit. What a wasted date. You should feel lucky to be on this date with me. Good thing the crew's in a different car. Can you imagine how embarrassing this conversation would be for you if it aired on TV?"

I bit the insides of my mouth to keep from reminding him that our conversation was still being recorded and that *I* wouldn't be the one to look like the fool. He wasn't worth protecting.

If I didn't know that I was awesome, I might have cried. Except, some days, it was hard to hold on to my self-confidence. Some days, it was easy to believe others who said that I was less. That I was only good for what I could *give* to someone else.

Used for a fake engagement, for money.

Cheapened to a pretty body for short-term distractions.

Discarded when others saw no more value in keeping me around…

The limo pulled to a stop. The door opened, and Greta popped her head in. "You two haven't talked about anything serious or interesting, right?"

"Just small talk, like you asked. Right, Pippa?" Pietr shot a nervous glance at me.

"Nothing of worth." Chuckling with bitter mirth, I bit my tongue on the lie. "Come to think of it, I'm not feeling so good today. I might not be able to handle the rocking of a boat. Pietr can go without me."

Greta might be paid to believe this nonsense about finding love on a show, but she was no idiot. She glanced at the distance between us in the back of the limo and said, "Okay, okay. We can work around this. Pietr, we'll pull another girl to join you. Maybe Hailey, she said she was interested in you. She can come here with the intention to crash your date, but since Pippa is gone, she can console you. You can take Hailey on the boat."

"She's the swimsuit model, right?" Delighted at the plan, Pietr nodded with enthusiasm. "Yes, I think she'll do just fine."

Disgust appeared and disappeared on Greta's face faster than my interest in Pietr. Ignoring him, she instructed me, "Pippa, someone will take you home after you do an ITM talking about how sick you feel. Act sad, okay?"

Thirty minutes, five redos, and some fake tears and clutching my stomach later, I was finally allowed to leave. Greta packed me up with another handler in a small sedan back to our Sugar Beach resort. With a fifth of the contestants on dates, the rest had taken advantage of the downtime to nap in the cottages or cabanas scattered around the beach.

A few of the crew sat by the beach bar, eating a late lunch. Several examined their equipment underneath a cluster of palm trees. One climbed a ladder, checking one of the many "hidden" cameras stashed in bushes and trees around the resort. After only a couple of days with cameras and the crew everywhere, it was a weird feeling to arrive at a quiet beach with no one waving a camera in my face.

With nothing to do and no access to TV, internet, or books, I forced myself to unpack my suitcases. Annie had already folded her clothes in neat piles in the drawers and hung a single dress in the closet. Unless she kept a stash of clothes elsewhere, she didn't seem to have packed enough for two and a half weeks. On top of it, outside of the single floral dress, a couple pairs of jeans and four shirts and a toothbrush, there were no other personal belongings.

I hated the fact that my mind focused on this useless, mundane non-mystery.

I hated being alone, and I hated the thought that others would arrive back, excited about their dates. Even more, I couldn't get away from the ick that the non-date with Pietr had left me.

Talk about a dud. He couldn't even last a limo ride before dropping the facade.

Was August having a good time with Annie?

Unlike Pietr, I couldn't imagine August picking someone because of her fuckability or how she'd help him with his nonexistent social media followers. He probably genuinely thought Annie was interesting and wanted to get to know her more. The thought that they would return from some fabulous date, holding hands or giggling with secret joy, made me want to quit the show.

Not that I was interested in August. Not in *that* way.

It was only that I wanted company in my misery. Not that I wanted August or Annie to be sad.

It was only… fuck, I didn't know what I wanted. Just not Pietr, with the brown eyes that weren't the *right* shade of brown.

Tired of cleaning my suitcases, I ripped off my mic pack and headed down to the beach.

CHAPTER SEVEN

~PIPPA~

ITM filming, Day 2, 1 p.m.:

Greta: Okay, let's try again, Pippa. Look more in pain. Tell me what's happening.

Pippa: My stomach hurts. I don't think I can continue the date with Pietr.

Greta: Tell me how disappointed you are.

Pippa: I'm so sad.

Greta: You're a terrible liar. Fine. Are you worried about Pietr hitting it off with Hailey?

Pippa: Hell, no. She can have him.

Greta: Are you worried about August hitting it off with Annie?

Pippa: Why do you keep asking me about August? It's not as if I care. Why, did you hear something about their date? Where are they going?

Like some utter loser, I roamed the beach, wandering farther and farther out into the ocean until the waves lapped at my knees. I might have been on the shortest date in the history of *The Journey of Love*, but at least I would have toned calves from walking on the sandy beach. In the grand scheme of things, toned calves weren't a terrible consolation prize.

Halfway to toned calves, I stopped my aimless roaming, realizing that I had walked within sight of the resort again. On the beach in front of the cottages, I could see tiny figures moving around as the other contestants returned from their dates or woke up from naps.

Not wanting to face them, I turned to stare at the line separating the depths of the ocean from the sky. The sun started to dip into the horizon, its light bathing the ocean in hues of brilliant orange and yellow. The shifting colors touched the water where I stood, pulling and pushing the sand underneath my feet.

Funny how I couldn't remember the last time I had watched the sun set or rise. When was the last time I had enough time to stand still?

The splish-splash of water behind me perked up my ears. Without turning, I knew who it would be. Was it because I wished him here with me?

"Hey, are you okay, Pippa?"

August's voice bathed me in warmth. He must have seen me on the beach and come to check on me. Again.

Or maybe he had heard about my disaster of a date, and pity drove him here. Again.

Embarrassed, I didn't turn around, though I heard the swirls of the water as he came closer. "I don't know. How was your date?"

"Fine," he said, giving nothing away.

Fine as in, it sucked but redeemed by the nice scenery of the island? Or fine as in, it was amazing, but he didn't want to boast about it?

Burying my questions in the silence, we stood together in the cooling water. His body behind me cast a long shadow, shimmering in the water. He stood only a wingspan away.

Our feet rested in the water. Our bodies swayed with the push and pull of the waves. August didn't press, and I stayed quiet, locked into my frustrations, and fighting back questions about his date with Annie.

I kicked at the water hard enough to wet the ends of my long hair. Again to spray my face. Over and over again, until water coursed down my body, the coolness of the ocean just barely dulling my inner irritation.

Ignoring my mini tantrum, August spoke again, "Annie and I hiked up the Gros Piton. There's no—I don't—Annie and I are just friends, if you are curious."

I *wasn't* curious. The cheering inside of me meant nothing. It definitely didn't mean I cared about connections August was or wasn't making on the beach.

Liar.

Splish-splash. He was close enough behind me that the swirls created by his steps reached me. If I leaned back, he could have caught me. Instead, straightening my spine, I leaned away from him.

"How was your, um, date with Pietr?" August cleared his throat. "He came back with Hailey. Are you okay?"

Breathing hard, I kept my back to August. I didn't want to see or hear his pity. Yet, a part of me was too tired to care. After someone had fed you ice chips in the bathroom to calm your alcohol-rocking stomach, was there any lower you could sink?

"Pietr picked me because he thought I was hot and he could use me to make money. I overreacted. Silly to complain, right?"

"No," August said firmly, anger tinting his voice. "You're not foolish to expect more. Pietr is an ass for trying to use you."

Even though I didn't need August to fight my battles, warmth seeped into me at his incredulity. I turned around, ready to face him.

Except... I wasn't ready. I couldn't have prepared for the visceral way my body reacted to him. To how his brows furrowed in anger on my behalf, to the kindness radiating from his brown eyes. *The right shade of brown.*

"I don't understand. How would he make money from you?" he bristled.

Despite the warnings firing off within me, I couldn't stop my feet from stepping toward him. Did he not understand the turmoil within me, that I was one kind gesture away from throwing myself at him? Or burrowing myself against his chest... to gain a moment of rest?

That impulse was cheesy to the max. Instead, I responded, "Social media sponsorships. Parlaying this experience into gigs. Selling the ring. Have those not crossed your mind while on the show?"

"No. I wouldn't get engaged for a free ring, no matter how nice it is. When I ask someone to marry me, it'll be because I can't imagine a world without her." His eyes had darkened with unidentified intensity. What would it be like to be in a relationship with someone who felt this deeply? "And she wouldn't care that the ring isn't fancy."

As an afterthought, he added, "I don't have social media, remember?"

"I still think it's weirdly old-fashioned of you. It makes me question if you even have a phone or send messages via the telegram," I teased.

"Dear Miss Fleming, I'll have you know that I caved—stop—and got a cell phone when I turned eighteen. Stop."

That's how the world felt at that moment. *Stopped.*

I beamed up at August, watching him imitate typing a telegram. Hands in midair, he grinned down at me. He was undeniably a little weird.

And charming.

And quick-witted, but not at the expense of others, as so many jokes were.

And… if I listed any further, I might just realize that he wasn't the staid Boy Scout I had assumed earlier, but someone so beguiling that I'd let my walls down before I spotted the danger. Something was shifting or had already shifted within me. It was at that moment, against the background of the sun flaring with light right before it dipped into the ocean, I realized I might like him.

Just a smidge.

Without a word, August took off his baseball tee and draped it around my shoulders. His hands skimmed my arms and back, leaving a trail of sensations, as he adjusted the shirt around me to ward off the evening chill.

I drank in the solidness and kindness of him. Shirtless, August's naked chest contrasted with the incoming coldness and darkness, like a beacon calling me. I moved closer, drawn by his warmth and strength, until we stood inches away from each other.

Naked chests were the de facto uniforms for guys on this show, and I was no inexperienced virgin seeing scandalous skin for the first time. Still, the sight of August's chest sparked a thrill through me. His skin was made for touching, for lingering. Brown, curly hair on his chest tapered down to a trim waist, with hints of ab lines that begged me to explore him.

Because touching him felt more intimate than I could handle, I broke the silence. "I needed to sulk and throw a tantrum after a bad date, and the ocean is the only place they allow you to take off your mics before midnight. Why are you here instead of with the rest?"

"I wanted to make sure you were okay," August said after a pause.

"Why?" I asked. "There are dozens of people from production and the resort monitoring us, in case I get attacked by a rabid crab or revengeful jellyfish."

With a sigh, August shook his head in frustration. "Their job is to create a show with high ratings, even if it's at the expense of people. They're not thinking about how you're doing, only what drama they could get you to stir up. Or how to goad you into doing something for the sake of promos. I don't want—I want you to be okay."

"Why?" I asked again. I should leave his statement be, let it rest as a nice gesture from a kind man. But, after the mess of today, with Pietr's turnabout, I felt particularly ornery, and maybe a little scared of my attraction to him.

"What's it to you? Are you trying to look like a good guy in front of the cameras?"

"Looking after you isn't a performative gesture." Though his expression remained unreadable, he spoke with conviction.

After a minute, he muttered under his breath; the words carried to me by the ocean waves. "I don't know what it is about you that makes me want to protect you. Is it too much to believe that I might not like seeing you sad?"

His hands reached out to pull me closer by my shoulders, his fingers feathering along my skin. He was so focused on my face that I wasn't sure if he realized what he was doing.

On the receiving end, I was all too aware of how much I needed this moment to be real. How long had it been since someone cared about how I felt, not just how I made them feel?

Too intrigued and too tired to resist, my hands brushed against him. Feathery light explorations of his warm chest, of the gentle sloping and dipping of his chest and stomach, juxtaposed against the hardness of muscles underneath my fingers.

My breaths raced ahead, galloping even as my fingers moved leisurely over him, reveling in the uneven, raspy breaths torn from his chest. August dropped his hands from my shoulders to grasp my waist, his fingers imprinting on my skin.

Our breaths mingled together, excitement and desire bouncing off each other. He held me still—away from his body—even when his fingers tightened on my waist, the pressure heightening the pleasure.

In the course of today, I had been burned by one pretty face and his lies. There was every reason to feel trepidation.

Except, I could only feel yearning. The hint of danger flamed a primitive need that spun higher the longer we both fought it.

With a tortured groan, August flexed his hands on my waist. My heart sank. He was going to push me away.

I dredged through my brain for a joke to shield against my utter disappointment. Before I could open my mouth, August yanked me flush against the hard length of him. Both of us sucked in a breath at the shock of pleasure. My limbs lost any ability to hold themselves up as I sank against August's body.

Lips parted, I tipped my head up. In blatant offering. *Take me.* Forget why he was doing what he was doing. As long as he kept me with him until this wave of desire receded.

August bent toward me an imperceptible inch. Hunger blazed across his face. He bent another inch toward me, so close that his warm, minty breath caressed my skin in a promise of *more*.

My eyelids fluttered shut. Waiting.

Anticipating.

In a burst of movement, August wrapped his arms around me. At the same time, instead of kissing me senseless, he twisted his head to the side to fall toward my shoulder. Breathing hard, he growled against my hair, "You shouldn't welcome my advances. Tell me to go away."

The words should have been at the tip of my tongue. We were completely wrong for each other. He wanted a serious relationship. I wanted fun. Right?

Yet, even though we were complete opposites, I didn't want him to go away. Though I had only met August, he felt familiar. As if some deep part of me recognized him.

What the hell was I going to do about him?

"August, Pippa!"

At the sound of our names, we stumbled apart. Fifty feet away, Nate stood on the sand, yelling our names through a megaphone. He waved one arm toward the main cluster of palapas where the other contestants were partying under string lights. "Pippa, August, come on over!"

Laughing to hide my disappointment, I joked, "Saved by the bell. Let's go before—"

"Pippa, August!"

Nate had his megaphone in one hand, his flip-flops kicking up sand as he headed toward us on the beach. Careful to avoid the waves, with an inpatient frown, he called out, "C'mon, guys. You can't keep taking off your mics and running away. There's time to hookup later. You can even be the first couple to go to the private room."

Private room.

The one place on this resort without cameras. It was supposed to be where couples could go to talk, but everyone knew it was a meeting spot for banging. Blushing, I glanced at August, as he protested in vain, "No, Nate, it's not what you think."

Ignoring the protest, the smirk stayed on Nate's face as he continued to wave us over. Laughing, all traces of the dark hunger wiped, August returned to his usual friendliness. "C'mon, let's go before Nate calls security guards to carry us back."

He held out his hand toward me, his hair blowing in the breeze. He looked so carefree, yet so solid.

In contrast, I only felt turmoil. On one side lay possibility, an opening of *something* with August. But memories of failing so catastrophically with Pietr kept on intruding.

I had never had good luck with men. Why would anything change now? Exploring a relationship with August would only be a world of unknowns and places for me to stumble. It terrified me.

On the other side lay safety, a place for me to keep my distance while I figured out my attraction to August. Here, I could protect myself. You couldn't get hurt if you didn't put yourself out there, right?

Like a coward, I ignored August's outstretched hand. A frown replaced his smile, and his eyes cooled as he looked away. Shoulders straight, he strode back to the beach, leaving me behind in the water.

Damn, if I didn't feel like crying at the loss of something I never had.

CHAPTER EIGHT

~AUGUST~

ITM filming, Day 3, 8:47 a.m.:

Greta: *You went on a date with Annie. You also ran after Pippa twice, and both times, you spent a solid amount of time alone with her. Did you imagine that you'd be in the middle of a love triangle?*

August: *I'm not in a triangle. Annie and I are friends.*

Greta: *Oh, a love line with Pippa then?*

August: *No. I thought there could be something, but something happened. She retreated... it doesn't matter anymore. I mean, she matters... it doesn't matter how I feel.*

"Remind me how digging in the sand will show who's here for the right reasons?" I asked, thrusting my hands back into the mounds of sand in front of me.

Ten minutes ago, a six-foot-tall sandcastle stood at the edge of the beach. Now, with an influx of people digging around, searching for coveted keys, the sandcastle resembled the sandbox at my twin ten-month-old nephews' favorite playground.

An hour ago, Mark had gathered the contestants in the main gazebo to announce a challenge, with a special guest judge. Adding to the surrealism of the entire reality experience, one of my favorite comedians, Nico Manganiello, had entered to loud cheers. Nico had informed us that the challenge would be featured in a future episode of his show, *Talking with the Face*.

Now, Nico and Mark sat behind a makeshift anchor table with a colorful banner hung on the side—"Talking with the Face Love Challenge." Laughing, Mark yelled into his megaphone, "Who's going to get to the finish line first and win a coveted date? I see Pietr is still at the beginning trying to grab a crab."

"His ability to catch a football is only slightly better than his ability to capture crabs," chimed in Nico.

"At the second station, we have Otis still with the spicy tacos," Mark said.

"I can't tell if he's crying from the spice or crying because it's the first time he's eaten carbs. Don't worry," Nico shouted, waving at Otis to continue, "your abs will still be there! On the next part of the challenge, we have Jake and Annie still trying to ride their unicycles to the sandcastle. Have they never ridden a unicycle before? What kind of deprived childhood did they have?"

"Much safer ones," quipped Mark. Nico laughed, and the two hosts joked while they sipped on their cocktails.

Dressed in a blue polka-dot bikini top with tiny shorts that showed off her long legs, Pippa dug in the sand next to me. Since our almost-kiss last night in the ocean, she had ignored me as if I were the pox.

Ugly jealousy had reared up at how happy Pippa seemed while chatting with everyone else except me. Last night, after Nate had pulled us back to the beach, she had held court. Guys had interrupted each other to steal her away. She had even rewarded Pietr, with Hailey hanging off of him, with laughter at his weak jokes.

The misplaced sense of possession had shot up when my roommate, Garrett, a Chinese-American banker-turned-country-music-singer-hopeful, had pulled her away to a cabana to "get to know her." It didn't matter that they had picked a cabana in full view of everyone. Or that she had done nothing more than talk. Or that they were soon surrounded by more of her admirers.

The moment in the ocean had meant nothing to Pippa. The way her eyes had softened, the way she had leaned toward me and touched my chest—it meant nothing.

That realization was reinforced this morning. Once again, she talked with everyone else except me. The sandbox was small enough that I could hear her laughter. We were close enough that her avoidance of me could only be deliberate.

Frustrated, I shoved aside the last remaining tower of the sandcastle. A key glinted in the sunlight. Without thinking, I dove toward it.

Instead of cool metal, my hands clasped around warm skin. Pippa's face was inches away, her hand in mine. Her lips formed an O of surprise. My brain forgot that she had ignored me. Instead, it became frozen with pleasure at our proximity.

There was nothing and no one else in front of me except her. My vision tunneled to her face, to the way her eyes widened with awareness, before fluttering down, casting shadows on her reddening cheeks. To the light dusting of freckles in the middle of her straight nose. And to the glow of her skin, so soft that I dared not to touch.

Except, it was impossible for me to not touch. My thumb drifted over the delicate skin at her wrist, feeling her pulse jump. When her eyes lifted back to mine, the banked fire in them pulled me closer.

"Oy, Pippa's got one of the keys!"

At Garrett's excited exclamation, Pippa and I sprung back. She unfurled her hand to reveal one of the keys. Turning away from me, she jumped up with the key held high. The sparks that lingered between us crashed down, leaving me wanting more.

"What a turn of events!" boomed Nico over the megaphone. He stood up from behind the booth to see better. "Pippa's got one of only three keys hidden in the sandcastle. She's the first one to get to the last station. Oh, wait, Callie and Drew found the other two keys. For everyone else, you've been eliminated!"

Ignoring the chorus of disappointed groans from the contestants, Nico pointed to the final station with excitement. "Now, these three finalists have to face the spinning bat. That's right, Pippa, stop glaring at me, put your head on the bat, and spin twenty times. No cheating, folks. Mark and I finished kindergarten and know how to count to twenty."

With her red hair flying, Pippa spun around the bat like one of those swings at carnivals. When Nico yelled out, "Twenty," she threw the bat to one side to sprint toward the finish line.

Barely two steps in, she tumbled head over heels, rolling forward a few feet. Giggling, she hurled herself back up. Her arms stretched out like the wings of an airplane for stability. With the other two finalists, Callie and Drew, zigzagging behind her, Pippa wobble-ran toward the finish line.

Amazed, amused, and turned on, I cheered Pippa as she teetered like a drunk seagull across the flimsy banner at the finish line. A few seconds later, Callie and Drew tottered through the finish line before collapsing in a dizzy heap.

Firing confetti guns, Nico and Mark ran toward her, whooping with delight. As if an invisible barrier had been broken, the rest of us non-finalists rushed over to the finish line. Cheers exploded around me. I couldn't tell if people were genuinely happy for Pippa or relieved they didn't have to finish the obstacle course.

Outside of Mark, Nico, and the other two worn-out finalists, I was the first to reach Pippa. Hair strewn all over her face, sprawled on the sand, she called out, "Help me get up."

Not caring whether she thought I was someone else, I grabbed her hands, lifting her up. Pippa was covered with confetti, sand, and the streamers from the finish line. Her tangled hair blew like kite strings across her face. Guileless, joyful, she pushed the mischievous strands away, laughing when they came whipping back around.

Something primitive within me reacted to her. Not so much physical hunger for her as soul-stirring, emotional longing for this woman. All-consuming craving for more of her infectious sunshine.

She stared back at me, with her brows furrowed in question. Before she could ask, Garrett rushed in between us, swinging her around in an excited hug.

Stepping back, I walked a few feet away from the crowd surrounding Pippa. Half listening, I caught a few snatches of the boisterous chatter on the challenges from my fellow contestants, eager to share their thoughts and jokes now that the challenges were behind us.

"You let her win," said Nico, coming to stand next to me. "Don't deny it, you let her take the key. And, you kept peeking at her during the entire challenge. You like her."

When I woke up this morning, if you gave me a hundred guesses, I wouldn't have believed that Nico Manganiello would walk onto the beach. Now, for him to ask about my lack of dating life… it was so surreal that it was absurd.

My eyes still stuck on Pippa in the distance, I answered, "It's hard not to like her. She surprises me. Just when I think she's one way, she shows me another side to her."

"Yet, you look sad instead of happy that you found someone who fascinates you," mused Nico. One hand reached behind him to turn off his mic.

"I thought we'd shared a moment last night, but she's barely said a word to me since." Bitterness rose up at the back of my throat. "In two weeks, we won't see each other again, so what's the point?"

"Who says you can't make it work outside of the beach?"

"Have you met her?" My words came out harsher than I expected. Couldn't he see how different Pippa and I were?

Instead of taking offense, Nico laughed, drawing the admiring gazes of some of the contestants. "Yes. Earlier, we had a nice talk."

"Then you know she's way out of my league," I said.

When Nico stayed silent, I expanded, "I'm the odd duck out on this show. She's… she's her."

"Here's a story for you. Once upon a time, there was a boy. Let's call him Boy A. There was a girl, Girl A. They met as kids. Boy A fell in love with Girl A but didn't think he was good enough. Plus, some… circumstances. Boy A left to chase his dreams. I'd like to think that Boy A did okay for himself. But you know what?"

"What?" I asked, wondering where this hypothetical story was going.

"Even though Boy A met lots of other girls—B, C, D, E, etc.—and eventually led a glamorous life, he never forgot Girl A. It wasn't that Girl A was the most beautiful girl or would fit the best in his life or help his career the most or whatever. Our boy here couldn't forget her, because she was the only person who ever felt like home to him. Who knows why, when there are eight billion other people? For some reason, Girl A was our boy's safe haven, where he could be himself."

His expression softening, Nico glanced down at his left hand. For the first time, I noticed the ring on his finger and searched my memories until it landed on a prior episode of his show, when a blond woman had proposed in her underwear. At the time, I had assumed it was a joke, a pre-planned skit…

"Congratulations, it sounds like Boy A and Girl A lived happily ever after in your case," I said.

"I'd like to think so." Nico nodded. "Is it possible that Pippa doesn't need a male replica of herself? Maybe she needs someone to feel safe around, who appreciates every facet of her. Maybe she needs someone to feel like home, just the way Elizabeth has been my home. Is that not worth the possibility of heartbreak? As for her ignoring you, is it possible that she's equally scared and confused? Elizabeth wasn't my biggest fan for a long time. Think about it."

Without waiting for my response, Nico winked at me and turned his mic back on before walking back into the crowd. He raised Pippa's arm in the air. "Ladies and gentlemen, let me present you the winner of the coveted date, Pippa Fleming! Unicycle riding, spicy food eating, sand digging, bat spinning extraordinaire! Which lucky person are you going to whisk away on a date? I heard you might even get AC."

Even though I knew she wasn't going to say my name, a sliver of hope snuck in. If Nico was right that she might be interested in me, then a date was the best chance for us to get to know each other.

Sneaking a peek in my direction, she flushed. Tearing her eyes away, she announced, "Garrett."

With a holler, Garrett leaned down to kiss Pippa's cheeks. His dark hair lay against the warm sunshine red of hers. They looked good together. Jealousy fisted within me, followed by sadness.

One of the handlers ushered them up the steps to the cottages to change. With them gone, the crowd started to spread out. A few feet away, Nico glanced over at me, tilting his head toward Garrett's and Pippa's retreating backs. What did he expect me to do? Knock Garrett out so he couldn't go on the date with Pippa?

I shook my head, glaring at Nico. He mouthed something. I shook my head again.

Who knew one of the biggest comedians liked to play matchmaker? It was too bad that he had misread the situation between Pippa and me. For a moment, his story had given me hope.

"Hey, August," Annie said, coming over to stand next to me. "Are you okay about…" She waved toward the cottages. "They could have a terrible time. Not that I'd wish a boring time on Pippa. Maybe just an okay time."

I laughed at her attempt to cheer me up. Noting her anxious expression, I said, "Don't worry about me. How do you feel after the challenges?"

"A little embarrassed that I did so poorly," she started, wrinkling her nose. "Do you think we should help clean up? There's a giant mess on the beach from the challenges. I know there's a crew to take down everything, but messes bother me."

"Why not?" I said, glad for some distraction, even if it meant cleaning up confetti on the beach. "It's not as if either of us has a date to prepare for."

CHAPTER NINE

~PIPPA~

ITM filming, Day 3, 2:20 p.m.:

Greta: *Interesting choice to pick Garrett for the date. What do you like about him?*

Pippa: *He seems like a fun guy. He's very sophisticated and well traveled. The jingles he plays are amusing.*

Greta: *I'm surprised you didn't pick August.*

Pippa: *Why would I pick him? Did he say something?*

Greta: *Are you serious? You've disappeared multiple times with him and taken off your mics. When the other contestants disappear, they're usually having a... private party.*

Pippa: *No, it's not like that at all. I don't—never mind.*

Greta: *Did something happen?*

Pippa: *No.*

Greta: *Pippa, what happened?*

Pippa: *I don't know. It's just that guys like Pietr or Garrett feel familiar. I don't know what to do with a guy like August.*

With a final glance at the mirror, I headed back down the steps toward the beach. It had only taken a few minutes to decide on a simple white sundress, but forty-five minutes to tease out the glitter and confetti from my hair. And another fifteen minutes to drum up excitement for the date with Garrett.

There was nothing objectively wrong with Garrett. In fact, he was quite perfect: impeccable education, successful career as a banker, great singer, supportive during the challenges, articulate, witty. He had been born in Hong Kong and had traveled to all seven continents, including an epic trip to Antarctica in business school while carrying a penguin costume.

Since he had already accomplished so much, he had told me that he was on bucket list number four after finishing everything off prior lists. Skydiving, bungee jumping, playing poker in Vegas, dancing to the moon in Thailand's Koh Pha Ngan, skiing at night in Aspen, sailing off of Tahiti—Garrett was a walking, talking hot mix of cool adventures.

Unlike *someone else*, Garrett took the initiative to seek me out.

However, the sand and sun had whacked my good senses upside down. For, instead of being smitten with Garrett, my mind stubbornly drifted to someone else who was so different from the guys I'd dated in the past.

Someone who made me feel safe enough to open up and be myself. Someone kind and even-keeled—

A few yards away from the main part of the beach and bar, I stopped in my tracks. That even-keeled guy that I was most definitely *not* wishing I was going on a date with was shirtless, in the middle of a crowd, engaged in a shouting match with Garrett.

Or rather, Garrett was shouting at August, while August tried to ignore him. I shook my head just in case I was suffering through the side effects of spinning around a bat.

Nope, August and Garrett still circled each other while the other contestants watched. Instead of defusing the situation, the production crew pointed their cameras and extended their boom mic toward the escalation.

Too far for me to hear, August said something that set off Garrett. August turned to walk away. When Garrett raised one arm to swing at August, I unfroze to fly down the steps.

The production crew tailed me. I threw up my hands in a futile attempt to hide from the cameras. In the crowd, I couldn't see what was happening with August and Garrett. I could only hear the discordant shouting and surging crowd circling me.

Was August okay after the punch? Damn Garrett for listing black belt on his bucket list. Double damn him for boasting that he had crossed that off his list last year.

Shoving aside two crew members who did nothing except continue filming, I burst into the edge of the clearing. August and Garrett stood in the middle, facing off. Relief washed over me at the sight of August still standing, with bones intact.

Garrett threw out a jab, which August blocked easily. August called out, "C'mon, man, I don't want to fight you. Just tell her the truth."

He blocked another punch, knocking Garrett's arm away. "Why don't you take a swim and cool off?"

Foolish, dear man. I almost laughed at August telling the red-faced, not-calm Garrett to chill out. August's attempts to defuse the situation only served to piss off Garrett. Yelling like a William Wallace follower in *Braveheart*, Garrett charged toward August.

Without thinking, I made my decision and raced into the midst.

Toward August.

Eyes widening at the sight of me, August pushed me behind him. Garrett, who noticed me too late, came barreling toward us, tumbling all three of us onto the sand, with me as the bottom layer.

My first thought was that, if not for the public nature of this situation, I wouldn't mind lying under the weight of a shirtless August.

My second thought, which might have been my *first* if my body hadn't thrown all of its wits out the door at the touch of August's naked chest, was that my earlier efforts to dust sand off were moot.

My third thought, which *should* have been my *real first* thought if my brain hadn't been fried by the Caribbean sun, was that the fighting had stopped.

Somewhere half buried in my brain was the real question. Why did I run to August instead of the guy I chose for a date?

Apologizing profusely, August and Garrett scrambled off me. Both extended their hands to help me get up.

I batted their hands away. With a flourish, I got up myself.

"What the hell got into you two?" I demanded, frowning at both of them.

August said nothing. Even as I stared at him, he resisted my mental-persuasion glare. In contrast, Garrett twisted his lips in his signature megawatt smile that had been attractive until he swung at August behind his back.

"Don't worry, Pippa, it was nothing. Some guys don't handle jealousy well," he said in a too-loud, too-jovial voice. He looked pointedly at August, whose jaw clenched tighter.

"Really?" I asked, surprised. If August hadn't even approached me last night after the moment in the ocean, lashing out today because he was jealous seemed… improbable.

Garrett nodded. "Yeah, I don't know if he was upset that he didn't win or upset that we're going on a date, but that dude was nuts, making up stupid shit. You should have heard the accusations that he was throwing out."

"Oh, like what?" I asked, trying not to look too curious.

"That I wasn't here for the right reasons, that I wasn't into you. He's the one not here for the right reasons," Garrett said with a smirk. "He's tired of being a teacher and wants a free vacation on the beach. Or wants to be an influencer. You should stay away from that loser."

"You're covering up. You know that's not true," August protested. He stepped toward Garrett.

I cut in front of August to avoid another tussle, laying a hand on his tense arm. I shouldn't have worried. Even as he bristled under my palm, he held all that coiled energy in check.

Noting where my hand was, Garrett scoffed. "Pippa, you can't be serious. Are you taking this nobody's side? He's the one using you—"

"No, you're lying!" cried out a voice. Annie marched up. Her petite body shook with emotion, determination, and maybe fear. "After Nico left, August and I overheard you saying you wanted to leave your job to be a full-time singer. You told Pietr that Pippa could get her friend Ashton James to get you a music deal."

I stared at Annie, who blushed furiously like a tomato, and August, who stared at the ocean, as if detached from this whole situation. Then I swiveled to face Garrett, who blustered about trying to convince some of the other contestants to come to his defense.

No one did.

Someone even chimed in from the back of the crowd, "I heard Garrett asking people for their follower counts and engagement rates while we were playing beer pong last night."

For some reason, the image of Garrett casually dropping questions about social media analytics while lobbing ping-pong balls at red Solo cups cracked me up. Laughter bubbled up. Did he have a secret Excel sheet calculating present-time values for each partner he evaluated?

"How did you know I was friends with Ashton?" I asked.

Glancing around at the angry crowd and the cameras, Garrett admitted, "The cast list was released right when we got to the resort. The resort lobby had a newspaper article describing everyone. It had a photo of you and Ashton."

A second image of Garrett sneaking a newspaper article behind a potted plant broke the dam of laughter within me.

"You flirted with me last night and stuck around me during the challenges because of my friend?" My voice cracked with mirth.

Another image floated through my mind, of Garrett dressed in a blazer looking pensively out of his window, strumming his guitar. Fake Garrett in my imagination was way better than the real asshole.

Hiccups punctuated my giggles—*giggle, hiccup, giggle, hiccup*. August placed a hand on the small of my back, rubbing soothing circles.

"I was interested in you," Garrett said, his eyes defiant. "It wasn't all an act. You have to believe me, Pippa."

Damn, if he wasn't somewhat believable. If he hadn't glanced at the cameras to make sure they caught his words, I might have forgiven him.

"On second thought, I'm uninviting you on my date." Straightening to maximize my five-foot-nine-inch height, I tilted my head back to glare at him. "I don't think you're a good look for *my* image. I'm taking August on the date instead. Go on, Garrett, I'm bored with you."

With a confused, stunned expression, Garrett froze until Pietr grabbed him, yanking him away. I thought I heard Pietr mutter, "Let's find you someone better."

The crowd dissipated around us. The production crew followed them, pulling a few to the side to get their reactions in ITMs. I was pretty sure after the fiasco with Pietr and now the much more public fiasco with Garrett, my fellow contestants thought I was an ice-princess, reputation-ruining, bad luck charm to stay away from.

I should start buttering up the producers to ensure that my edit turned out okay. I should… but my heart wouldn't be in it. Plus, was it that bad if my villain edit on TV served as a warning to other assholes to check their fuckboy ways before approaching me?

With the beach cleared up, only August and Annie remained by my side. What an unexpected motley crew I found myself in. And I wouldn't change it for all the confetti on the beach.

"C'mon, August," I said, breaking the silence, "you have a date to get ready for."

"You're serious? I thought that was for show." He waved in the direction of the still-fuming Garrett.

Nerves fluttered in my stomach. Why should August bail me out? I had gone out of my way to ignore him since our… moment in the water. Except now, in broad daylight, I couldn't remember why I had been so scared of my feelings last night. I was an adult, fully in control of my emotions. We could hang out as friends on a date, right?

Giving him my most winsome smile, I answered, "Yes, you. Turns out, I'm not in the mood for bankers-turned-country-musicians today. Don't worry, I'm not using you for your lack of social media or your high school teacher uniform of khakis and button-down shirts."

Looping his thumbs in the front pockets of his jeans, August laughed. "That never crossed my mind. No one has ever been attracted to high school teacher uniforms, and I should know since I teach history. Though, I must admit my discounts are pretty good at Target. Who could resist that?"

"If you say so. I've never been to a Target."

"What?" August exclaimed.

"Haven't you seen their one-dollar or three-dollar bins at the front? They have great, cheap options for decorations or toys," chimed in Annie.

I shook my head, trying to hide my discomfort. "Is it weird that I haven't been inside? I've heard about Target, of course. Their private brands, like Cat & Jack, are the fastest growing part of their business."

"You must be the only person I know who has never visited the store but has read up on their investor reports." August grinned, shaking his head in disbelief.

"Not investor reports, *Wall Street Journal*. It's not that weird." I shrugged again. What was wrong with my shoulders? "My mom got me a subscription when I turned eighteen. It's on auto-renew. What are you laughing about?"

"Nothing. I better go get ready. I have to go find a business journal to read, so we have something to talk about on our date. Should I search for it in the same place that Garrett found his tabloid?"

Without waiting for my answer, laughing, August turned around to walk slowly back to the cottages. When he passed by Annie, he patted her on the shoulder. "Thank you for standing up for me. I know it wasn't easy." Then, he jogged back toward the steps that led up to the cottages.

"I'm sorry I interfered."

"Hm?" I asked, distracted by the sight of August running shirtless across the beach.

Annie started again, "I'm sorry I interfered. I just couldn't stand that Garrett was lying to you. I hate liars."

Startled at her vehemence, I hugged her. "Thank you, I appreciate it. You're a good friend."

"Really?" She stilled. Awkwardly, she patted me on my back, as she sniffed. "No one's ever said that before."

"What?" I stepped back.

Avoiding my gaze, she kicked at the sand beneath her feet. Whatever was in her past, she wasn't ready to share with me. Why should she? We had only known each other for three days, and we hadn't officially met until the second day.

Was it only three days? The lack of phones and the internet messed with my internal clock.

"You must have known some terrible people in the past," I half-joked. "If you're ever in the Boston area after this show, you have to let me know. When we're in the same place, my best friend, Tia, and I try to get together on Saturdays for boozy tea and to paint. I'll even let you in on a secret. The painting is just a disguise to hang out—venting, gossiping, plotting diabolical revenge—you know, all the important things in life."

With her fairy glow coming back, Annie nodded. "I'm quite good at painting. For a period of time, I thought I wanted to be an interior designer or create art. Unfortunately, you know, that requires training, and training needs money."

"If you ever decide to pursue it, I'm all ears. First, tell me, what happened to August's shirt?" I looped my arm around her elbow, prodding us toward the steps.

"He had confetti on it, so he took it off. I thought you weren't interested?"

"Hmm, it's hard not to notice when his abs are in my face. Or rather, when I was squished under his naked chest. I had no choice but to notice."

"Sure." Annie smirked with barely suppressed laughter.

"Don't tell him I said 'naked' when talking about him. Wow, it's hot today." I flapped my hands like fans in front of my face. "Anyways, you have to help me decide on an outfit to wear. I seem to have torn part of my dress in the scuffle. Let's hope that I make it on to a date this time and experience the coveted AC they keep touting for dates. It better be some damn champagne-level AC for all this trouble that I keep getting myself into."

CHAPTER TEN

~AUGUST~

ITM filming, Day 3, 3:45 p.m.:

    Greta: *Tell us about the fight with Garrett.*

    August: *What's there to tell? You caught it on film.*

    Greta: *We want to hear it from you. Garrett told Pietr that he hoped that Pippa would introduce him to Ashton James, to help his music career. Why did you decide to call Garrett out?*

    August: *I don't know.*

    Greta: *You told me before that you're not interested in Pippa. You could have ignored Garrett.*

    August: *Sure.*

    Greta: *C'mon, give us something, August. How do you feel about taking Garrett's place on the date with Pippa?*

    August: *I'd rather be picked first.*

    Greta: *Ah, now we're getting somewhere.*

The helicopter zoomed over the lush green treetops of the rainforest before turning to reveal the expanse of shimmering ocean. The water glowed from the sun. The light added to the richness of the blues and deep greens of the ocean.

The ocean curved around the land, carving out small beaches and bays, harbors for small white boats and swimmers. Colorful homes nestled together in small villages, with larger resorts sprawled nearby, all connected by windy roads. Ever present, the Petit and Gros Pitons jutted out to form the end posts, as the land in between sloped down to form a valley. For a small island, St. Lucia had something for everyone: ocean and sandy beaches for those trying to escape the heat, famous mountains for the adventurous, rainforest for the explorers, and cities for day trips.

On yesterday's hiking date, I had caught a glimpse of the island. But no amount of preparation could compare with experiencing this all with Pippa by my side.

I unstuck my forehead from the heavy windows of the helicopter and turned toward Pippa. "This is awesome!"

Away from the other contestants, away from the earlier drama, Pippa relaxed, her body slouching in the seat. At this moment, it didn't matter that she had ignored me last night or that I wasn't her first choice. I was already under her spell.

Because it was the most natural thing in the world, I reached over to squeeze her hand. Whether she was caught up in the moment too or felt the pull between us, her fingers twisted until they linked with mine.

Palm to palm. Fingers wrapped around each other.

My thumb brushed against the soft valley between her thumb and pointer finger. Her lips parted in surprise. Her deep intake of breath brought her closer to me.

The helicopter bumped in the air, throwing both of us back. I missed her hand in mine.

Swaying back and forth, the helicopter started its descent to land in a field of rock overlays with some sparse grass. The rocks gave way to pools of mud and separate pools of water, while steam blew low on the ground.

Once on the ground, with the noise of the helicopter dying down, I yanked off my protective earmuffs. In a much gentler gesture, I removed Pippa's. My fingers lingered to brush her hair back behind her ears.

"That was awesome, wasn't it?" I yelled again, before realizing that I didn't have to. Lowering my voice to a normal volume, I continued, "Wow, you're so low in the helicopter. To fly right above the tree lines and be close enough to see the ocean waves from up top… thank you, Pippa."

Blushing, she waved my thank-you away. "You should thank the producers for planning this. I just showed up."

"More than showed up." I grinned. "You beat everyone else at the challenges to win this. Who knew you would be so multitalented?"

"What can I say? I'm competitive and hope for the best."

"I aim not to disappoint then."

At that moment, Greta opened the helicopter door. The stench of rotten eggs from the nearby rocks and steam poured in.

"Hey guys, come on down," she called. "Don't worry, the sulfur smell from the hot springs is particularly bad here, but the mud bath area smells fine. We'll shoot you two introducing Sulphur Springs, and then we have a couple activities set up. Follow me, but stay a few feet away so the cameras can get you two walking alone."

Pippa and I nodded. I jumped down from the helicopter first. Craving an excuse to touch her, I lifted her and swung her down. Following Greta, I held on to Pippa's hand as we made our way across the rocks to a screened area.

Similar to the Gros Piton hike, the producers must have worked out a deal to make sure we were the only ones here. With no other tourists in sight, Pippa and I became the focal point for the production crew who trailed after us.

"Go on in, get into your bathing suits." By the screened area, held up by colorful cloths draped from poles, Greta waved us inside.

The six-by-three-foot makeshift changing room had no additional dividers. Blushing, Pippa turned away from me. Though I had seen her in swimsuits before, watching her disrobe felt too intimate, too intrusive. Mimicking her, I turned around and yanked off my shirt and shorts, leaving me in blue and white striped swim trunks.

Even with my back to her, I could hear her pull off her shorts and shirt. Movements, followed by the sound of the zipper coming down. The swoosh of fabric falling to the floor. Closing my eyes, I fought against the image of soft cotton caressing her skin. Did she bend down to grab her clothes from the floor?

I cleared my throat. "Ready?"

I didn't know if the question was for Pippa or for me. Bracing, I turned around and bit my tongue at the sight of her tiny white bikini. I was ridiculous. For the past three days, I had seen her in various swimsuits. She shouldn't have affected me this much.

Yet, there was something thrilling, dark, knowing that she had disrobed for a date with *me*. If she noticed my tongue-tiedness, she didn't comment. Instead, she seemed fixated on my chest. For my own preservation, I shifted my hands to cover the front of my trunks.

Way to be not obvious.

Before I could do something too scandalous for even a reality TV show, I pulled open the cloth screen and headed out. It took reciting the entire Red Sox lineup twice before I was appropriate.

Once outside, one of the handlers checked our mics again before Greta prompted us to talk about the Sulphur Springs. Speaking quicker than normal, Pippa rattled off facts about geothermal energy and volcanic eruptions. Words tumbled over each other in eagerness to get out.

I had never heard half the things she mentioned, but still, I couldn't help but be impressed. When had geology become so sexy? If she kept talking, volcanic eruptions wouldn't be limited to just… okay, terrible joke.

At my grin, Pippa's words slowed. When she stayed silent, Greta jumped in with prompts about our helicopter ride and weren't mud springs the perfect place to explore love? Though Greta threw more questions at both of us, Pippa kept her mouth shut, while I covered the awkwardness with bland responses.

"Okay, that's good for now," said Greta during a lull. "We set up an area next to the mud baths with champagne and chocolate strawberries for you to enjoy. Talk. Flirt. Pretend we're not here. Stay away from dissertations on rocks, okay?"

Like dutiful soldiers, Pippa and I headed down the steps into a shallow, rectangular pool of gray mud. Despite the heat of the Caribbean sun, the mud was at least ten degrees cooler.

Waist-deep in mud, on one edge of the pool with Pippa on the other side, I asked, "What was that about?"

"What was what?"

"The abrupt freeze back there. Don't leave me hanging. What was the conclusion of the paper you had read about soil richness?"

Pippa's head snapped up. "Are you making fun of me? I read a lot. It's not weird."

"No, why would I make fun of you? Half my job is convincing my students to read."

"Oh, well… sometimes, people get thrown off…"

For a minute, I said nothing, my mind cataloguing the prompt shutdown earlier, and how she barely spoke about her career on the beach. Suspicion rose.

"Who told you to hide your intelligence?" I guessed.

"It was a long time ago," she said, waving a hand in dismissal.

"Sometimes people try to make themselves feel superior by putting others down. No one should ever make you doubt yourself. You're—" I stopped before I revealed anything further.

"What?" she prompted.

Before I could reply, Greta ran over, a frown in place. "Pippa, August, as lovely as this conversation is, it's a bit… not so exciting. Why don't you talk about volcanoes and dirt on the ride home? Right now, try giving each other massages. Maybe rub some mud on each other? It's supposed to have health benefits."

With a flourish of her hands for us to proceed, Greta ran back. Half behind a bush, she waved at us again, this time miming a back massage.

Ignoring Greta, I asked, not able to wait any longer, "Why did you pick me for this date?"

"Why not?" Pippa countered.

"Even without Pietr and Garrett, there are others who would be ecstatic to be here with you. Others whom you haven't been avoiding. Why me?"

A shadow crossed her face. She slanted her head to study me. "You could have turned me down if you didn't want to be here. I wouldn't throw a hissy fit if you said no."

"I do—" I paused, unsure how much to reveal, unsure where this would take us. "I do want to be here. More than anything. But I don't want to be the last resort."

"You're not." She paused for a moment before adding, "You didn't have to fight Garrett for me. I don't want you to get in trouble with your school."

"Don't worry about it. I can explain if any parents or administrators have concerns."

"I haven't been very nice to you." A flush crept up her cheeks. She refused to meet my eyes. "I'm sorry for ignoring you last night. It's just that… I got a little scared."

"Scared of me?" My pulse picked up, hating the idea.

"Not in that way." Blowing out a loud breath, she studied her nails. "I'm scared of how I feel about you. You're so different from other guys I've met."

"Is that bad?"

"I don't know yet."

"I would never hurt you," I promised.

"Not on purpose, but this"—she waved a hand in between us—"could lead to something where you have the power to hurt me. I don't want to be vulnerable if all you think of me is a pity project or some amusing entertainment."

My legs carried me through the heavy mud until I stood in front of her. I tilted her face toward me. "*Nothing* I do with you is out of pity. Foolishness maybe. I feel so many things for you, but pity has never been one of them. I'm here because I want to be around you, because I can't stop thinking about you. Because the thought of you going on another date with someone else brings out jealousy that I didn't know I could feel."

Her breathing raspy, Pippa covered my hands with her mud-stained ones. Whether to keep me there, or pull me off, I didn't know.

"I'm scared of what I'm starting to feel for you, too. I want to be around you all the time. Even when you ignored me last night, all I wanted was to find you and steal you away," I continued.

"You don't have to pretend or rewrite history." She shook her head.

"I'm not. I had ordered some fries to tempt you away from your admirers when you came to the bar and grabbed Beckett instead."

"Oh."

I thought back to the bar scene. How Pippa popped up on my right as I waited with Annie for the fries. How Pippa had frozen and then turned to grab Beckett.

Realization jolted through me. "You know that Annie is just a friend? I meant it when I said Annie and I had a platonic date. What I feel for you is *not* friend-like."

I commanded, my voice dipping deep, "Come here."

Eyes widened, Pippa stepped forward until our bodies touched, the motion bringing the tips of her breasts against my bare chest. Every breath that we sucked in became a teasing caress.

I was grateful for the mud to hide the tent in my swim trunks. However, the mud did nothing to decrease the desperation that seized me, or the light-headedness from my blood rushing down there. Demanding, hungry for her.

Wordlessly, I slid my hands down her neck to rest above her hips. With more control than I felt, I turned her to face away from me before pulling her closer. This close, there was no way she couldn't feel what she did to me.

How easy it would be to bend her forward, to press into her. Tease *her*. Tease *us*, until we caved into this storm brewing between us. She was temptation incarnate.

Letting out a shaky breath, I dropped my hands. Pippa swayed, and my hands flew to her waist to steady her. My fingers grazed the bare skin not covered by her bikini.

"Would you like a massage?"

CHAPTER ELEVEN

~PIPPA~

ITM filming, Day 3, 3:50 p.m.:

Greta: *Third time is the charm, right? Hopefully today is the day you actually go on a date. We have a very exciting date planned. How do you feel about the switcheroo?*

Pippa: *Honestly, good. With Garrett, I felt as if I had to compete with him and his bucket lists. Like, he would say he climbed the Grand Teton, and I had to say something similarly impressive.*

Greta: *Not with August? You don't want to impress him?*

Pippa: *Hm, it's different. I mean, I just want him to be impressed with regular me. That's scary, right? What if he doesn't like regular me?*

"Would you like a massage?"

My body jumped at the strum of his words, but I was held in place by his hands on my waist. Each breath felt wrenching, each second closer to some invisible cliff.

I nodded, even though what I wanted was… more.

I wanted to beg for something else. Hell, I'd take a massage… somewhere lower and needier, somewhere strung tighter. I clenched against the wave of desire, little shocks of electricity coursing through me.

August's hands moved up to my shoulders. His strong fingers kneaded tension I didn't realize I carried, nerves that I didn't know existed. I had never contemplated my shoulders before this moment, beyond a connector for my arms.

The dichotomy of strength and gentleness in his touch as he explored spots of stiffness were heady revelations. How had I never realized how erotic shoulders were? The joke was on me.

Wanting more, I stepped back toward August. With his hardness pressed against me fully, I froze. His hands on my shoulders stilled. Sucking in air, I pushed against him, my body on fire, demanding to… *move.*

His hands gripped my shoulders so tight that they would leave indents on my skin. With August, I wanted him to mark me as his… for tonight.

I craved his possession and domination. I needed August to carry me, carry us, through this haze of pleasure.

To use me. And for me to use him.

I had kidded myself when I thought I could control my feelings. There was no way to put what I was starting to feel in a neat little box. The intensity of my need scared me. I could grow attached to him, and that opened me up to the possibility of getting hurt. I wanted to run away again, even as I wanted to rub against him.

Instead, I did the only thing that made sense at the moment. I drew back and threw a handful of mud at August's bare chest. And another splash of mud on those fucking sexy hands of his.

The mud did nothing to hide the memories of them on me. Instead, his dirt-stained hands seemed that much naughtier.

If he made any move, my resolve would tumble. But his surprised laugh broke the spell, before I could do something foolish, like bite him.

"If they want drama, let's give them the best mud fight out there," I teased, relieved that my words seemed to make sense. Or at least, August wasn't staring at me like I was a weirdo.

Maybe a little.

But he said nothing, as if he instinctively knew that I needed to retreat to regain my bearings. With one of his familiar crooked grins, he approached me slowly, those hands of his folded behind his back.

I tried to step back. *Not quickly enough.* Before I could protest, I was horizontal in August's arms. One of his arms was behind my back and the other under my knees. I might have enjoyed this position, *too damn much,* if not for the glint in his eyes.

"One mud fight ready," August said, laughing, a second before he threw me into the pool of mud.

One long shower and an entire bottle of shampoo later, I stepped out of the hotel room where I got cleaned up after the afternoon portion of the date. My sparkly golden minidress swished around me as I followed Greta down winding stairs.

"Go through those doors, and you'll see a lit path to follow." Greta pointed to a set of heavy doors. "Don't worry, you won't get lost."

Of course not. Not with two crew members walking backward with a camera and sound boom. Not obvious at all.

Taking a deep breath, I headed to the dinner area the producers had set up. The mud fight seemed to have restored August's and my relationship back to a comfortable zone. Outside of him tossing me into the mud, he had kept a careful distance between us.

Regret flared up.

Just a tiny, *tiny* bit of regret, really, so small that it was probably just hangriness. It was only that August had looked as if he had truly desired me. I knew I was giving him mixed signals. At some point, he would get tired of this limbo. Even mentally knowing that, I couldn't lower my walls.

Too many men had lied to me or revealed an uglier nature after I let my guard down. Even on this show, within the first three days, two men had tried to charm me while they had ulterior motives. The idea of August having an ulterior motive terrified me.

Yet, I couldn't stay away.

At the end of the lit path lay a shallow pool. A rose-covered table stood in the middle of the water. When I rounded the bend, August came into view. He had changed into a pair of khakis, rolled up around his ankles to avoid getting wet in the water, and a blue-green plaid button-down.

Too nervous to call out a greeting, I smiled shyly before slipping off my heels at the edge of the ankle-deep water. Before this summer, I had never had a date with someone while barefoot. Now, it seemed that I was constantly with August while standing in a body of water, sans shoes.

His eyes widened and drifted down my body. *Shit, I look like a Christmas decoration with my flaming red hair and sequins.* While he fit right in for a casual island date, I was ready for a disco party at Studio 54.

"You are beautiful." He held out a hand to help me into my chair.

"Not like a Christmas tree topper?" I snarked.

August tilted his head to contemplate my question. "Not sure what toppers you're used to, but mine is a discarded angel from my parents that's missing a wing. I blame my sister, and she blames our childhood cat, Luna Broccoli. Dear Luna Broccoli couldn't talk, but I imagine she'd back me up. It's a mystery to this day."

He cleared his throat. "No… I was thinking that I was too underdressed, and you look like you walked out of my dream."

"Oh. You clean up good." Right, I was a master of eloquence. Seriously, how was I supposed to react to this man knocking me sideways with his words?

"I might still have some mud in my hair. It's like glitter," he laughed. "Darn thing seems to get everywhere."

"I wouldn't know," I said, picking up my fork to play with the food. Greta had given me a sandwich to eat in the hotel room and warned me not to eat with my mic on—interference with the sound and all. "My parents weren't into arts and crafts."

"What were they into?" he asked.

"Academics, sports, violin, my learning about their business, finding internships, discussing future plans, networking… you know, things that they thought would help me get into college and find a job." My childhood sounded even more constrictive saying it out loud.

"I babysat a buddy's kid one day. She had a tub of glitter. I found glitter everywhere for months in places you wouldn't believe—on my clothes, hair, socks. So, to your parents' credit, they had foresight in keeping your home clean, and you probably have an unbeatable résumé."

"Sure, let's call it that," I said. "Yes, our home was always clean. My mom didn't like messes. She liked having everything in place."

We poked at the food that we couldn't eat. I fidgeted in my seat while August looked too thoughtful for my sense of peace.

What did he think of me? I didn't care about most people's perceptions of me, but to my surprise and discomfort, I cared about his. Cared *too* much about his. I was too chicken to ask.

"Have you been here before?" August broke the silence.

"Where? St. Lucia or in a helicopter?"

"Both, either, neither."

"Both," I admitted. Feeling an inexplicable need to explain, I added, "I came to St. Lucia on a school volunteering project. As for helicopters, my dad used to charter them to avoid traffic. He said the time saved justified the cost."

August stared at me.

I stared back.

My whole body flushed, and not from whatever magical spell he had woven around me earlier in the mud baths with his hands. I sounded like a spoiled brat, even with the explanation. I sucked in a breath to calm down, to slow down my thoughts, before I got too riled up.

I knew I was lucky that my parents' investment company was successful. I was incredibly fortunate to have had experiences that many people would never have the time or budget to have. But, I didn't want August to believe that *I* thought I was better than him, because I wasn't.

August shook his head in disbelief. To my surprise, instead of calling me snotty, he leaned forward, his forearms resting on his knees. "Outside of being a world traveler, riding in helicopters, and being anti-glitter, tell me about yourself. What sort of volunteering project did you do? Where did you grow up? What's your family like? What would you have done instead of reading financial newspapers as a kid?"

"I grew up all over the place, went to college, went to law school, now split my time between Manhattan and Boston. I like traveling, fashion, matcha lattes, boozy tea parties with my best friend, keeping busy. I don't know what I would have done as a kid if I had free time." Relieved that he was still here, I blurted out my whole life story in a single, fast breath.

"You told me the first night that you left your law firm and were trying to figure out what to do. Why did you leave your firm?" he asked.

"I made partner in February. I thought that was my dream," I mumbled, raising my hands up in mock celebration. "I had worked hard all throughout school, joined one of the top firms in New York, and was part of the team that started its Boston office. I thought nothing of doing eighty or ninety hours a week. I was *really* good at my job."

"What happened?" he asked, reaching out to hold my hands in his.

The gesture probably meant nothing to him. It was so small that August likely didn't realize that he held my hands. Yet, his instinct to comfort me pulled forth my embarrassing confession.

"When I found out that I had made partner—the youngest partner in the company's history and only the second female partner—I cried."

"Not happy tears, I'm guessing." August squeezed my hand.

I barked out a laugh, the sound bitter even to my own ears. "No, I felt empty. My parents don't understand why I quit, or rather, officially, I'm on a sabbatical. Everyone thinks making partner should be the pinnacle of my life. For years, I had worked toward a goal, whether it was SATs, LSATs, passing the bar, making partner. What happens after making partner? What's next?"

Before he could answer, I asked, "Do you know why I 'chose' to be a lawyer?"

August frowned. He was probably regretting asking about my life. "Why?"

"Believe it or not, I didn't have a real boyfriend until my freshman year of college," I started.

Might as well word-vomit my whole life at him. Even if August ran away after this, I couldn't stop the train of words and memories from crashing on.

"He was a senior and president of his fraternity. Everyone said I was so lucky he picked me. A few months into dating, he got upset that I chose to study instead of going to some frat party with him. He told me, with 'my looks' and my parents' money, I should go for an MRS degree instead—"

Dropping my hands, August shot off his chair. He turned away from me, but not before I registered the thunder darkening his expression. Cursing under his breath, he ran a hand through his hair, pulling it up into tousled ends. I caught the words, "sexist fool."

Overly pleased with August's reaction on my behalf, I grabbed his fisted hands to pull him back to his seat. As much as the production crew would love for August to punch a palm tree or fling the table in anger, I didn't want him portrayed as angry on TV, especially not after he had stood up for me with Garrett.

"I dumped his ass. After I aced my finals, he was rejected from Yale Law. Like some parody of *Legally Blonde*, I made Yale Law my next goal," I declared.

"Soon, that decision became less about revenge and more about having a predefined road map to follow. The more that people thought I couldn't do it, because of my looks or that I didn't seem serious enough, the more I wanted to prove them wrong. Plus, it had the added benefit of my parents' approval. You probably think I'm ridiculous for deciding my career based on an ex and some naysayers."

"I agree that your ex and those naysayers are jerks. I don't agree that you're ridiculous," he said, shaking his head. "What you've done is remarkable. Your discipline, your intelligence, your motivation, even your bravery to quit rather than continue something you don't love. You may not have found your next goal yet, but you still have all the qualities that led to you crushing your prior goals. Those don't go away."

"That's the nicest thing someone has ever said to me," I whispered, blinking rapidly to avoid embarrassing myself in front of this kind man. Someone was cutting a bushel of onions. That was the only explanation for the sting of tears crowding behind my eyes.

Maybe August sensed that I couldn't handle any more emotional conversation. Or maybe to give me a moment to gather myself, he joked, "Here I thought, Kaiden's comment the first night, that you and your alcohol-created twin were hotties, would win the prize."

"You heard that?" I asked, surprise taking over the need to sob in self-pity.

"Hard not to, with the way he was yelling and pawing at you that night."

I stared at August's mouth, set in a grim line. Just like that, the decision to come to this silly show felt right. Some—*most*—parts of this show were ridiculous, cheesy, or both. At the same time, the overly produced, forced isolation from the real world had also led to genuine interactions with this surprising man.

"Don't tell me you were jealous, August?" I teased. "Were you watching me?"

His face reddened. He was cute when he blushed.

Okay, okay, I'll admit it, he was cute all the time. Handsome, steady, comforting… with sexy hands. What would he kiss like?

Remember how he could hurt you?

Consensual spanking never hurt anyone.

Forget it. We're friends.

Do we have to be just friends?

"Take heart," I said. My lips widened into a smile so big that my cheeks hurt. "At least, you were the only one to see me sprawled on a bathroom floor like a bad eighties shag rug. You should feel privileged. I don't usually allow guys to see that until the fifth date, at least."

"I'm sure someone else would have checked in on you," said August. "It was nothing."

I shook my head. "It *did* mean something to me. You'd be surprised. Not everyone lives in a magical small town where neighbors bake you cakes and everyone gathers at the village diner for gossip and tea."

"You should visit one day." August stiffened, as the invitation left him.

I froze.

He coughed. "Shock my neighbors or something."

We both knew that was a cover-up. His original offer surprised both of us—a crack of that proverbial door, to open up the possibility of seeing each other outside of this island paradise.

It didn't sound like an awful idea. In fact, not seeing him after the show felt... I shifted in my seat, trying to get comfortable.

"I'll have to think of something truly scandalous to do... like sit on your lap and make out with you at the diner." My voice came out raspy and low, as if someone else was in control of my words.

August's jaw clenched. In seeming disbelief, he searched me. When I held steady, refusing to back down from my offer—or was it a circuitous acceptance of his offer?—even as I wanted to throw myself into a bush to hide, August leaned forward.

We were inches away from each other. Chills raced down my back. As if he had made some critical decision, a slow smile spread across August's face. Anticipation sizzled between us.

"Maybe we should practice?" he teased.

Before I could agree by launching myself at him, August hauled me over to his lap, his kiss cutting off my words. We had been building up to this exact moment with every conversation, every touch.

I thought I knew what to expect, and at the same time, nothing could have prepared me for the reality of it. The first touch of his lips against mine electrified me. I was reduced to sensation upon delicious sensation, at his mercy.

His tongue sought me, teasing until I opened up. August sucked on my bottom lip, wringing out a low moan from me. How could I have ever thought he was Mr. Nice Guy, when he made me feel anything but nice?

Needy, yes.

Naughty, definitely yes.

I wrapped my legs around his waist, my hands thrust into his thick hair, pulling his face impossibly closer. I could tell myself that this kiss was simply to satisfy my curiosity, but I would be lying to myself. There was nothing *simply* about this.

In this impossibly vivid moment, I breathed in the faint smell of the ocean in the background, the hint of mint from August. And breathed out my worries.

I wanted to shout: Here I am, for maybe the first time, here I am, just me, in all of my raw, unpolished, unglamorous form. *Please, see me. Please, like me for me.*

Kissing him… waiting this long to kiss him, after knowing the kind of guy he was… a maelstrom of emotions gathered, pushing me toward some invisible cliff that I didn't understand. The earlier feeling of things shifting intensified except now change didn't seem as scary when cocooned within August's embrace. Instinctively, I knew he would hold me up if I tumbled, even if *he* was the reason for my fall.

August devoured me, plunging us into a heady whirlwind of senses. My body felt none of the coldness of the coming night or the chill of the wind picking up. Instead, I was on fire for his kisses, for his touch… for him.

Yet, it still wasn't enough.

His hands moved up, brushing against my thighs, finding bare skin. His hands lingered, caressing, branding me with his mark. My heart skipped and skedaddled every time his fingers brushed teasingly against the edge of my dress, never dipping underneath.

Where were wardrobe malfunctions when you needed them? Shouldn't it be time for my dress to rip or, better yet, disappear?

I gyrated on his lap, almost exploding, when I felt his hardness against my flimsy underwear. His hands gripped my hips as I teased us, his hips pumping upward toward me, sending shocks of pain-pleasure to that needy spot.

Frantic, I grabbed at his shirt, trying to rip open the buttons. I didn't want barriers between us. Who the hell decided to put buttons on button-down shirts? Some day in the future, I promised to buy him shirts with Velcro for easier access.

"No, Pippa."

I blinked rapidly, trying to process his words. August's hands came up to cover mine, stopping my progress with his buttons.

Had I come on too strong? Embarrassed, I jumped off his lap. Biting my still-swollen lips, I took deep breaths to calm down.

"Pippa, not like that. I don't want to do this with cameras around." August stood up. His whiskey-voice was still raw with desire. He wrapped his arms around me, pulling me against his still-clothed chest. The pounding of his heart and the shakiness of his breath soothed me.

I hadn't been alone in the storm. That thought saved me from despair and brought me back.

Light from the nearby cameras winked in the starlight. If I squinted, I could see the half-hidden faces of the production crew, spread out in a semicircle around the bushes and trees, barely twenty feet away.

"How was that practice?" I joked, trying to save face at the thought of how close we were to having sex on camera. "Will your town's diner throw us into jail for public indecency?"

With a gentle kiss on my forehead, August growled, "You would be worth it."

CHAPTER TWELVE

~AUGUST~

ITM filming, Day 4, 8:30 a.m.:

    Greta*: You look like you had a good night.*

    August*: I plead the fifth.*

    Greta*: You can't. We have cameras everywhere. The nice teacher turns out to have a naughty side.*

    August*: I'm not sure I can look my students or colleagues in the eyes again.*

    Greta*: A khaki-wearing teacher with an edge. Think about it, you could be the coolest teacher around.*

Sweet. Dark and intoxicating.

I could explore her for the rest of my life and always want more. Pippa answered with eagerness. My hands brushed along the sides of her lithe body. Her legs tangled up with mine, her body arching toward me, seeking me.

Mine.

I yanked her tighter to me. Her softness against my hardness. Her warmth a siren call for me to sink into.

If her lips tasted so sweet, what did her pussy taste like? Ignoring her invitation and my straining cock, I slid down. Her hum of pleasure made me want to beat my chest, claiming victory.

I didn't want low moans. I wanted her screaming my name. I wanted her begging for me, the anticipation so acute, the final pleasure so devastating that she couldn't think of anything besides me.

Only me.

Her moans grew, escalating up.

Too loud? I wanted Pippa to scream, not sound like she was a helicopter whirling over loudspeakers.

How did we end up going from my bed to a bunk bed in a helicopter?

Pippa's face retreated as the helicopter blades came closer. I reached out to grab her. Instead of her softness, my hands found air and cotton.

Male laughter and the sound of a thousand blenders kicked out the last vestige of my dream. Disappointed and groggy, I rolled out of bed. The only thing that hadn't been my imagination was my morning cock-stand.

"How was that practice? Will your town's diner throw us into jail for public indecency?"

"You would be worth it."

The memory of last night came flooding back. If nothing else, I had discovered that my cock had hidden levels of hardness. Almost like a video game, though instead of unlocking a secret power, Pippa introduced me to ten levels of blue balls. Amused at the image of me dressed as Mario chasing a Pippa-looking coin, I dressed and stepped into the living space of the cottage.

Ten shirtless guys hovered around the kitchen island. It looked like the chemistry classroom at school. However, instead of beakers and chemicals, tubs of protein powder and used blenders scattered across the counters. Beckett analyzed a recipe book, writing notes in the columns.

Ten pairs of eyes, plus a camera, panned to me.

"Hi," I called out.

Never had I felt more like a teacher than at this moment. I had half a mind to dole out grades on the various glasses of shakes in front of me. Did twenty- and thirty-something-year-old men like scratch and sniff stickers as much as my high schoolers?

"How was your date with Pippa?" Pietr called out, with a condescending smirk. "You were her third choice, right? After me and Garrett."

A haze of defensiveness swept over me. I thrust my hands inside my shorts to keep them from doing something moronic, like punch the ass.

The camera crept closer. None of the other guys laughed, except Pietr and Garrett. I was reminded that most of these guys weren't bad. Minus Pietr and Garrett, who had hurt Pippa, and didn't even have the gall to pretend shame.

"Was I her third choice?" I asked, feigning confusion. "Here I thought I was the first one Pippa *stayed* on a date with. I guess her first two choices weren't worth her time."

Without waiting for Pietr and Garrett to stop sputtering profanities, I walked out of the cottage. I knew their egos were hurt. Even if Garrett claimed he didn't care or Pietr was shacked up with Hailey, it was still a blow to be dumped.

Yet, I couldn't help but wonder. *Third choice. Was I* still *her third choice?* Did she respond to her third choices the same way that she had responded to me last night?

I was almost sure she hadn't faked any of her responses with me. Her vulnerability was too real when she shared glimpses into her life. Or the way she reserved a secret smile for me, one that glowed from the inside.

Plus, her *other* responses to me were too wild to fake. The way her skin had heated under my hands, the way her eyes had glazed, the way she had twisted in my lap... No, those moments were real. I had to believe that.

Though we were separated for only a night, I missed her. If it was weak to feel this strongly for someone so fast, I didn't care. Nothing mattered except that Pippa might possibly be interested in me. That this might be real.

For the first time, the decision to be on this show wasn't a ridiculous escape from my mundane world. It was the path to meet Pippa.

I laughed. I sounded cheesy even to me. Greta and Nate would be proud of how much I had bought into this experience. Not because of the fancy dates or paradise-like location, but because of Pippa.

Instead of heading to the breakfast bar, I veered toward the producers to explain my idea. An hour later, I finished preparations and headed away from the beach toward Pippa's cottage.

"Good morning, August!"

In the distance, Pippa popped out from her cottage. Watching her jog toward me, my heart thumped hard against my chest. It took all my self-control not to run up to her, throw her over my shoulder, and claim her as mine.

Instead, I settled for wrapping her in my arms, letting her feel how fast and strong my heart beat for her. Pippa burrowed against my shirt while her hands stroked my back.

"Hi," I said to the top of her head. Whatever nerves remained from Pietr's taunt or my own doubts about seeing her again vanished.

Her red hair glinted in the sunlight, capturing the rays. The humidity of the

Caribbean sun in the summer curled her hair into gentle waves that fell around her shoulders, down her back.

Because I couldn't help myself, I ran my hands through her hair and tugged, encouraging her to tilt up toward me. Her eyes clouded with desire that mirrored my own.

No, not mirrored mine. There was no way she could feel the same as me. A fraction of what I felt was sufficient.

For now.

Pippa was the first to break the mounting tension. She loosened her arms around my back, and with great reluctance, I let her go.

"Will you come with me?" I asked, my hand reaching out to her.

"Where are we going?"

"It's a surprise."

After only a minor hesitation, she put her hand in mine. That small gesture sent my heart soaring. Possession swelled at the sight of her small hand in mine. This morning, she wasn't running away.

"Why are you looking at me like that?"

"Like what?" I asked as I led her up to the top of a rock outcropping.

She tilted her head to her left. I bent down to brush my mouth against hers. My breaths shook from the restraint of not yanking her to me so she could feel just what she was doing to me. But I reined in the need to possess, to taste. The feelings I had for Pippa went beyond lust, and I wanted to show her.

When I pulled away, Pippa let out a frustrated sigh. Her hands fisted in my shirt to keep me close. Against her ear, I murmured, "Go on another date with me?"

Without waiting for her response, I turned her around to face the sand beyond the rocks. Colorful blankets and bright pillows spread out across this part of the sand, hidden from the rest of the resort by the rocks we stood on. Earlier, I had convinced Greta to let me schlep a few pots of flowers from the main gazebo and bungalow area. A platter of fruit, eggs, baked goods, and a cup of matcha latte lay at the center of the blankets.

Pippa let go of my shirt to stare at the makeshift picnic. "You did this?"

At her hesitation, the picnic now seemed pitiful compared to the extravagance of the dates on this show. Instead of lugging plants and pillows around, I should have asked Greta for a boat ride.

"I know it's not as glamorous as a helicopter ride—"

"*You*, not the producers, thought of this date? For *me*? You remembered that I like matcha lattes?"

"The food is edible and not glued down."

Despite how she had snuggled against my chest earlier, she now kept her hands fastened in front of her. "I don't understand. Why would you do this? I know you didn't mean anything serious when you invited me to your town. I don't expect anything. Don't worry, I'm not going to just show up in Beach Falls. We were both caught up."

"Hold on." Alarms rang through me. Nervousness radiated from Pippa, punctuated by the rapid cadence of her words. "What if I want you to expect something from me? What if the invitation is real? Would you visit me?"

"As friends?"

"No, as someone more than a friend. I'd like to introduce you to my friends and family." There. The ball was in her court.

Wistfulness softened her face before she turned away from me. Her shoulders shook with emotion. As she gathered herself, the last twenty-four hours played in my head. Somewhere, I had misinterpreted her. Somewhere, I had been so overwhelmed by my feelings for her that I missed something important.

"I haven't met anyone's parents in a long time." Her voice sounded far away, almost robotic. "For the past few years, I didn't have time to be serious with anyone. So it didn't matter that every guy I went on a date with was terrible. I can do flings and undefined *entanglements*, but I don't know how to be in a relationship."

"That's okay. I haven't been in a serious one in years. We can learn together."

"You don't understand." She turned to face me, fear dulling her eyes. "What if I'm *terrible* at relationships? I don't know how to do second dates and sweet gestures. What if I ruin this? I like being good at things and being in control. You... this whole thing makes me feel... I don't know..."

As she spoke, her hands quickened with frantic motions. One hand reached up to brush her hair back, the other rose in midair before dropping. With a grunt of frustration, she picked up a small pebble and threw it toward the ocean.

I had never seen her restless like this before. Not after the failed attempts at dates with Pietr and Garrett. Not even last night when she admitted she was nervous about being hurt.

She had also said that I was different. Maybe this morning, she had decided that different was bad; different was too much.

Taking a deep breath in, I watched Pippa fidget with her hair. "How does it make you feel? How do I make you feel?"

A lock of waves blew into her face, hiding her from me. She pushed off the hair and tucked it behind her ear. Blinking too fast, she said, "I'm terrified of getting hurt, and that you'll have the power to hurt me. I'm terrified of what I'm starting to feel, of sucking at dating you, of doing something wrong, of jumping in too quickly, or not quickly enough… the list goes on.

"One moment, I'm on fire for you and want to know more about you. The next, I question why I'm so invested and want to hide until I figure it out. I don't want to ruin this *thing* between us by moving too fast. You see, I'm no good at this."

That knot in my heart loosened. She wouldn't be terrified about getting hurt if she didn't care, right?

If Pippa erected too many walls of protection between us, I might lose her.

If I pushed now, Pippa would run.

Making a quick decision, I said, keeping my voice even to not alarm her, "Know that last night meant something to me. *You* mean something to me. But we don't have to rush. We can go slow."

She nodded, exhaling the tense breath she held.

The timer started now. I had two more weeks of this experience to show her that I was worth the risk. *Better get busy.*

"Would you rather be a zombie or be a human, running from the zombies?"

I considered Pippa's question with the seriousness a zombie apocalypse deserved. "Stay a human. It's possible that we have zombies all wrong. What if they have a conscience and could become good if we give them a chance?"

"While you're trying to feed stray zombies, I'll be the zombie eating your head," she mused, breaking off the outside edges of her cookie. She popped the soft middle into her mouth. "Running from zombies seems tiring. Though, maybe someone will invent a zombie vaccine. Technology tends to progress faster in times of crisis, and what is a bigger crisis than zombies trying to eat your head? Want the crunchy parts of my cookie?"

I took the best parts of the cookie, as Pippa did some back-of-the-envelope math on when zombies could overtake humans if no cure was discovered. Like so often in the past two weeks, I stared at her with a mix of frustration and fascination.

Since our talk on the beach, the days had passed in a confusion-filled, disorienting blur of no labels. I didn't push, didn't attempt to kiss her, or hold her in the way that I craved.

The effort to let her set the pace was driving me up the wall, especially since her swimsuits seemed to get smaller each day. I had gotten very good at reciting baseball team rosters in my head to cool off.

Couldn't Pippa see that I'd let her zombie-self eat me in an apocalypse? If that wasn't the ultimate sign of *liking* her, then I didn't know what was.

Every few days, the contestants competed in some ridiculous competition to win dates—from who could eat the most tacos to paintball to scavenger hunts. There was even one where we all had to wear mermaid tails and race in the shallow ocean water before climbing onto an artificial Little Mermaid–like rock. The interns must have had a drunken laugh when they came up with that one.

Pippa and I won no more challenges. While others went on dates or canoodled in the cabanas, Pippa and I settled into a holding pattern. We were the first ones to wake up, outside of Beckett who took over the guys' cottage every morning, testing new recipes for a juice bar that he wanted to open. In the past few days, Annie had joined him as well, to my surprise. Leaving them to their food chemistry, Pippa and I went for long walks before the sun reached its peak.

In deliberate fashion, Pippa and I, by following her lead, kept the conversations light. No sentences strayed into the intimate. Our conversations were so broad-ranging, yet contained so little depth, that the camera crew stopped following us on our walks after a few days.

One cloudy morning, we debated whether Pluto was a regular planet—it wasn't. At lunch, we tossed around the merits of a zombie bunker. That night at dinner, we talked about what foods we would fill our bunker with, while Pippa lamented at the probable lack of lattes in bunkers. After dinner, when I found out that Pippa had never used a can opener, I found one so I could teach her that invaluable life lesson.

For the sake of the apocalypse, of course.

As a friend, Pippa was everything I could ask for: funny, smart, interesting. Each conversation, no matter how ridiculous, added a piece to the Pippa puzzle.

The zombie versus vampire debate showed her intense logical side. When she pretended to be a sports commentator during the other contestants' workout routines, I was in awe of her quick-wittedness.

This retreat back to friendship might be what she needed to get comfortable with the idea of us. However, every moment as *just*-friends rankled me. "Friend" was too light for what she became to me. Since we spent all of our waking moments with each other, with no distractions from technology or the outside world, she became my closest companion, partner, the other part of me whom I missed when she wasn't around.

If only friendship was enough.

Instead of this limbo, I craved all of her.

I wanted Pippa, the friend, and Pippa, the shy, beguiling, self-deprecating woman who was trying to find her way. I wanted *my* Pippa back, who looked at me as if she truly desired me. As if she couldn't wait to tear off my shirt, even as she tore the walls off around my heart.

With each day, I was running out of time, waiting for her to be ready.

CHAPTER THIRTEEN

~PIPPA~

ITM filming, Day 17, 10:45 a.m.:

Greta: *Tomorrow is the last day of this experience! Couples can break up or leave the island engaged.*

Pippa: *Engaged is extreme.*

Greta: *What do you mean? You two have been inseparable since your date. I think you have the strongest bond of all the remaining couples.*

Pippa: *Maybe at one point. I think I ruined it, though, when I told him it was all going too fast. He hasn't made any moves since the morning after the mud baths.*

Greta: *Just because you're not shagging in the private room all the time— *cough* Pietr and Hailey—doesn't mean you don't have something between you two. You have been able to build a true foundation. You should go for it and lay out your feelings. Don't leave with regrets.*

Pippa: *What if it's too late?*

"Congratulations, you are one step closer to getting engaged!"

Mark smiled like a benevolent king at the crowd of contestants sitting in the gazebo, waiting for us to clap. Most of my fellow contestants looked around nervously, though a few cheered loudly.

Out of thirty contestants, there were three true couples. Pietr and Hailey ping-ponged from drunk shouting matches to make-up sex marathons in the private room. The second couple—Drew and Amelie—had floated from partner to partner, until two days ago, when they'd declared each other their soul mates. Lastly, to everyone's surprise, Kaiden and Vidhya acted like an old married couple, spending most of their time taking naps together in a cabana.

Now, as if on cue, like synchronized swimmers, the three couples leaned toward each other to make out in victory.

Gag.

Outside of those couples, there were two other *pairings*. After the first few days, Annie had struck a friendship with Beckett, a vegan hipster from Austin who dreamed of starting a juice bar.

Then, there was August and myself... whatever we were. If my whole body could sigh in frustration, it would have at that moment.

Handsome, levelheaded August.

The same August who had become a close friend. The same August who respected me enough to give me space. In fact, he had slowed our relationship so much that I wondered if he was still interested.

In the past, too often, I had mistaken a guy's interest in me, only to find that his interest didn't go deeper than the physical. I didn't want August and me to be a lust-fueled, quick romp, especially when I felt more than lust.

However, when I told him no pressure the morning after the helicopter date, I didn't mean for him to treat me like one of his fishing buddies. The key words were *slow down.* As in, let's not jump to mad sex on camera. Or let's hold off making rash decisions to move to a Hallmark town and bake pies for neighbors.

But please proceed to kiss me or debauch me... in a more temperate manner, while I figured out how not to be terrified.

Did the dense man understand what was so obvious? No. The dense man remained dense.

Or oblivious. He hadn't even blinked at my bikinis. Yes, my swimsuits had gotten skimpier as the days had gone by, in an attempt to try to get him to make a move.

At this rate, I could prance around him with flashing nipple rings, and August would continue philosophizing the politics of a post-zombie world of underground bunkers. Forget how to divvy up canned food equally. I'd like to throw one of those hypothetical canned beans at his thick head.

There was only one other explanation for this utter standstill. Somewhere between planning a picnic breakfast for me and debating whether werewolves or vampires would win in a fight, August had decided I wasn't worth it. I had pushed him too far away, especially after he had taken the initiative to plan something so sweet for us.

Maybe his initial curiosity about me had waned. After all, a globe-trotting, loud person with no clue what to do next with her life simply didn't mesh with his comfy, meaningful life.

My body emitted another sigh.

Nudging me gently with his shoulders, August mouthed, "Are you okay?"

His hand landed on mine to offer comfort before pulling away as if burned. I nodded, forcing my cheeks into a not-so-grimace-like smile.

"The next twenty-four hours will be life changing," said Mark, waving his arms to get the attention of the make-out bunnies. "Tomorrow morning, each of you will need to make a choice about your relationship. Leave the island single or get engaged."

No middle ground? Panic flared. Next to me, August let out a ragged breath.

"I have something that will help you with your decision. For any couple who needs more time, you can choose to spend a Final Night *together*, away from the cameras. Talk about the future, share what's in your heart, and you know, protectives are provided." Mark smirked as the three couples giggled.

"Okay, please go pack your bags," directed Mark. "For the couples who want to spend the Final Night together, meet me here in thirty minutes with your luggage. For the rest of you, say your goodbyes. Your journey to find love has ended."

"What do you think about spending the Final Night together?" August asked as the other contestants started to move toward the cottages.

"Hm," I squeaked, unable to meet his gaze. "Um, I have to pack."

Like a coward, I ran off, my long legs allowing me to pass the other contestants. Inside my shared room in the cottage, I slumped down on the bed. *Fuck.*

Last night with August.

I knew *The Journey of Love* wouldn't film forever. But tomorrow? I would never see August again after *tomorrow*? Even if we weren't a real couple, the idea of losing him wracked me with sadness.

Regret washed over me. What would have happened if I hadn't been too scared to explore a relationship with August? Now, it was too late.

"Hey, Pippa." Annie entered our shared room. Grabbing her suitcase from inside the closet to pack, she asked, "Are you going to spend the night with August?"

"We're just friends," I said, saddened by how true that statement was.

"Sure." Sarcasm oozed from her voice.

"It's true."

"Uh-huh. Because friends look at each other like they want to… you know… do naughty things," she whispered, her face flushing with discomfort. Clearing her throat, she changed path. "Or, August is terrible at flirting. Whenever I talk with him, his mind is on you. Whenever you walk into sight, he gets distracted. The tension between you two is so intense that it feels like we're invading your privacy."

I stayed silent. Maybe the tension could have developed into *more*, but it had been two weeks without August making any moves.

Finished with packing, she stared at me, as if weighing a problem. Inside her small suitcase, her neatly folded clothes, shoes, and toiletries didn't fill the space.

With a sigh, Annie finally said, "Here's my advice, take it or leave it. I've lived most of my life scared. Oh, not of being physically hurt. Just scared to do the wrong thing, say the wrong thing, *be* the wrong person.

"On the flip side, having freedom is scary too. If I choose the wrong thing, I can only blame myself, versus when I didn't have choices, I could blame my circumstances. There's no riskless path. Still, I wouldn't trade my freedom for anything, no matter how frightened I am."

Her voice strengthened with conviction. "You've been holding back. Is the fear of putting yourself out there worth losing August?"

"If he's still interested in me, why hasn't he shown it?"

"Because you've rejected him every time," she pointed out, without judgment. "You told me you two had a moment on the beach, and then you ignored him for a day. Instead of picking August, you picked Garrett originally for the date. Then, after an amazing date and him planning a surprise picnic, you told him to slow it down. What's he supposed to think?"

She was right. Yet, the thought of making the first move and being rejected frightened me. On the other hand, the thought of never seeing August again overwhelmed me.

Besides, even if tonight went amazing, was there even a point when we only had a day left together? There was no way we could work outside of this beach.

Right?

August had his perfect town and life to go back to. There was bound to be a perky young teacher who joined the school, or a new gardener who came back to her hometown to take care of a sick parent and would fall into his lap.

I was never going to let Tia suck me into watching Hallmark movies again.

A knock sounded on the door of our room before it swung open. "Hey, can I talk to you?"

I spun around, my face breaking into a wide smile at the sight of August. Then remembering how he was supposed to fall in love under the mistletoe on a Christmas tree farm with the owner of a cute bakery, my smile dropped.

"Um, I'll leave you two alone," said Annie in a bright voice, backing out of the room with her suitcase. "Good luck!"

August opened the door wider to let Annie through, leaving us by ourselves. He sauntered into the room. Red flagging his cheeks, his eyes landed briefly on my bed.

"Why are you here?" I asked.

"You ran off before we could discuss the Final Night. We're supposed to decide if we want to spend the night together or leave the island." August tilted his head back, giving nothing away.

Shit.

I had assumed he'd want to spend the night together, at least as friends. Maybe he was eager to get back home. I should be unselfish and let him date the cute single mom who organizes Girl Scout cookie booths outside of her quaint bookshop.

I should.

We were never going to see each other after this. A relationship formed on a reality TV show was too improbable.

"We don't have to spend a night together if it makes you uncomfortable," August continued. His fingers tapped against his khaki shorts in a rare nervous gesture.

"Is that what you want? To part ways now?" I asked.

August stilled. Even his hands stopped tapping. "No. I like spending time with you."

For a declaration, this was akin to soggy toast from the night before. So why did I blurt out, "Me too"? Why did my face shift into a cheek-hurting smile mirroring his?

"Okay, good. Good," repeated August. "I want to make clear that there's no pressure at all to do anything else but hang out and talk."

Damn. His soggy toast of a declaration was still platonic bread. I nodded as we stared at each other.

Was he thinking of some hypothetical debate we could have? An epic second round of discussion of whether Pluto was the ninth planet? It was, by the way, by the laws of solar system grandfathering logic, or something to that effect. Or whether a blueberry bagel was legit? It wasn't.

Whee me. While the other remaining couples played horny bunnies, we'd debate whether a bunny made for a good pet.

I had royally screwed up by telling him to slow down. It was only now, at the near end of this experience, that I realized what I had missed by hiding behind my fear. The possibility of a genuine relationship. Of hope.

Fuck. Time to pull up my big girl panties.

"August, what—"

"Hold on. Before you say… Hear me out," August interrupted. His hands tapping again against his legs, August rushed on. "I've been thinking. The past couple of weeks have been awesome. Don't get me wrong. I've tried to give you space, to go with the flow. But that's not who I am. I don't like undefined relationships, especially not with you.

"As much as I enjoy being your friend, I don't want to spend the last night debating whether Pluto is a planet again—it's not, by the way. I meant what I said two weeks ago. You mean something to me… more than something. I like you, Pippa. Not just as a friend."

"What?" My head did not compute what he was saying.

"I like you, in a naked way." His face flushed tomato red.

In a flurry, he sank down on my bottom bunk bed, shoving his face into his hands. Mumbling from his hands, he muttered, "No, that's weird. I want more than the funny conversations. I'd like to see you naked. With me naked at the same time. Does the word 'naked' sound weird to your ears? Naked, naked…"

He stood up in a rush. "I'm going to leave right now."

"Are we naked together?" I asked, trying to keep my laughter at bay.

"That would be preferable. Yes. You, me at the same time. In the same space. Naked. Or partially clothed, that's fun too. Naked, naked. Are you sure that word doesn't sound weird to you?"

Poor guy.

I pulled at his T-shirt to keep him from backing out of the room, relief pouring over me, mixed with regret that we waited until the last day to have this conversation. Still, one night with him was better than nothing.

"When I said that I didn't want any pressure in this relationship, I didn't mean to push you away completely," I said. "I've been regretting my words that day. In truth, I'm still petrified… and more than the petrified tree I played in sixth grade. I don't know where this is going after the beach. But at least while we're here in St. Lucia, I would like something more. Very possibly the naked kind too."

Groaning, August leaned into my hand, backing me up against the wall. My breath quickened at his nearness. The air in the room shifted. Anticipation and hot exhilaration wrapped us in an intimate cocoon.

I could feel the heat of his body against mine. The rise of his chest barely brushed against the needy tips of my nipples. The fall of his chest as my body felt its loss.

This tension was different from the prior two weeks. Our attempts at a platonic relationship had caused an awkwardness in our interactions. But this here, this straining, physical longing… this felt right. As if we were in our natural state of being, with the push and pull of familiarity and excitement.

"Pippa, would you like to go on a date with me tonight?" His voice deepened, caressing me. "No pretending, just us."

Shutting off the questions about tomorrow, I agreed, "Just us. Just tonight."

CHAPTER FOURTEEN

~AUGUST~

ITM filming, Day 17, 4:11 p.m.:
    Greta: *What do you expect to happen during the Final Night?*
    August: *I don't know, somewhere between amazing and terrible.*
    Greta: *That's a wide spectrum.*
    August: *Do you think you could help me with an idea? I want to set up some-*
thing special for Pippa. Let's hope it turns out better than the breakfast picnic.

Nerves shaking, I breathed in and out. It was no use. My imagination ricocheted from one extreme to another—Pippa leaving forever, Pippa undressing, and everything in between.

Greta had guided me earlier to wait at a villa. It was in a different part of the resort than the cottages we had stayed in or the main resort building. Far from other buildings, nestled in lush foliage, the single-story hideaway was a retreat from the world.

The dense trees and blooms muffled sounds. The windy path to the villa made it hard for any guests to wander over by accident. Outside, a terrace over-looked treetops and a sliver of the darkening ocean. Just to the side of the terrace lay a hot tub, strewn with rose petals.

For the first time since I landed on this resort, Pippa and I had a guaranteed chunk of alone time without mics, producers, or cameras over our shoulders. Did I really say it out loud that I wanted her naked?

With me naked too.

The word *naked* would never not sound weird to me again.

It had taken every part of me not to devour every part of her, to save this for tonight. That and the copious amounts of noise from the other side of the door from the other contestants packing.

Here I was, for what amounted to a pre-agreed-upon hookup with no strings attached beyond tonight. Unease and excitement twisted within me with a strong dose of adrenaline.

A soft tap sounded on the door, followed by another one, this time louder.

I patted my white button-down and khaki pants, both of which had been on the receiving end of an aggressive iron earlier this afternoon. Then, bracing myself, I opened the door.

"Hi."

There was no amount of bracing that could prepare me for Pippa. She glowed in a flowy forest green dress. Soft lamplight from outside backlit her, giving her a halo effect. Her eyes were luminescent in the dark—my north stars.

It was one thing to think of tonight as just sex, but another when the object of the "sexing" was in front of you. No matter how prepared I thought I was, it was still Pippa. Part of me would never treat anything with her as casual.

"Hi," she mimicked back, before leaning up to brush her lips against mine. An all-too-brief greeting.

"What's that for?" I asked, pulling her into the villa and closing the door behind us.

"I'm trying to get over my fear and just allow myself to do whatever I want with you. Right now, I want to kiss you. Is that okay with you? Oh, what's this?" She stared at the scene behind me. "Did you rob a candle store?"

I followed her gaze to the candles covering the inside of the villa. They were different sizes, different colors, resting in different containers. There were candles on the side tables, by the large leather couch in the living room, and grouped together on the kitchen island. Behind the door to the bedroom, I had lit more candles.

"I asked Greta to take me shopping earlier. I might have gone overboard. Is this okay? I wanted something special for you tonight."

Pippa didn't say anything, instead turning away from me. One hand rose to cover her mouth. When she did speak, her voice sounded raspy. "This is lovely. You didn't have to."

"I wanted to, because it's you." I flushed as the words left me. I sounded cheesier than cheese. Pivoting, I stared into the darkened sky outside the French doors to the terrace.

Because it's you. The words beat against my heart. So strong, so right.

I knew what the Final Night was for, and one part of me grew harder thinking about Pippa, underneath me, riding me, taking my cock in her red lips…

Yet, Pippa didn't feel like a one-night stand. She felt like more. She was *more*. I wanted it all, fears be damned.

"Do you want some wine or chocolate?" I asked.

At her nod, I poured two glasses of Bordeaux and dipped a strawberry into the chocolate fondue. Careful not to make sudden movements, I held the strawberry up to Pippa.

When her red lips took in the strawberry, my cock sprung up as if she was taking me into her warm mouth. *Lucky strawberry.* When she licked her lips, it was as if she stroked my hardness.

Mimicking me, Pippa dipped another strawberry into the chocolate. She raised it toward me in a silent offer. I bit into the sweetness of the chocolate and the tartness of the berry.

Pippa's eyes widened. Her pupils dilated. Smoldering hunger replaced any signs of nerves. Never mind the hundreds of flames surrounding us, this woman lit me up.

I burned for her. I wanted Pippa to be on fire for me, in that same gasping-for-air, restless, confounding way I felt.

"I'm going to think of you whenever I see chocolate-covered strawberries," I growled. Tension vibrated between us, escalating until I couldn't stand it anymore.

"What are your plans after this show?" She cleared her throat, not meeting my gaze.

I forced my brain to function. "Go back to teaching and coaching, build a deck. The same old, same old."

The same old boring life. Especially after knowing the vivacity of Pippa, Beach Falls paled. On the tip of my tongue was the question, did she remember my offer on our first date?

But the words never formed. If dating on this show scared Pippa, a relationship outside of this show would send her running before I got the question out.

Instead, I asked, "What about you?"

"I still have to decide if I go back to my law firm, or if there's something else I'm interested in. A few years ago, my best friend and I founded a start-up based on an AI engine she built. We eventually sold it, but those couple of years were some of the hardest and most interesting times that I've had. As a patent lawyer, I reviewed so many technologies—there are so many interesting ideas out there, so many talented people. I'd love to stay in that space somehow."

She shrugged. "In the meantime, I'll have plenty of time. I had a bucket list of things that I made a while ago, maybe I'll do that. Like take a road trip around Iceland or a sailing retreat off the shores of Tahiti. Garrett went to Antarctica last year. I don't know about the cold, but I guess it's a neat experience to add to my list."

Of course. Her plans didn't include me or Beach Falls. Why should they? "Your bucket list seems vast. Much more exciting than mine."

"I don't know if it's exciting, just something to do." She grimaced. "What's on your bucket list?"

"Finding someone to spend the rest of my life with. Kids to love. Continuing to teach and coach. Pretty mundane, right?"

I started to pace, running one hand through my hair, tugging at the ends. I thought of the right words to say, the right question to ask. What could I say to keep her with me?

Now that it was clear Pippa's life post-show didn't include me, was it time to protect myself? If I knew how Pippa felt gripping me in her body, if I knew how she looked when she found her pleasure, if I had a night of her moans and crying out my name, it wouldn't be enough to last me. I would always crave more.

The memories of her would torment me. They would drive me up a wall, until I jumped out of my skin with want, with *need* for her.

I couldn't do only one night with her. I hated the part of me that wanted more, that reached for stars that I couldn't have.

"Do you think tonight"—I gestured between us—"is a good idea?"

Pippa's mouth opened to form a small O. Before I could withdraw, she threw herself at me. Despite my own confusion, and despite my earlier desire to retreat, my resolve crumbled.

"August, I want you," whispered Pippa. "Kiss me. Touch me. Please."

My heart tumbled at her vulnerability. Screw tomorrow. Future me could figure it out.

I kissed her, yanking her flush against me. My cock throbbed against her, heavy, needy, blood pounding to take her. Now.

My hands cupped her face as I drew her toward me. She tasted like berries. I commanded her to open up, to give in to this maelstrom of feelings. When I sucked at her lower lip, she groaned and moved one hand down to rub against me. My cock jumped at her touch, growing harder with every stroke. Pleasure rumbled from my chest.

I yanked my shirt out of my pants. Diving under my button-down, Pippa touched my bare skin, her fingers hot, branding me to her. I pulled up her dress, parting her underwear to find her fucking wet for me.

Something switched inside of me at the sign of her arousal. Triumph surged. I moved over her face, down her neck, kissing and sucking, whispering frenzied encouragements as my fingers explored her, teasing her, spreading her wetness.

"Fucking wicked, wicked man," she moaned, her hips lifting as I sunk two fingers in her. She clenched around me, holding me to her.

Pulling out of her, I sucked on my fingers, tasting her wetness. Offering my fingers to her, for her to taste herself.

Her moans enveloped us. The way her tongue licked at my fingers, the way her mouth sucked on her own sign of arousal… it was too much. And not enough.

She let her head fall to the side. At her offering, I leaned down to kiss her neck, nipping at her sensitive skin with my teeth, before soothing her with my tongue. Her legs opened even wider as she leaned up on her tippy-toes to rub against me, seeking relief.

Groaning at how good it felt, I lined my hard-as-steel cock against that wet center of her and pressed. A whimper escaped from her.

"Pippa, you're going to kill me." My eyes closed at the pleasure as I grabbed her ass and held her in place for two heartbeats… before my hands started kneading her flesh, lifting… separating…squeezing her ass.

It wasn't enough. I wanted to see all of her.

Wrapping her legs around my waist, I carried Pippa into the bedroom. At the foot of the bed, I tossed her onto the mattress. Before she could protest, I followed, bracing my weight on my arms.

Too much space still separated us. She wouldn't be close enough until I was buried in her warmth.

As if she read my mind, Pippa wrapped her legs around my waist. With a dark laugh, I settled myself against her and rocked. I whispered against her ear, "Is this what you're looking for?"

Her breath caught. With a whimper, she nodded.

I pulled her tight against me, her wetness against my hardness, and thrust against her… again… and again…

There were too many clothes between us still. I yanked off her dress. Growling in pleasure, I found no bra and only a skimpy red thong. My movements faltered at seeing Pippa laid out in front of me like a feast.

"I came to play," she teased.

Before I could tell her that I was *this* close, Pippa circled her hips against me. She whimpered, "That felt good, August. So good… I'm so close…"

The room filled with her moans and whimpers. Her nails clawed at my back. My movements were wild and unrefined now. I needed her to lose control with me.

With her cries getting louder, I bent my head to take one of her hard nipples into my mouth. Sucking on the nipple at the same time, I circled her. With a hitch of her breath, Pippa spasmed, waves of pleasure rolling over her. Her whimpers breathy, she clutched at me.

My cock throbbed, a reminder that I was still clothed. I wanted to be inside of her, needed to be inside her next time.

I craved her. Craved this intimacy, this moment with her, and would for the rest of my life.

Even as she journeyed around the world. Without me.

I had a bucket list of things that I made a while ago, maybe I'll do that. After tonight, Pippa planned to travel the world. My earlier doubts rushed back.

"Fuck!" I threw myself off of her, hurling toward the opposite wall.

Behind me, Pippa asked, "Do you want some help… you know… um, I'd be happy to help."

Yes!

Yet, the image of her at the Blue Lagoon in Iceland or trekking through Antarctica held me in place. "Does this look like I need *more* help? I'm trying to unhelp it."

"Oh. Why?" She reached for my pants.

Pippa was temptation incarnate. If I wasn't careful, I would fall too far to climb back out.

"I didn't mean to *take* it this far. I'm sorry, Pippa. I thought I could do casual. Just tonight. I want to. You can't know how much I want to. But I can't. I don't do one-night stands, and I can't have sex knowing that there's no future… not even for you."

The shock and hurt on her face as my words registered gutted me until I couldn't take the clawing panic rising within me. Everything in me was shouting that this was all wrong, that I had made a mistake.

Before my resolve could crumble, without another word, I strode out of the bedroom, into the cool air on the terrace. The image of the woman of my dreams, naked, flushed from the aftermath of pleasure, imprinted on my mind.

Despair gripped me. How easy it would have been to forget tomorrow and sink into her, fuck us both mindless. I could have lied to myself, and to her, that I can handle one-night with her. But, as much as I wanted to, I wouldn't be able to separate sex from my feelings. Even with my cock throbbing, I couldn't go any further, knowing that by tomorrow, I'd be left with nothing but memories.

If we had sex tonight, it would be too easy for her to run away tomorrow, discarding our connection as only physical or exaggerated by the show. If I wanted her to take a chance on us outside of this show, I needed to convince Pippa first that I wasn't like the other men in her past.

Backing off was the biggest gamble of my life. But the upside… the chance at a future with Pippa… she was worth the risk.

So no, I couldn't have a one-night stand. Especially not with her.

Not when I wanted the *world* with her.

CHAPTER FIFTEEN

~PIPPA~

ITM filming, Day 18, 7:22 a.m.:

Greta: *It's the final day! Each couple will meet on the beach to decide whether they break up or get engaged. What do you think will happen with you and August? Have you made up your mind?*

Pippa: *Could we do this ITM later? I have to get ready.*

Greta: *You've already changed seven times.*

Pippa: *Do you think I would look better in the white dress? I don't think I brought enough clothes here. Why is it that I simultaneously have too many clothes and not the right clothes when I need it?*

Greta: *Are you okay? Did you sleep last night?*

Pippa: *I don't know. I don't know what to do. He said he liked me, but he didn't want to have sex with me last night. Why?*

Greta: *Really? I was so sure. We were all so sure that none of the other producers wanted to bet against it.*

Pippa: *Wait, you tried to bet on us? What else have you bet on? Nevermind. I think he's not as interested in me as he said and doesn't want to lead me on. I'm going to lose him, aren't I? Maybe I should leave instead? Gahhh, do you think I should wear this green dress? Help me.*

"Are you ready, Pippa, for your life to change?"

Déjà vu settled over me. For a quick moment, I froze, disoriented.

"Are you ready, Pippa, for your life to change?" Mark asked again.

This wasn't my first day on the beach. This was the end. Mark wasn't in his loud Hawaiian shirt and swim trunks like the first day. Today, he appeared out of place in a crisp black suit.

After trying on every single piece of clothing I had brought to the beach multiple times, I settled on a lime green dress. In hindsight, it wasn't the best choice. The color reminded me too much of last night's green dress. The dress that he tore off of me. The dress that I had to pick up from the floor, in humiliation, after he stopped.

Today's green dress had a tight satin sheath that turned me into a fancy, unripe banana, if banana peels rode up your legs and had a built-in bustier. My boobs looked fantastic.

My ability to breathe or walk—not so much.

That's what I got for my lack of concentration. That's what I got for wallowing in sadness over never seeing August after this, when I should have realized that I was dressed up as a business casual-phallic fruit.

"You and August are the last couple to go through the special ceremony," Mark said, oblivious to my inner turmoil. "I'm delighted to say that Pietr and Hailey, Drew and Amelie, Kaiden and Vidhya, and to everyone's surprise, Annie and Beckett are now engaged!"

"What?" I shouted, scaring poor Mark. "Annie and Beckett are engaged? I thought they were just friends."

"You and me and everyone else," he muttered. "Yet, Beckett got on one knee, and Annie said yes. They've won a trip to Tahiti and are the proud owners of a quarter-of-a-million-dollar diamond engagement ring, which is theirs to keep if they stay engaged for at least six months."

"Wow." Had I been so in my head and self-absorbed with August that I had failed to notice Annie and Beckett's romance? Sure, they spent a lot of time together, but the only thing that I had heard them talk about was juice recipes. On the other hand, who was I to judge the power of juice?

"It could be five for five." Mark wriggled his fingers at me.

"No, it won't."

Startled, Mark raised his arms, the same way someone might approach a startled beast. "It's okay to have doubts. You have to *let* yourself trust this journey."

"No, I won't be getting engaged. You'll have to make do with four engagements," I repeated. For added effect, I crossed my arms.

Bad decision. The unripe banana dress stretched across my back, in danger of popping. Too late to shift positions. I was making a point, wardrobe accident or not.

"If you're not getting engaged, are you saying that you are planning to break up with August?" His voice rose with excitement. "It would be a first, but if that's the way you feel… quite a dramatic ending."

Excited murmurs rose around me. I could hear Greta's fast-clipped whispers from behind the potted plants. This was a fucking game to them.

"It's okay to let your emotions out during the conversation at the ceremony," counseled Mark. "Whatever *you* decide, we—I mean, August—would appreciate hearing why you dumped him at the last moment, especially after going to the Final Night with him. Don't hold anything back. It's good to let it all out, leave everything on the table. Cry if you need to. Okay? Good luck."

I was dismissed.

I picked my way down the steep stairs to the beach. Behind me, I heard Greta bark out commands. "Evan, check the sound. Steph, get a couple more camera guys down to the beach. I want more angles. I want *everything* to be caught."

Greta and the crew were going to be disappointed. This was going to be the most amicable breakup between a non-couple they ever recorded.

I don't do one-night stands, and I can't have sex knowing that there's no future… not even for you.

August's words roiled through me. Yesterday, I had shoved down my walls and had decided to follow my feelings. For a too-brief, mind-blowing moment, I thought it would be all worth it. We would use the Final Night to catapult us into the real world. Or at least, give me one night to store in my memory.

Then he pulled away. Despite him telling me I meant something to him, I clearly wasn't enough. If I wasn't enough for a serious relationship or a fling, then what was I good enough for?

The irony wasn't lost on me. I had asked him to slow down earlier, and when I was ready for him to catch up to me, he couldn't get there.

Hurt prickled underneath my skin. I wanted this show to be over. The whole experience was a failure on multiple fronts. This "vacation" was not a mindless break from real life for me to think about what to do next.

All this "journey" accomplished was to make me question what I wanted, instead of propelling me to the next part of my life. Instead of feeling excitement about planning a trip to climb in Patagonia or magical confirmation to go back to law, I dreaded the emptiness that would follow leaving this island.

Instead of feeling rejuvenated, I would leave with a broken heart.

Not a broken *heart*. That would mean that I had fallen—no, I would leave with a broken *something*.

Maybe Tia would let me stay with her and her husband, Andrew, for a while. My best friend liked to feed people as a sign of love. The thought of wallowing in homemade dumplings, the only thing Tia could make without burning pots, and ice cream sounded like the perfect recipe to eat away my sadness.

The ever-romantic Tia would tell me to chase after August. On the other hand, practical Andrew, whom I had gone to law school with, would likely tell me to dust myself off and forget about August.

In his terse way, Andrew could be trusted to list out why any relationship with August would be doomed to fail: First, our personalities were too different. August was too good, too kind, too trusting. I was a jaded floater who had seen too many people use others for their own benefits. He could never be happy with someone like me, and his goodness would bore me after a while.

Except, I hadn't been bored at all. I hadn't missed my phone or sought distractions. Before meeting August, I hadn't realized how much my mind wandered. Around him, I felt present.

In my mind, Andrew would poo-poo my counterargument and read off the second item from his fake memo: August was stuck to his perfect town. He had deep roots there in the community, while community, to me, meant brunches with different friends in different parts of the country whenever our schedules collided. I loved traveling, loved new experiences, loved being independent. I could never give up those parts of myself for a guy.

Except, could August be my new adventure? August mentioned his bucket list consisted of waking up to a beloved and enjoying the daily small joys. Was freezing in Antarctica or party hopping that much better than going to sleep next to someone you felt safe with?

Third, and the most important argument, August had a date with destiny, in the form of a soft-spoken knitter who made sweaters for dogs in shelters and fostered too many pets. Who was I to stand in the way of his true happiness?

Okay, okay. Andrew would never include the last one. But his other hypothetical points were valid. At the end of the day, August and I weren't compatible.

Instead of cursing August in my head, I should thank him for stopping us before sex made our *friendship* too messy. Once I left St. Lucia, I would wake up and realize my good fortune that we stopped before my feelings developed into something irreversible.

The only thing left to do was tell August thank you for keeping me company on the island, and… goodbye. Then, I would be free to cry in private.

At the bottom of the steps, I sucked in a deep breath at the edge of the beige, fine sand. I scanned the horizon for August. Far off, near the crashing waves, stood a wooden platform. Even from this distance, I could make out the plethora of flowers surrounding a lone figure—August.

My breath hitched for completely different reasons than this banana bustier.

The four engaged couples milled around on the sand between August and me. When I approached, they clapped and yelled encouragements. Annie squeezed my hand as I passed her, the diamond of her new ring glinting in the sunlight.

"Good luck. Whatever happens." Her brows dipped with concern.

Fuck.

What a fucking spectacle.

The romance of the island, the fancy dates, and forced proximity were meant to encourage people to forget their minds. The recipe worked for four couples who had definitely lost their senses if they had gotten engaged after knowing someone for two weeks.

Did they even know each other's phone numbers?

Taking as deep of a breath as my banana dress allowed, I marched ahead. I was determined to rip the Band-Aid off. Better to break up with August than be broken up with.

Up close, August didn't look like his usual self. He was dressed in a dark blue suit, with a white button-down shirt and a black tie. Someone had even put products in his hair to tame it. August resembled the lawyer and finance bros from my regular life.

I wanted to tear his tie off and rumple his clothes. This man in front of me was too put together. Too cool and unapproachable.

Too devastating.

When I stepped up onto the wooden platform, August's eyes dropped to the top of my dress, his hands clenched by his side.

Okay, not too cool. Maybe the banana dress was redeemable if I didn't faint from lack of air. I had something urgent to tell him… what was it?

"Hi, Pippa." My name rumbled from his chest, sending my heart aflutter.

August reached a hand up to adjust his tie before forging on. "I've been doing a lot of thinking about us."

I remembered what I was going to say—my breakup speech. Except, August was already breaking up with me. The pain twisted my insides up, cutting off my thoughts.

"We come from very different backgrounds, with very different goals. I don't know how we could work outside of this. Yet, I can't help but feel as if there's something between us."

"I feel it too." *What the hell did I say?* I was supposed to dump him. Wait. Wasn't he supposed to dump me? How I'm cool but he doesn't see a future, yada yada.

August froze at my words. It was clear he hadn't expected me to agree so readily. One of his hands reached up again to play with his tie. He looked a fraction more rumpled, more like the August that I had gotten to know in the past few weeks.

"I don't want to have a fling, or be friends with benefits," blurted out August. "Pippa, I want it all—all of you."

The twisting in my chest stopped, replaced by a single question. "Why did you stop last night?"

"Pulling away from you last night was the hardest thing I'd ever done." With a sigh, August ripped off his tie and stuffed it in his pocket. "I knew if we had sex when we hadn't talked about our relationship, there was a good chance you'd write me off as a one-night stand. Or you'd convince yourself that our connection was just physical. Or reason it as horniness due to two consenting adults stuck together on an island."

"Or that we'd lost our minds after being out in the sun for too long without AC." Jokes aside, I admitted, "You're right. I probably would have come up with an excuse… and then later, regretted my cowardice."

"You're not a coward for wanting to protect yourself," he started, the tenderness in his eyes holding mine captive. "I backed off last night in part to protect myself too. A relationship formed on a show has almost no chance of surviving in the real world. Yet, practicality doesn't seem to matter for once. Every time I'm with you, I find another interesting thing about you that makes me eager to learn more.

"I like when you tease me. I like quiet times when we're both in our heads, because I feel comfortable with you. I like how you challenge me and make me see things in new ways. I like the intelligence you try to hide because you don't want to show off. Don't hide with me, because everything I've seen is sexy. So, yeah, I like you way too much, Pippa. Let's throw out rationality and see what we could be outside of this."

My chest expanded. I could breathe again. My mind whirled in a million directions, sorting through his words, trying to find any pitfalls. Why was I elated, instead of protesting, that we would fail so badly that we shouldn't even try?

I like you way too much, Pippa.

August stuck his hands in his pockets, shifting onto one leg.

Oh, *fuck*. The producers got to him and overrode his common sense.

"You're going to propose?"

Alarm crossed August's face. He pulled out his hands. To my relief, they were empty. "No." Suspiciousness warred with more alarm. "Are you hoping for a proposal?"

I laughed, breathing out relief. "No. It's just the other couples are engaged, even Annie. I didn't know if you got caught up."

"I am not a romantic who falls in love at first sight. Nor will I get engaged to someone whose phone number I don't know," he said, his lips quirking up in amusement. Then, in a more serious tone, he stared at me. "What do you think about trying to date outside of this?"

Longing filled me. All the words inside of me that I couldn't place yet, all the feelings inside that I didn't dare name yet—they fluttered, daring me to define them.

Yet another part held me back in the name of self-preservation. I was already too *in like* with August. What would happen to my heart if we pursued something outside of this island? What would I do if he broke it when he inevitably realized that we didn't suit?

"We are very different," I stalled.

"Yes, without a doubt."

"Our lives are very different," I added.

"Also true."

"We'll probably clash in the real world."

"True. Wow, Miss Fleming, you are acing this test," August bit out, sarcasm coating his every word. He paced to the far side of the platform, overlooking the ocean. The waves crept closer, the white foam touching the wooden structure.

The tension had left his body. Instead of anger or frustration, he seemed tired.

The hope behind those expressive eyes burned away, turning them into a bleak, unapproachable abyss.

I sped up my words. "I memorized a speech. I wanted to sound fair but firm —something where we could still be friends after this. After all, what's the chance a reality show romance would work in the real world? Rip off the Band-Aid. It was a very good speech."

"Pippa…" My name ripped out of him on a tortured breath. August raised his hands to frame my face, his thumbs brushing against my cheeks. With a groan, he tore back his hands and stuffed them into his pockets.

I didn't want him to withdraw. I wanted him to keep touching me, his strong hands on my smooth skin. I placed a hand on his chest. Even through his suit coat and shirt, I could feel the responding jump to my touch. At that moment, standing close enough that I could hear his heartbeat, I made my decision, the decision that had always been waiting for me to grab onto.

This time, I grabbed his face in my hands to keep him with me, to keep him from retreating. My words tumbled over each other in a rush to be heard. "For reasons I don't fully understand, the idea of staying to date you is more exciting than the idea of gallivanting around the world. Let's do it. Let's date outside of this. Is your offer to visit you in Beach Falls still on the table?"

August cocked his head to one side. I almost laughed at his look of confusion as the words slowly sank in. As his expression transitioned from confusion to hopeful, calmness lodged in my chest.

At the end of the day, I didn't want to leave him. That desire to be with him overshadowed my fears. When I looked at it that way, I had no other choice. My earlier pain had shifted to a mix of anticipation and a sense of… *rightness*. Like the feeling I had when I took off my power suits after work or a too-glamorous dress after a night out to snuggle into my oldest pajamas.

My mind was clear for the first time on this island. I was no longer muddling through this reality experiment, trying to figure out my next steps. August *was* the next step. The other pieces of my life would just have to fall into place or wait until I was done exploring this relationship with August.

"Hm, I just realized that I don't know your last name."

"Weather."

"August Weather? Really?"

Mr. August Weather grinned. "My parents thought it was funny. My older sister is June."

"Are you at least born in August, and your sister in June?"

"She is," he replied, his eyes twinkling in that way that preceded one of his dad jokes. *Remind me not to bring this guy to poker games.* "My birthday is September 5. My parents thought it was close enough to August to name their son that. They still think it's hilarious."

His eyes softened at the mention of his parents. My heart beat faster. This was what he looked like when he talked about someone he loved. I wanted to capture his expression and point it to me.

What an odd thing to think.

"I seem to have forgotten what I was going to say… again," I blurted out.

August's mouth twisted up. He pulled my body closer until we were almost touching. Forget what we were talking about—the tease of his body against mine was too much.

"I swear," I whispered, "I'm not usually so forgetful. Around you though, I seem to be a little scattered."

"You were saying what a great idea it is to date outside of this beach." August bent to kiss my cheek.

His breath sent tingles down my spine. I clutched at his shirt. It was only because I was wearing heels that I needed to hold on to someone. It wasn't at all because my knees were wobbly from a single chaste kiss on my cheek.

Not so chaste when he sucked on my nipples last night.

"Yes. That's the answer to your earlier question. The offer to visit me is still on the table for you." He kissed my nose. As if sensing that my ground was shifting—because of the damn heels, what else?—August wrapped his arms around me, bringing me flush against him.

I leaned back to give myself a few inches to gather my thoughts. "Stop kissing me. You're distracting me."

"That's the point." August cradled my face. "Stop overthinking and kiss me back, before you decide chasing penguins in Antarctica is more exciting than breakfasts in small-town diners. Come home with me."

"Diners don't sound bad. I wasn't so keen on lugging freeze-dried food and my own waste bags around. August, be serious. I'm not joking." I grabbed his face.

As much as I had decided that I wanted to leave this island in a relationship with August, I needed him to know what he was getting himself into. If you set your expectations, then there were fewer chances to be disappointed. The last thing that I wanted was for August to be disappointed or regret me.

"I'm scared that I'll get hurt, that I'll suck at dating you… I don't know how to be a good girlfriend. I haven't had much practice. But I *want* to try. Are you sure *you* know what you're getting into with me?

His voice serious and steady, he said, "You don't need practice being a girlfriend. You've had a lifetime of being you, and *you* are what I want."

His words soothed a part of me I hadn't realized had been crying out for recognition, for assurance. He *saw* me. There was a possibility that he could want me for *me*. The idea was heady.

"Don't worry, I know what I'm getting into. I've told you I'm not a romantic. We've only known each other for two and a half weeks. I don't expect a lifetime commitment now. You can leave anytime you feel restless or this"—he gestured in between us—"isn't what you need. Promise me, though, you'll give us a fair chance."

He looked so earnest, so confident, so hopeful that I could do nothing except believe him. I nodded.

When his face lit up, I felt like I had climbed a summit. Wasn't that just a cheesy thought?

"Now, kiss me, August Weather," I demanded.

Did I ever find August not my type? For that slow smile spreading across his face had become my type. His exact shade of warm brown eyes had become the only right shade of brown. His goodness, his patience, his ability to appreciate me for me… he was unexpectedly everything I needed.

Anticipation brewing, I leaned forward to meet him halfway. My last thought before he kissed me senseless was that his expression had been a mix of tenderness and wonder.

As if he cared deeply about me.

Then he bit my lower lip, sucking on it, and all of my thoughts flew out. For the first time since I could remember, I embraced what my heart wanted.

PART 2

BEACH FALLS, (THE MONTH OF) AUGUST

CHAPTER SIXTEEN

~AUGUST~

"Finally! The twins are down for a nap. Let's enjoy five minutes of peace."

My sister, June, slumped down on the couch and closed her eyes. Her husband, Ben, reached over to rub her shoulders before he went back to scrubbing spilled milk from a corner of the living room rug.

Playing my part, I dropped down to look underneath a gray love seat. Triumphant, I grabbed a hidden Cheerio and added it to my pile of Cheerios that my twin nephews had tossed.

For ten-month-olds who couldn't walk yet, the twins had reached an expert level of chaos. In the thirty minutes that I had been at their house, the twins had managed to feed the carpet their cereal, water plants with their milk, and render their toy containers useless.

The rug underneath me was worn. The room was an obstacle to navigate, with stuffed animals and toys that made sounds strewn everywhere. One of the photo frames on the wall was askew.

It was one of my favorite places to be.

June and I had grown up in this house, with its creaky stairs, odd floor plan, and smell of cookies baking. When my parents moved to Maine a few years ago to live out their dreams of painting by the ocean cliffs, June and her husband had purchased the house.

Even though June and Ben had changed some of the furniture, the home felt the same—approachable and full of love. On top of my own happy memories as a kid here, I had new memories of spending time with June and Ben, and now these two twin tornadoes with the faces of angels.

June and I were only fifteen months apart. Our next-door neighbor, Ben, was in between our ages. Our parents had called us the three musketeers growing up since we were always together.

It had seemed inevitable for June and Ben to start dating at some point. For years, I hadn't minded being their third wheel, not when I had plenty of other single buddies to hang out with.

Except, one by one, my buddies got married. I was happy for each of them. Heck, I had been a wingman for several of them, a groomsman at six weddings, and celebrated their babies and new homes. However, with each wedding invitation came the nagging question of, when will I find my person?

Since Zara, I had dated plenty of women—sweet, kind, smart women that I didn't let too close to me. None of them stirred emotions stronger than "like" or "deep caring." None of them made me want to risk heartbreak.

Until my heart had zeroed in on an unsuitable, impractical woman who was fated to break it.

There was no denying my heart beat faster around Pippa. There was no rational explanation for the feelings she stirred within me; feelings that I didn't think I could ever feel for someone. Or how I hungered for her every touch, driven to know every part of her, and filled with deep-seated craving to be around her. It was as if I had lived in pastel until I met Pippa and now experienced the full spectrum of colors.

She had become too pivotal for me. When she had agreed to date outside of St. Lucia, she had shattered the last defense around my heart, leaving me a raw ball of need for her.

"I can't believe you're dating someone from a show. I can barely get you to date one of my friends," remarked June.

"That's because I've known all your friends since we played in the mud as kids," I retorted.

"Still," she mused, "it doesn't seem like you. I know you told us all about it last week, but I still can't wrap my head around the fact that my little brother went on a reality dating show and came back with a girlfriend. This is wild! My book club already has plans for watch parties when the show comes out in January."

"You did sign him up," Ben remarked.

Jackknifing up, June pointed to me. "It's August." As if that explained everything. "I half expected you to ditch the show to go read history books in a dusty library somewhere."

"I'm more interesting than that."

"Are you, little brother?" she teased. "Did you wow Pippa with your talk about picking the right fishing bait or a dissertation on the Hundred Years' War?"

"Nah, zombies and Pluto."

Laughing, she chugged her coffee before sinking back onto the couch. "Maybe that's what you youngins are calling it these days."

"This youngin is only a year younger than you," I drawled.

"*Fifteen* months. Those extra months give me infinite wisdom over you. It says so in the *Official Handbook of Older, Wiser Sisters*. C'mon, tell me your plans. When are you going to see Pippa again? How'd you leave it off?"

Shaking my head in amusement at her impatience, I answered, "This week, she's staying at her parents' house in Boston and hanging out with some friends. But, in half an hour, she's going to come to my house to hang out for the day."

"Ah, is that why you bought a cup of matcha latte at The Flying Squirrel at 8:00 a.m.?" My sister sat up again. Nothing energized her like gossip.

"It could be for me."

"You don't drink lattes. Besides, Rose said you brought a thermos to pour it into. Why would you need a thermos unless you wanted to keep it warm for someone else who is coming later?"

"Here I was, hoping Rose would keep it to herself."

"Sure." She smirked. "For a few minutes."

Ben chimed in, "I heard it from Bill at the hardware store this morning when I was picking up screws for the baby gate. He heard it from his wife, who heard it when she was picking up breakfast at The Diner."

"Why don't I take a page out in the *Beach Falls Times* with our full itinerary to save everyone the time?" In big red letters, I was ready to mark Pippa with the words "she's mine." Was that too caveman of me?

"That's mean of you. You'll deprive us of our gossip," chided June. "What are you planning to do for the day? Are you taking her to dinner?"

"I'm surprised you don't know already," I said, spotting another Cheerio behind a board book. Those devious babies, it was a wonder that any food made it into them given the amount they "shared" with the furniture.

Looking at my sister's and Ben's expectant faces, I grumbled, "After she sees my house, I'll show her around town. First The Diner. Then, I borrowed Rob's boat to take her out on the lake. For dinner, I made a reservation at Maestro's. Don't worry, *Mom* and *Dad*, I'll have her home by midnight. Do you approve?"

June stuck her tongue at me. "Maestro's is fancy."

I nodded. I got up to throw the handful of Cheerios away. Sure, there might still be a dozen floating around behind toys, but wasn't I being the best uncle by leaving some surprises for the twins to find later?

"You like her, then?" June's eyes sharpened.

I grunted in what I hoped was a noncommittal way. Speaking of grunting, when had I started doing that? *Same time as you started growling and thinking like a barbaric caveman about Pippa.* Damn, was I in trouble.

"August's a grown-up—" Ben started.

June tsked. "Even so, he's my little brother. It's my responsibility to annoy him with unneeded advice, especially when I'm worried for him."

Scratch that. There was something else that energized June besides gossip—butting into my business.

And nothing ticked her off more than me telling her to butt out. "I don't mind. I know you mean well, but I don't need any help."

"I do mean well. Does Pippa mean well?" she demanded, sticking her hands on her waist. I had heard this tone and seen this look a thousand times as a kid. But this time, she didn't know best.

Not about Pippa.

"Pippa's different, true. I like her. I *really* like her."

As if she hadn't heard me, June marched on. "I joked about the show, but to be honest, I thought I was signing you up for a much-needed vacation. I didn't expect you to *like* someone. How much do you know about her? A quick Google search returns hundreds of articles about her.

"Did you know she cofounded a company that created an AI fraud detection solution and sold it to E&Y? Did you know her parents are serial entrepreneurs who own homes all over the world? Or that she dated Mikey Olsen back in college? The same Mikey Olsen who is the heir to some bazillion-dollar tech company and running for Congress? Or that she dated *The* Alex Turgenev, the hockey player? Here, let me show you—"

I covered her phone with my hand to stop her. When June looked up with indignation, I said, keeping my voice firm and steady, "I don't need to read what random internet strangers say about her. They don't know her."

"You think you do?" June probed. "You spent two weeks with her while the cameras were on. Of course, she was on her best behavior. At best, you two got carried away by being forced to be together all the time in a beautiful place—same thing as camp or vacation flings. You have the biggest heart, and after Zara, you shut your heart to any possible relationship. I don't want you to open up, only to be heartbroken again."

That was the downside to having an older sister who knew you too well. June wasn't wrong in her concerns. In fact, she voiced the same doubts that crept up at night for me. If Pippa left, concluding that we weren't compatible outside of the show bubble, where did that leave me?

I couldn't go back to living half a life, after knowing what life could be like with her in it. I couldn't live a lifetime of knowing what I was missing.

For my own sanity, I pushed that ugly doubt away. If I gave it too much space, that doubt would create an unmovable seed in my mind. The seed would grow, overshadowing everything else, poisoning me from the inside, ruining whatever time I had left with Pippa.

During the last ceremony, she had promised to try. For now, that was good enough.

Drumming up confidence that I didn't quite feel, I said, "Then today will be a test. There will be no reason to pretend in Beach Falls."

For once, June had no words. She stared at me, blinking rapidly as if tears threatened her. Ben stopped with his carpet cleaning and wrapped an arm around her. "What your sister is trying to say in her own way is that we love you and want the best for you."

"I want you to be careful," she added.

"We also trust your judgment," Ben continued, with a pointed look at my sister.

"When your judgment matches mine." June nodded, looking so earnest that I laughed. "I love you, you big goofball. Now, please make me more coffee so I have the energy to show the munchkins who's the boss when they wake up."

Just like that, the tension dissipated in the room. Whatever came of this experiment with Pippa, I had family and friends to pick me up. Saying my quick goodbyes, I hurried home to get ready.

It had been a week since St. Lucia. To my surprise, after the final ceremony, Pippa and I hadn't had a lot of alone time together. All the final contestants had to participate in hours of filming *in the moments* and B-roll. While the show wouldn't air until early next year, we also received media training and were forced into multiple photo shoots to support upcoming publicity.

Every time I had tried to sneak in private time with Pippa, a producer pulled one of us away. Then the tropical storm warning hit, and there had been no time for any further discussion outside of exchanging phone numbers and figuring out how to get off the island.

Since coming home, Pippa and I had exchanged a few impersonal texts that focused on logistics of our first date in the real world. I hadn't expected love essays. Even then, I had an aunt three times removed, whom I had met once, who still sent me birthday cards with more enthusiasm.

Sweet Caroline, good times never seemed so good. Sweet Caroline.

The doorbell warbled the familiar lyrics ingrained in every Boston Red Sox fan. I turned off the YouTube video of a suit-wearing real estate agent karate chopping his pillows to prepare for an open house. My single pillow slumped down on the couch.

Taking a deep breath, I opened the door and swallowed hard.

Pippa wore an electric-blue silk dress that clung to her curves and showed off a tantalizing amount of pale skin. A ponytail pulled her hair away from her face that was half covered with giant sunglasses. Her sexy heels brought her to my height.

She looked out of place in Beach Falls. Too glamorous, too sexy. What the heck was I thinking when I suggested a date in my hometown? I should have taken her somewhere fancy in Boston instead of asking her to brunch at a diner known more for giant portions than finesse, or to schlep around in my friend's twenty-year-old boat.

Before I could suggest that we drive to Boston, she took off her sunglasses. Her brows drew together in a slight frown. As her breaths came out in an uneven pattern, she studied me.

"Hi, August."

Her unsteadiness was a balm to my doubts. Pippa was just as unsure about this as me. Yet she had shown up.

I pulled her inside and brought her into my arms. "Hi, Pippa."

The tension melted away from her as she sank against me. I played with her ponytail and tugged at it to tilt her face up. "I'm going to kiss you, okay?"

She nodded, her lashes fluttering down as her lips parted. I meant it to be a gentle kiss. But somewhere between my intentions and my need for Pippa, I lost control. My mouth moved over hers, teasing and insistent. When I lifted my head to catch my breath, Pippa chased me.

Growling—when did I learn to growl?—I pulled her inside. I backed her up against the wall, trapping her between my legs. Her hands flew to wrap them-selves around my neck, pulling me closer to her.

I kissed her soft cheek, down her neck, and sucked. Her hips rocked against mine. A moan escaped from her lips when she felt my cock, hard and ready. That sexy sound reminded me of the sounds she made when she had fallen apart in my arms in St. Lucia. They would forever be tattooed in my mind.

Every time I was around her, I thought I could control myself. Every time, I underestimated my control. Wild with need, I reached up to touch the sides of her breasts, and nearly came undone at the full weight of them. They filled my hands, her peaks hard in anticipation. I bent my head, eager to taste them, to tease her.

Pippa pulled my head up, stopping my exploration. She leaned back against the door, her eyes glazed and her lips swollen. In a breathy voice, she whispered, "Do you greet all your house guests like that?"

As if emerging from a Pippa-induced lust fog, I yanked away my hands. My manners or common sense didn't seem to exist where Pippa was concerned. I had been about to maul her in my hallway with my front door open. If she stayed long enough, I might regress to a caveman.

You. Me. Fuck. Now.

Because that image was too tempting, I stepped back from Pippa. "No, only you."

I meant to match her joking tone. Except where Pippa was concerned, nothing about how I felt was a joke. If she was startled by my intensity, she kept silent. Instead, she peered behind me with curiosity.

"Let me show you the house," I said. "This, um, is the hallway."

"Oh, yes, I won't forget the hallway." She winked at me.

What was this woman doing to me? I had never met anyone who had the ability to fluster me and put me at ease at the same time.

Trying not to stare at her long legs or ass as she walked around my house, I led Pippa through the first floor. When I had purchased this yellow Cape with black shutters earlier this year, I had been delighted to find something within my budget in my hometown. It was walking distance to the high school, soccer fields, and The Diner. There was half an acre of lawn in front of the house and another two acres behind the house of conservation land, where huge pine trees rose into the sky, providing shade in the summer.

Before I had left for St. Lucia, I had repainted the walls in an off-white color that June had recommended, and I had used a chunk of my savings to pay for nice, sturdy furniture. Books covered the shelves in the living room, and my parents' artwork hung on the walls.

Now, when I tried to look at it from Pippa's perspective, my long list of to-dos jumped to the foreground. Even though the rooms were clean, I had to admit that this looked like a bachelor pad—a bachelor-on-a-teacher's-budget pad.

"This is the kitchen. It's outdated, but on my list for future renovations. Here, I bought you a cup of matcha latte, with vanilla soy milk. It should still be hot." I handed her the thermos. "Want me to froth your latte like the way you like it?"

Heat rose up my neck and face. Pippa burst out laughing.

"Thank you," she said, her eyes sparkling. "I was worried that you would be different away from the cameras, that we would feel different. But you're still kind of weird and very, very thoughtful. And yes, please… froth it just the way I like it."

Mentally lecturing my cock not to respond to her husky voice and innuendo, I handed off the frothed latte. She took a sip and licked her lips. I needed to move before I did something impetuous like lift her up onto the kitchen counter to…

"Okay, um, let's keep going." I waved toward the back of the house before leading Pippa to the room that dominated the first floor. "This is the living room. It used to be two rooms, but my friend and I took down the wall to make it one bigger room."

When I bought the house, there had been a frilly formal living room and a sunny family room. Since there was only one of me, and I had no use for a room where I couldn't put my feet up, one giant room made the most sense. What did Pippa, who was used to the finer things in life, think of a room dominated by comfy couches and mismatched bookcases?

"It feels inviting and cozy. I like it," said Pippa, spinning around to take in the room. She reached out, nestling her hand in mine.

Didn't that feel right? Holding *my* woman's hand in my house in my home-town. What had been a project, it now felt like home with Pippa walking by my side.

Unable to stop the goofy grin spreading across my face, I squeezed her hand. "Here, let me show you the other parts. There's a half bath on the first floor. The previous owner liked the color teal, as you can see by the tiles. I want to renovate the kitchen and bathroom, but I haven't figured out what to do. Over here, you can see the backyard. I'd like to add a deck one day that spans the whole back of the house, put a grill there and some chairs. It would be great for summer barbecues, or just to read a book, watch the birds. You might even spot a deer… Boring, huh?"

"No. I've never stopped to watch the wildlife. It sounds lovely." She leaned up to kiss my cheek, lingering to nuzzle against my neck. "If you want, I could help you with renovation ideas. Not to intrude, but if you wanted ideas or for me to look at tiles."

"I'll take you up on that offer." Not letting go of her hand that I still held, I wrapped my other arm around her.

It was too easy to imagine Pippa and I working side by side, picking paint colors or bathroom sinks. Too easy to envision her with me on this to-be-built deck. As much as I didn't want to hope, my heart was determined to conjure up images of us. Tempting, *improbable* visions of what our lives could be.

Holding her tighter than necessary, I led her up the stairs. "Up on the second floor, there are three bedrooms and two bathrooms. Here's my bedroom."

"Have you brought anyone else up here? Forget it, forget I asked. It was stupid. It's not my business what you were up to before. Everybody has a history. I don't know why I asked." Pippa asked, her words rapid.

"Even so, are you jealous?"

"No."

Grinning, I wrapped my arms around her, pressing her back to my front. Pippa's head fell back against my shoulder, exposing her long neck. I brushed my lips against the pulse at her throat, reveling in the tremors coursing through her.

"Liar," I whispered. My mouth trailed up her neck and captured her for a kiss. There was no resistance from Pippa as she opened to welcome me in. Her tongue brushed against mine, sending a straight shot to my cock.

Where I was hard, Pippa was all softness and silk. Her body melted against mine, and her arms wrapped around my neck, holding me in place.

As if there was anywhere else I'd rather be.

I strummed my hands down her sides, coming up to brush against her straining breasts. Pippa arched back. Her ass ground against me, and her breasts pressed against my hands.

My vision blurred around the edges. No matter how much I wanted to bend her over, I wanted to tease her more. The beast in me demanded that she lose control first. Bite me, sink her nails into my skin to draw blood.

Forget about protecting myself from getting hurt. Forget future heartbreak when she walked away. Only this moment mattered.

Only Pippa mattered.

She was a drug. Her lips were sweeter than the peaches in my buddy's orchard in late summer. Every whimper and response from her fed my soul. Every frustrated sigh and movement to get me to touch her taut nipples pushed me closer to the edge.

I craved her with every part of me. Since we left St. Lucia, how many times had I fantasized of her in my bedroom? The images of her had infiltrated my dreams, and every morning, I had woken up, hard as steel, wanting her.

Here she was.

Desire overwhelming me, I pushed Pippa down onto my bed. I followed her, breaking my fall with my elbows, so as not to crush her. In my dreams, her red hair had been spread over my sheets as she lay naked, writhing in my arms.

My hand trembled as I reached to untie her ponytail. I fanned her hair out. She wasn't even naked, and yet, I had never felt this intensity of pleasure at seeing her bright red hair against the cool, white sheets.

My bed.

My woman.

Mine.

Pippa leaned up to kiss me. A soft kiss that did nothing to cool me down. The contrast enflamed me. It took everything in me to go slow, to not tear her dress off and fuck her until she screamed my name.

She slid the straps of her blue dress off her shoulders. Slowing the pace, she shimmied the silk inch by inch down her body until the dress caught on her nipples.

My breath turned ragged. There was not enough air in this room. Unable to wait any longer, I yanked her dress down. One of the shoulder straps broke. I didn't care. I would buy her a dozen shoulder straps later.

Light-headed, I stared at her skin-colored bra that didn't seem to have enough fabric to cover her breasts. I could see the darker color of her nipples peeping out from the lacy material.

My cock throbbed, an insistent reminder to hurry, to sink into her warmth. Claim her as mine. No wonder I couldn't think straight.

I tore my eyes from her breasts to see the rest of her. And almost came on the spot. Pippa wore no underwear.

With a siren's smile on her face, she spread her legs, an open invitation. "I came prepared, just in case."

"Fuck."

At my unexpected curse, a throaty laugh rumbled from her, shaking her body. Her nipples threatened to burst out of the lacy bra. Putting both of us out of this tortured anticipation, I pulled her bra down. Her breasts lay before me, an indecent feast, propped up by that sorry excuse of fabric.

"Fuck."

Pippa made me think, feel, say things that I didn't recognize. I should want to be gentle with her. Refined lovemaking. Instead, all I could think about was thrusting my cock between her tits, her pink tongue licking me each time. Erotic visions of Pippa playing with herself, while I feasted on her.

She had created a monster of need within me.

I leaned down to kiss her straining nipple. A low moan escaped from her. The moan escalated. Why was her moan vibrating from my pants?

I lifted my head from Pippa's chest and scanned the room for the noise. On autopilot, I reached into my jeans pocket. I threw my buzzing phone across the room and bent my head again.

A minute later, another phone rang, this time more jarring.

"You have a house phone?" Pippa's voice was still raspy and uneven, but her eyes were clear. "You're the first person I've met our age with a house phone."

"I regret it with every inch of me."

"That's a lot of inches." With a naughty lick of her tongue over her kiss-reddened lips, she nudged me with her hips, driving me fucking crazy. "You should answer it. No one calls on two different phone lines if they don't have something urgent."

With a groan of protest, I got up to grab the phone from the top of my drawers. "Hello?"

A few minutes later, I hung up. Pippa still lay on my bed, her hair a rumpled mess, her bra pushing up her naked breasts. How easy it would be to fall right back down. My cock would thank me. Maybe it would even stop hoarding all the blood and share with the rest of me, like my brain.

But I couldn't ignore the call.

With reluctance, I said, "Sorry, Pippa, change of plans. One of my buddies, Bryan, just called. He asked if I could look after his two-year-old for a few hours. His mom fell, and his wife isn't home yet from her shift. I don't know how long I'll be. Do you want to reschedule our date?"

Pippa sat up. She pulled up her bra and reached for her dress. "Why reschedule? Let's go."

Incredulous, I shook my head. "You're coming with me, to babysit?"

"How hard can it be to look after a toddler? Don't they sleep most of the day?"

CHAPTER SEVENTEEN

~PIPPA~

As it turned out, two-year-olds don't sleep for most of the day.

Within fifteen minutes of Bryan's call, August and I had arrived at his friend's house. I didn't know what prompted me to say yes to babysitting at ten o'clock in the morning—a time when I would normally have still been sleeping on the weekends. I wasn't particularly maternal. Not that I was against kids; I simply hadn't given them much thought before.

Yet, for some nipple play, I had followed a guy to babysit.

Fucking amazing nipple play.

Seven hours later, I was so exhausted that if August fell on my boobs, I wouldn't even react. Okay, okay, *maybe* a little.

I didn't know how parents or teachers looked after kids all day. It was more exhausting than being stuck in an airport with the fussiest law partner. At least my law partners could feed themselves and wipe their own butts.

From the moment Bryan opened the door and rushed out to help his mom, his daughter, Ellie, had run into August's arms with a big smooch and glared at me. Kid was smart. If I were her, I would be all over August too.

Unlike the tiny terror though, I would nap all day like a squirrel hoarding sleep before adulthood came about. I would not whizz about the house, changing my mind every two seconds.

By the end of the day, I was intimately familiar with Bryan's house. I knew where all the snacks were, as evidenced by Ellie trying every single one of them.

I knew where all her toys were, including those wrapped on the upper shelf of the bathroom closet for her upcoming birthday.

I had read every single *first* page of her bazillion books. We had taken five three-minute walks outside, each of which included thirty minutes of getting ready *before* going outside. As a last resort to tire her out, I had even tried ideas inspired by Pinterest for toddler art.

To my surprise, every single Pinterest-er was lying. None of those artworks were created by kids, not if Ellie was an example. No matter how the art project started, we ended up with a soggy piece of paper with various shades of brown. Who knew that if you mixed enough colors together, the mixture always resulted in mud?

At one point, I had even attempted to rock her to sleep while singing random songs. With nary a yawn in sight, Ellie had told me, "No, no, no, maaah do it."

Then, she had proceeded to warble at the top of her lungs the ABCs. Or rather, the ABUs, because she "no like *c*." When I tried to argue with her that *c* followed *b*, she had asked why. At that moment, with all of my education and work experience, in the face of toddler logic, I had no answer.

Surrounded by something that I learned was called Duplos, I sprawled on the floor in the living room, in a dress with a broken strap temporarily held together by a hair tie. In the hallway a few feet away, August fed Ellie yogurt from a pouch, while she perused a book upside down.

Why was she eating in the hallway? Who knew. I was simply grateful that she wasn't on any carpet. Or hadn't snuck the yogurt to feed the plants, as she had seven messes ago.

"Unda, unda." Ellie tugged at August's hand. "More snackie, snackie! Peeeeze."

"Sorry, munchkin, it's almost dinnertime. How about some milk?" He leaned over to wipe yogurt from her tutu.

"Cho'lay?"

"No chocolate milk."

"A weetle?" Ellie crawled into August's lap and gave him a slobbery kiss.

Glancing at me sheepishly, August shrugged. "I better find chocolate milk then." He laughed as the bouncing toddler threw her arms around him. With her clinging to his neck, August strolled into the kitchen in pursuit of more sugar.

Their banter in the background as a lullaby, I stared up at the ceiling, my eyes half closed. I couldn't remember a better day. Sure, we were all covered with food and paint, and my hair might be a rat's nest after she had decorated me with "pwetty" hair clips.

But Ellie was alive. Plus, she had even given me her doll to hold—as I'd learned, a clear toddler sign that I was in her good graces.

Beyond Ellie's *gracious* acceptance of me, August had been a revelation. Yet again.

Mentally, I knew he would be good with kids. After all, he taught and coached kids nine months out of the year. But seeing him with a kid—seeing him fake wrestle or soothe an imaginary boo-boo caused by a squished blueberry—it did something to me.

The earlier feelings of my world shifting intensified, and today, the ground cracked into visible lines. What lay underneath was too nebulous to see clearly.

The possibility that I could be bad at being a girlfriend didn't settle well after years of pursuing perfection. Just like in St. Lucia, that unknown, coupled with the potential to get hurt, frightened me. After all, I had stuck to a lawyer road map way past my desire for revenge on the ex, precisely *because* it was a road map.

Plus, what was the chance that a relationship born on a reality dating show would survive? I would be foolish to think we stood a chance.

Yet, curiosity, tinged with anticipation, coursed through me. If August stood at the end of the darkness and jumped with me, could the possibility of flying outweigh the pain of crashing?

"Is she asleep?" August walked back into the living room, still carrying Ellie. He pointed to her head, which lay on his shoulder, her face turned away from him.

With a dubious look, I unglued myself from the floor and checked her little face. To my shock, Ellie was asleep. Her dark eyelashes cast a shadow on her chubby cheeks. Not to my surprise, her drool created a tiny wet spot on August's shirt.

I brushed the back of my hand against her soft cheeks. Tenderness—or was it relief?—welled within me.

"Should we put her in her crib?" I whispered, taking a half-eaten animal cracker from her hand. The cookie came with me easily, a clear sign that Ellie was sound asleep. After a day with her, I had decided that whoever came up with the phrase "taking candy from a baby" had never met a real kid.

"No." Shaking his head, August sat down on the couch. "From what I've heard, kids have the magical *inability* to sleep in cribs. Let's not risk it."

Eager to get closer to August, I scootched aside a row of stuffed animals on the couch to make room for myself. Careful not to disturb Ellie, I rested my head against his other shoulder.

"Hey, I'm glad you're here," he whispered.

Despite his chocolate milk mustache, I leaned up to kiss him. "Me too."

When his lips turned up in a tired but utterly content smile, acute longing twisted in my heart. *This is what it could be for us.*

Even though I had supported Tia when she went through her drama, I hadn't understood why she had wanted to break off her engagement to try again with her ex-but-not-so-ex-husband… besides that her sort-of-ex, Andrew, made her horny. At the time, I hadn't envied her. After all, was one man worth the hassle? The whole situation had been too messy.

Now, I understood. In Tia's heart, Andrew hadn't just been an eligible, smoking hot guy. He had been the *only* guy who fit just right.

Opposite of what TV or movies depicted, you didn't need fireworks or chasing after your beloved in a speeding train to realize that you stood on the precipice of something marvelous. Or maybe I had never needed the grand gestures and had only now realized that I'd looked in the wrong places my whole adult life.

In the quietness of dusk, basked with waning sunlight from the open windows, August and I stared like goofballs at each other. My legs rested on his. We were cocooned in the intimacy of this absurdly normal moment after the chaos of earlier.

The same divergence of paths opened up for me as last week on the beach. On one side lay August, his forehead resting against my hair. He held the keys to an unknown, risky world of *potential*. On the other side lay self-protection and self-doubt.

When I agreed to date August, I had made the decision to dip my toes into the unknown. Only to find that I was fully submerged. Without knowing where the path would lead me, my heart was already running toward him.

Willingly.

Deliriously.

At the same time, terror crowded in with taunts that August wasn't by my side. The possibility, that we moved on parallel paths that would never meet, dismayed me.

Still, I made no attempt to brake.

August was my missing puzzle piece. I could cram hundreds or thousands of other pieces next to me. On most days, they would even fit okay. But I didn't want *okay*. I wanted my exact puzzle-match, no matter how wild the circumstances were in which we had met.

"Pippa—"

"August—"

Nervousness crept in. I whispered, "No, you go ahead first."

Against my body, his muscles tensed up. As if in pain, August closed his eyes.

I waited for him to continue. I waited for him to show me where I was running toward, if we would intersect. To tell me he was with me in dismantling our individual lives in order to fall toward each other.

Or, I thought with panic pinching at me, burn the path underneath me if he didn't feel the same.

When he opened his eyes, the depth of feeling threw me off-kilter.

"Pippa."

My name fell from his lips, exhaled on a ragged breath. With hope bubbling up, for his longing felt like a mirror of my heart, I cradled his face.

I fought my instinct to hide. Instead, I willed him to look… to really see me. See what I couldn't yet put into words, on my face, in my touch, beating in my heart.

"August, I—"

"I'm home—oh, did I interrupt something?"

A perky Asian woman entered the living room, carrying a clear container of muffins. She wore pink scrubs covered with Disney princesses. My mind registered her surprised face—the exact same as Ellie's when I found her in my heels. She dropped the box of muffins near the front steps.

"Hey, Min, we just got Ellie to fall asleep. Here, let me hand her to you." August stood up in slow motion and transferred Ellie to her mom's arms.

Even deep in sleep, Ellie wrapped her arms around her mom's neck, as if her sleeping body recognized her mom. When Min nuzzled her daughter's cheeks, Ellie gave a loud, indelicate snore.

"You must be Pippa," said Min, her dark brown eyes wide with curiosity. "I've heard so much about you… ahem, I've heard an adequate, non-gossipy, amount about you."

Red tinged August's cheeks. He placed a hand on the small of my back. "Pippa, this is Min, Ellie's mom. She's a nurse at the senior center in town. How's Bryan's mom?"

"Hi." I waved. "I hope she's okay."

Shifting Ellie to one side, Min reached over to pull me into a surprise one-arm hug. "Oh, yeah, she's fine. She'll be discharged tomorrow morning, and already she's complaining about hospital food. Thank you for watching Ellie while Bryan went to check on his mom. I'm so sorry to have ruined your date."

With a glance at the muffins on the steps, she continued, "Those muffins are for you. I heard August was planning to take you to The Diner, so I brought you some muffins from there on the way home."

"Thank you," I said, picking up the box of muffins. The box was still warm, and the smell of fresh muffins reminded me that I had only eaten green and purple kid yogurt and Cheerios today.

"June texted your plans to our book club," said Min, with a sheepish smile.

"There are forty of you in that club." August glared at Min, even as he reached for me. His arm wrapped firmly around my waist, anchoring me along the length of him. As if I belonged with him.

Min stared at my face, my broken dress strap and then the lack of space between August and me. For a brief second, I thought she would make us stand apart—room for Jesus, as my eighth-grade dance chaperones would say.

However, she beamed at my broken strap, in the same unguarded way her daughter beamed at sugar. At the rate that gossip moved in this small town, by dessert time, the news of my strap will have proliferated. I found I didn't mind August's friends knowing. Hell, I might even join them by shouting it from someone's colorful front door. He's mine!

Mine.

"If you're all set here, I'll take Pippa home," suggested August.

I scanned the first floor, wincing at the sight of toys scattered everywhere. "Yikes, why don't we help you clean up?"

Min waved my words away. "What are you talking about? Stepping on spiky toys and finding stuffed animals in my kitchen cabinets are the norm around here. You kept my kid alive, and you tired her out, so it must have been a great day for her. Go home, eat muffins, and finish… whatever led to your dress ripping."

With a wink, she hugged me again. When she got to August, she leaned up to whisper in his ears, "She's a keeper if she hasn't run out screaming after a day with Ellie. There is a reason we pay our babysitters more than the going rate."

"Shh, she's right over here."

"Pippa, if you didn't hear me earlier, you're a keeper!" Min called out, loud enough to elicit another snore from her daughter.

I laughed. If more happiness bloomed in my heart, I might need to add my heart to the list of body organs that needed examining, along with my neck.

"Pippa, let's go before her book club shows up to gawk at us." With an exaggerated sigh, August tugged my hand to lead me out of the house.

Without caring that we were in full view of Min who was furiously texting with one hand, I planted a loud smooch on August. "Okay, let's go home and make out."

CHAPTER EIGHTEEN

~PIPPA~

I had overestimated my ability to stay awake. Or underestimated how sneakily tiring chasing after a toddler would be. Somewhere on the ten-minute car ride back to August's house, I fell asleep after inhaling a still-warm chocolate chip muffin.

As much as I had grand plans to seduce him, I was more likely to topple over in exhaustion than participate. Or even remember.

When I woke up the next morning, soft dawn light flittered through the open curtains. Green leaves waved outside of the large window, and birds chattered in the distance.

It took me longer to register the heavy arm across my middle. *August*, I smiled to myself. I was in his bedroom, with my back pressed against his front. The last thing I remembered before falling asleep was taking off my clothes and putting on one of his comfy shirts. That shirt was now bunched around my hips.

Wriggling, I felt August's hardness against my bare ass. My breath caught in my throat, desire surging up, overwhelming me. I needed him inside of me, filling me up. Hard and fast, again… and again… until we lost ourselves.

I glanced behind me and groaned again. This time, in utter disappointment. August was still asleep.

Unless I wanted to wake him and demand cock, which I filed for later, my naked ass couldn't be near this shirtless man wearing gray sweats that hid *nothing*. In a dark mood, I slithered away from him.

Do you know the universal sign that you're one lick away from combusting? When slithering away from a hot guy made you horny too. Because slithering was rather close to wriggling, and wriggling was too close to… fuck, I had lost my mind.

Tiptoeing, though in my mind I stomped in frustration, I made my way to the bathroom to wash my face and brush my teeth with a new toothbrush I found in a drawer. With August still asleep, I headed downstairs to the kitchen.

What was the next best thing to mind-blowing sex? Okay, okay, fine, for me, a thousand steps below sex and guaranteed to cool my inner lusty bunny down?

Cooking.

"What are you doing?"

My heart thumped wildly at August's voice, raspy from sleep. Before I could turn around, he wrapped his arms around my waist from the back and kissed my cheek. The dichotomy from the casualness of the kiss and the sensations of being pressed against his naked chest threw my nerves into an ecstatic dance.

Or maybe I was standing too close to the stove, and my brain had fried.

"You ordered scrambled eggs every morning in St. Lucia." I lifted the lid of the pan on the stove. "So, I'm scrambling eggs for you."

August peered at the bright yellow mush in the pan. "Why is it steaming? Why do you have a lid on the pan?"

"I cracked the eggs into the pan, mixed it—"

"Mixed in the pan?"

"Yes." I turned around to stare at August's puzzled half-smile and couldn't help running a free hand through his tousled hair. His handsomeness disarmed me.

I squinted at him in suspicion. "Why, are you supposed to mix it somewhere else?"

His shoulders shook with what looked suspiciously like laughter.

"It seemed the most efficient to do it in the pan. Plus, no dirty dishes. Isn't there something called one-pan meals?" I explained. "Anyways, I mixed and waited, but the eggs got hard-looking. So I added some water."

August's chest rumbled.

I didn't understand what was so funny. My eggs were edible. Sort of. "The eggs still looked a bit dry and stiff. Then, I added some more water and put the lid on, like a sauna to hydrate the eggs. But they're not getting fluffier."

"You created an egg sauna?" He snorted.

I was definitely standing too close to the stove. Staring at him, I fanned myself with the spatula. It was a poor fan. Whoever invented spatulas with rectangular holes running through them had no foresight for my plight.

"Why not? I feel hydrated after going to the spa. Why wouldn't eggs? Hey, stop laughing." I glared at August as he let me go to double over. "You should have a word with your grocer for giving you defective eggs. These eggs aren't softening up, no matter how long I keep them in the sauna. They look like plastic."

I lifted the lid to poke at the eggs once more. There was no denying it. I had ruined the easiest dish to cook. There went any chance to impress August that I was a non-insider-trading Martha Stewart.

Frustrated, I turned off the stove. "Earlier, I found some yogurt and bread. Do you want that instead? Or I'm a champion food orderer. I could call a place."

August shook his head as he straightened up. Remnants of laughter remained in the curve of his wide mouth. He reached over to cradle my face, his expression impossibly tender.

"I love you, Pippa."

Forget about defective eggs.

This man loved me. This wonderful, down-to-earth, sexy man who didn't realize that he was too good for me, loved… me. Even after knowing that I was shit in the kitchen, hugged bathroom floors after drinking too much tequila, didn't know where I was going in life, and a thousand other imperfections, he loved me.

Me.

I threw myself into his arms, eager to get closer. To pinch me, him, to make sure he—

"Ow!" yelled August, nearly dropping me to rub the back of his head.

"Oh, sorry. I didn't mean to hit you with the lid," I whispered. Setting aside the blundering lid on the kitchen counter, I climbed back onto August, wrapping my legs around his waist.

My insides fluttered with delirious euphoria that flooded me with bursts of energy. I rained kisses over his face. So what if they were more scattered and enthusiastic than sexy?

August didn't seem to mind. His eyes crinkled. "I love you, Pippa Fleming, despite your attempt at sauna-ing eggs and the potential of eating shell-y eggs. I love you."

For the first time, my future was clear: leisurely Sunday mornings with this man, the courage to try new things, and laughter when we fell short. He was temptation incarnate—a vision of what could *be*.

Yet, despite how much I yearned for this vision, something held me back. I had run the length of this path toward August, only to find out that there was a final leap to reach him.

One tiny jump, yet a world of change.

No matter how much my heart longed for him, how much it compelled me to take the final leap, I froze. At this crucial moment, I couldn't erase a lifetime of taking the safe road, of careful planning. My brain filled with doubts that this was going too fast, that this was too good to be true, that he didn't know enough about me yet...

If I said those magical three words back, those words would become promises. A lifetime commitment to August.

In the end, I teetered back from the brink.

Rejection stole the joy from him. My hesitation caused him pain. I had disappointed him with my lack of response.

"You don't know how much your words mean, how much you mean to me," I whispered. I hated myself for hesitating. It wasn't as if I rejected his declaration. In fact, I was very, very in *like* with August. "Please be patient with me. I don't want to say anything... until I can make that promise without doubts."

"I told you before that I'll wait for you." Instead of judgment or anger, he nodded with understanding. He bent to kiss me, slow and patient. His hands stayed wrapped around me, as my legs and arms clung to him. Kiss by kiss, he soothed away the tension within me, replacing it with tenderness.

With his love.

With surety that we were going to be okay.

That whenever—because it was a matter of *when*—I took the final step, August would be with me. *When* I said those words, they would carry the full weight of my heart, free from doubts and fears.

"Why don't we buy some non-defective eggs, and I can try again? I could even make you eggs every weekend," I offered.

"No, I can think of something else for weekend mornings," he drawled, his voice dropping.

Just like that, his touch sped from gentle to dark and possessive. If I had underwear, it would have also dropped at the images that he conjured up with his whiskey-deep voice—our limbs entwined on the bed, his head bent at my breast, August lining himself up against my wetness, not to tease, but to *finally* possess me…

As if he could read my mind, his mouth twisted slowly into a wicked smile. Anticipation strummed through me. Before I could yell my enthusiastic agreement, August started walking up the stairs, with me still wrapped around his waist.

Inside his bedroom, he dropped me onto his bed. Before I could protest, he tore off my shirt, leaving me naked in the soft morning light for him. To devour at his leisure, as he cursed under his breath. To memorize my body. The open curtains and sunlight made my nakedness all the more stark, inappropriately naughty.

Off went his sweats in a fluid motion, baring him to me. My greedy eyes thanked him. Already hard, his cock jutted out at me. Whatever I expected from August was not this. Turned out Mr. Nice Guy hid one *large* secret.

"Stop that, Pippa," he growled, watching my tongue wet my lips.

His eyes darkened with desire and his hands fisted in the bedsheets. Above me on the bed, he looked half wild, as if any movement could snap his fierce hold of control.

Unleash it.

I reached up to flatten my palm against his heart. The touch unfroze August, because in the next moment, his hands moved down. He brushed against the sides of my breasts, palming them, lifting them up for his ravenous perusal. His fingers drew circles around the aching points, closer and closer… never touching where I needed him the most.

My heart skipped and skedaddled every time his fingers came close. I was on edge, and August had barely started.

"Touch me," I demanded.

"Where?"

"Touch me where I ache."

Except, I ached *everywhere*. My whole body had turned into a sensory overloaded instrument for August to play.

To wring out moans and pleas.

To tease.

Not tomorrow, not later. Now. I *needed* to be with him now.

"Please."

Who was this person begging for relief? It couldn't be me. She sounded too desperate, too at the whims of a man.

"Do you ache here?" With a wicked, wicked smirk, August took my nipple into his mouth, his tongue swirling on the hardened peak. His right hand flicked at my other nipple. The light movement combined with his mouth sent tremors throughout my body.

I couldn't help my body from arching up, in a wanton plea for more. I couldn't help the moans and pleadings from tumbling over each other. Neither could I help my hands from grabbing on to whatever I could of him, my movements growing more frantic with each flick of his tongue.

"Please, August… I need more…"

"More like this?" He released me and slid down.

Before I could register the coolness of air against my nipples, August was *there*. He lifted me, his eyes blazing with hunger as if he hadn't eaten in days. In my delirium, it wasn't farfetched to imagine that we were each other's feasts. Rewards for any heartache and loneliness before.

When he finally touched me *there*, where it ached for him, my body arched up in a helpless offer. In a plea for him to devour me.

The last vestige of my control snapped. I couldn't decipher nor prevent the pleading words—no, more like animalistic sounds—from tumbling out. My loud cries mixed with August's low laughter against my center. His movements, his tongue exploring before teasing that focal point of my desire, his fingers testing my wetness. Each touch sent me spiraling.

Every time I thought I reached a point where a breath could tip me over, August drew back, his hands holding my thighs open.

"August, please…" I begged, my voice coming out in puffs of air. "I was mistaken, you're not a nice man."

He lifted his head and propped my legs on his shoulder, widening me up even further. "Want me to stop?"

"No!" I demanded. My hands fluttered toward him, pushing his head, pulling him up. I needed him to move, and I wasn't picky which way.

"Good girl, scream my name," he growled, bending down again. This time, he sucked me into his mouth.

I shattered at the light pressure. My body arched. Spasms wracked me, radiating pleasure so intense I wanted to retreat, except August continued to hold me, keeping me in this moment. His name tumbled from me, over and over, until my throat was hoarse, and I could think of nothing else except him. *My August, my lover.*

"That's it, love, come for me," he muttered against me, as I bucked against his face, prolonging my orgasm, wringing out every tremor and incoherent demand. I felt as if I had run miles, leaped over mountains, tumbled over into an unknown world where only sensations dominated.

When the spasms slowed to gentle waves, August slid up and wrapped me up in his arms to kiss me. With all the desperation and lo-*like* I felt for him, I kissed him back.

My enthusiasm compensated for any lost techniques. My mouth, my body, every part of me, was still on fire and shaking too much for finesse. If August hadn't taken away my ability to string thoughts together besides "please" and "more," I might have realized earlier that something had been missing.

His pleasure.

Blinking, I leaned away from August. I peered at him from beneath heavy lids. Hunger, raw animalistic hunger, blazed across his handsome face, as he struggled to calm his breathing.

I shivered. Not out of fear or disgust, but in reaction to his fierce need. And to my own need for him. For, even after the mind-blowing orgasm, I still ached for him.

Our breaths mingled in the quiet room. Loud, broken breaths.

Anticipation strummed through me. The first orgasm took the edge off. Now, I was ready to play. The next time, August would be just as out of control as me.

"Hi there." I lifted my hips, bringing me flush against his hard cock. One of his hands shot down to hold me in place, his fingers digging into my skin.

"Hold on, I got some condoms." With reluctance, he reached over to his nightstand.

"I'm on the pill," I suggested. "And we were both thoroughly checked by the show's medical team, before St. Lucia."

"Are you sure?"

I nodded.

August moved back on top of me. "Hi, love." Though his words were gentle, the glint in his eyes was anything but. In challenge, August shifted and brought his cock closer to my entrance, sliding up and down.

So close.

The lewd sound of his naked cock against my wetness caused my body, still sensitive from his mouth and fingers, to clench in longing. If I thought I could stay in control, I was dead wrong. Seducing him backfired and threw me back in flight toward the edge.

This time, I was on a mission.

My mission was him.

Inside.

Of me.

Now.

Biting a moan back, I circled my hips, teasing him, teasing me. I brought my hands up to lift my breasts, flicking the still-sensitive nipples.

August's movements faltered. "Keep doing that."

I smiled at his guttural command. It only served him right to be driven a little wild, to make up for the fact that I was all sorts of irrational for him. "Tell me, August, what do you want?"

His eyes were liquid caramel in the glow of the sun streaming through the open windows. I had never had sex in the sunlight, and now I wondered why not. In the light, it was impossible to deny the love and stark longing in August's face, the way his hands fisted in the bedsheets, the corded tension in his muscles from holding himself in control.

He was a feast made for my starving heart.

"You. I want you, Pippa," he replied, without artifice, in that warm baritone that reached deep into my soul.

I stilled. "Then, take me."

The only warning was the shifting of the mattress underneath me as August's control snapped. *Finally.*

Before I could lift my hips to help him, August thrust inside, filling my emptiness, stretching me to accommodate him. I felt impossibly full, impossibly sensitive… impossibly next to the edge again. The welcome shock of him gave way to the *rightness* of this.

Maybe it was because it had been too long. Or because he had tormented me until my body craved his. Or just maybe, this was always meant to be.

August and me.

"Fuck."

Me and August.

"Fuck," he repeated. He kissed me, his tongue mimicking his intentions. "You feel so fucking good, Pippa."

I wriggled.

August bit my lower lip and pulsed, wringing a moan from me. This was no Barre class, with all of the micromovements. I wanted an onslaught… of him.

I clenched around his cock.

"Fuck."

Pulling out of me until only the tip remained, August whispered, "I love you, Pippa."

I l-lo-

He thrust hard. This time, he was truly fucking me, his strokes long and fierce. I cried out in relief, in pleasure. There was nothing to do but meet him head-on, match his ferocity with my need.

In and out.

In and out.

I wrapped my arms around his neck, my legs around his waist to spur him on. "Faster… I'm almost…"

August quickened his pace. The headboard behind me slammed against the wall with every thrust. Through the haze of pleasure, I could see him over me, his face contorted in concentration and hunger.

No longer the good-natured, handsome guy next door, he was a relentless warrior laying siege to me. Possessed by the same haze of desire that wove its way around me. Around *us*. Pulling us into the depths of a world where only we existed.

The pleasure built, ensnaring both of us in its grasp. There was nothing else that mattered. Nothing except this furious, frantic race to the edge.

August reached a hand between us and found my little nub. Shockwaves radiated from where his fingers touched. The light pressure was too much.

There were *too* many sensations.

"Too much…"

When he paused to withdraw his fingers, I grabbed on and held him close. Like a wild beast, I yelled, "Did I say stop? Don't you dare stop, you hear me? Oh… right there…"

"Like this?" He circled my center, his strokes never wavering. Yet, even as he fucked me senseless, even as his eyes glazed over, he had the gall to tease me.

That damn infuriating man. "Touch me, August… don't leave me hanging."

"I'm right here." His fingers moved.

That was all it took to set me off again. I spasmed around his cock, riding waves of pleasure more intense than before. With a triumphant shout, August came with me, sinking harder and deeper into me.

This—him inside of me, his movements wild as he lost all vestiges of control—had been missing earlier. Each thrust, each touch of his fingers, each kiss heightened my orgasm until my body didn't feel like my own.

There was no artistry to our movements, no choreographed dance. It was just us letting our bodies be. No judgment in how we looked or sounded.

We were simply us.

CHAPTER NINETEEN

~AUGUST~

I love you, Pippa.

Her awful eggs didn't make me fall in love with her. How could they? They looked more like slime with too much borax than anything edible. No, those words and the intensity of my feelings behind them had been building since the beach.

As unrealistic as finding your soul mate on a reality TV show was, we had needed the show. If I had met her at any other place, I wouldn't have stood a chance. Pippa would have remained an intrigue for me, someone unattainable.

Filming had created a bubble for me to get to know Pippa, and vice versa. Despite the eighteen-hour days filming while in forced proximity, the challenges, and producer demands, I would forever be thankful.

In those weeks, she had become more than beauty. She had rewritten what I thought I wanted in a partner to reflect her.

I had promised her earlier that I would wait. When I said that, we both knew it wasn't just for her to repeat the words back to me, but for her to choose a life with me. If she ever said those words, it would be a promise to mesh our lives together.

If she said those words.

If she felt safe enough to say them.

"Hey." She had fallen asleep earlier. Now, she stirred in my arms, turning around so we faced each other. Her voice was low and raspy. Immense satisfaction rooted within me at the memory of her screams from earlier.

A shy smile touched her lips, still reddened from earlier. I bit back a groan at the image of Pippa's mouth around my cock. My cock couldn't hide its delight at the possibility. Forget morning wood or noon wood, or whatever time it was now. I had perpetual Pippa wood.

With a knowing smirk, Pippa asked, "Do you have somewhere you need to be today?"

"No."

Experimenting, she arched closer. "I have some ideas."

I should let her rest. Or feed her, since she hadn't eaten anything since the muffin from last evening.

"We could go for a ride." Pippa rolled her hips, leaving no doubt to her intentions.

There went my resolve to be a gentleman host. "Do tell, Miss Fleming. I'm at your disposal." *Yes, ride me.* My hands reached up to cup her breasts.

"Or, I could really go for a shower."

Disappointed, I stopped my exploration. Of course, she'd want to get cleaned up. She agreed to a date. This was someone whose prior dates consisted of helicopters and fancy dinners. Instead, Pippa babysat yesterday, while a two-year-old princess threw glitter and Goldfish around.

Pippa rolled off of me. Entranced, I watched her hips sway as she walked to the en suite bathroom.

"Are you coming?"

"Me?" *Yeah, smooth going.*

Laughing, she walked out of sight. I heard water turn on, as Pippa called out, "I've never been fucked in the shower. Don't wait too long, or I'll start without you."

"Did I mention how much I appreciate your boldness?"

"It's not bold if I already know your answer." Pippa stole a Pop-Tart from the box in my pantry and examined it. "Do you know that I've never had a Pop-Tart before?"

My mind shifted from memories of the shower to the Pop-Tart. "Really? Then let me show you the complete experience." I threw two into the toaster.

"My mom said my grandmother gave her Pop-Tarts for breakfast every morning in high school, and for my entire life, she's hated them. They're on her shit list, along with people using the wrong utensils or not wearing makeup."

"I like you either way. Without makeup, I can see your freckles." I held her face between my hands and kissed the tiny brown spots on her nose. "They're cute."

"Ugh, they're weirdly shaped." But her smile undermined her words. "I would have brought makeup or clothes if I knew I was spending the night. Whose fault was that?"

"You." I grinned, tucking her head against my shoulder as I wrapped my arms around her. "I should have known you couldn't resist my manly hotness. Or khaki pants."

Pippa's shoulders shook in silent laughter. I couldn't pinpoint what about this banal scenario tugged at my heart. Heck, I used the same toaster every day and had never thought beyond whether I wanted bread or bagel with my eggs.

The difference must be Pippa.

With the full early afternoon sunlight as her backdrop, she felt *right* in this kitchen. *Right* in my arms. *Right* in my life.

By agreeing to date after St. Lucia, I had had no expectations beyond a few months of fun, a broken heart on my part, and then moving on to live a regular life with someone else. After all, the chances of a showmance becoming real were laughable. Now, at the thought of someone else… there was *no one* else.

There *couldn't* be anyone else for me. Ever.

Now, I just had to wait for her to realize it too.

Yearning beat in my heart, strong and loud. It seemed impossible that Pippa couldn't feel or hear the stark longing within me. Or the silent promise that I would give up anything and everything for a life with her.

Sweet Caroline, good times never seemed so good. Sweet Caroline.

Broken out of my tumultuous thoughts by the doorbell, I glanced toward my front door. "It must be my weekly vegetable delivery from a local farm."

"How adorable."

"You try resisting Mrs. Potter when she asks which vegetable box I want to sign up for. I haven't said no to her since she corralled me to help at her farm stand in high school."

"Admit it, you're a soft cinnamon roll."

"I think I've proved that I'm not soft. The opposite, in fact. Multiple times." I yanked Pippa flush against me, delighted with her squeal of laughter. "Want me to remind you again?"

"I'm too sore. Go, August. Your beets await." Pippa wriggled out of my arms and slapped my butt.

"City woman, beets aren't typically harvested in the late summer in this area. After I show you how to make eggs, I need to take you to a farm."

"Could I milk you?" she called out.

I stumbled over my feet. Winking, Pippa munched on a Pop-Tart she pulled out of the toaster. With great reluctance, I headed to the door, a giant, foolish grin still plastered on my face.

"Hi, Coach!"

Two of the rising seniors on the high school soccer team, Danny Jones and Jordan Lutz, waved in unison. They carried matching sports bags, and Jordan held a soccer ball in the crook of one arm.

"What are you doing here?"

"Remember, it's Sunday." They waited.

I shook my head.

"We have our first tryouts at two for freshmen?"

"You texted us last week to remind us to show up to help run drills?"

Recognition rushed in. Thank goodness for teenage boy oblivion, for neither remarked on my forgetfulness.

"Hey, Coach, you got any snacks?" Danny asked, peering behind me for magical snacks to run to him at his command.

"You live down the street. How did you get hungry from walking over here?"

Danny's shoulders slumped. "You would be too if your mom fed you kale-falafel for lunch and thinks spirulina rice cakes are desserts."

"Coach, those cakes don't even have sugar," chimed in Jordan in sympathy for his friend.

"Or flour."

"It's more like dried-up grass."

"Or hard mush."

Both boys nodded.

I suggested, "Why don't you walk on ahead to the fields? I'll be there in ten minutes."

"Okay, Coach. You'll bring some snacks? Like, real ones? I can't ask one of the other parents for snacks, because they'll tell my mom, and then she'll lecture me about processed foods."

I agreed to look around my house for acceptable processed snacks and waved those boys off.

Two hours later, I had seen enough of the incoming freshmen to pinpoint a couple boys who might make the varsity team. Several others would be good additions to the junior varsity team. The roster wouldn't be finalized until the longer tryouts during the first week of school.

Wrapping up the last drill and answering a few more questions from the players, I scoured the field for Pippa. In the distance, I found her under a large shady tree, surrounded by a dozen people. I couldn't wait to touch her, talk to her. My steps quickened in haste to reach her.

However, I had underestimated Beach Falls. Our telephone tree operated faster than a news organization. Paparazzi had nothing on small townites snooping for the possibility of gossip. Cars wrapped around the field as more people stopped by to see the commotion. The last time this field was this crowded was in 2004, when the Red Sox won the World Series after an eighty-six-year drought.

On any other day, the crowded field with coolers and pop-up chairs would have warmed my heart. The close-knit neighborhood feel was one of the biggest reasons I chose to move back here after a couple of years teaching in Boston. But today, when too many people that I had grown up with winked at me or crowded around to ask about *The Journey of Love*, moving far away didn't seem awful.

I mean, c'mon, the owner of the local convenience store even told me that they now stock ten different kinds of condoms. At some point, you had to draw the line.

"I like her. I was expecting someone who would look down her nose at us, but she fits right in."

Frustrated at another interruption, I tore my gaze away from Pippa. "June, why are you here? You don't even have kids old enough to play on my team."

"Can't I be a nice, supportive big sister?"

"Not unless it benefits you."

"Tiger mom trying to scope out future competition for the twins?"

"Your kids don't walk yet."

"Okay, fine, Rachel from The Chateau texted me that Vijay was leaving to help deliver fifty hot dogs to the soccer field for a red-headed stranger wearing three-inch heels. I hoped for the best." She didn't even pretend to act ashamed. Instead, she sipped her coffee.

I couldn't be mad at my sister. I couldn't be mad at anyone for their interest in Pippa. She had a magnetic quality about her that drew people to her.

But if you opened the door a sliver for June, she would barge in and take over. In mock exasperation, I commented, "At least Ben isn't supporting you on this."

"Oh, you're wrong. He suggested watching the twins at home while I scope it out, distraction free. He blusters, but deep inside, he has the heart of a nosy grandma." She waved at a group of ladies heading straight to Pippa before poking a finger at my shoulder. "August, of course, we're all curious. You haven't dated anyone seriously since the mess with Zara, and all of a sudden, boom! You come back from a TV show with a girlfriend. This is a huge deal in a tiny town! Everyone wants to meet your girlfriend. Who, apparently, slept over!"

My face reddened.

Half from my sister yelling it loud enough for the whole field to hear. There was a reason she had been the captain of our high school cheerleading squad, and it wasn't because she could dance.

The other half? Because memories of Pippa naked, her red curls spread over my white sheets, her body arching toward me, played on repeat in my mind. To the audio backdrop of her shouting my name, urging me on.

In preservation, I shifted my coaching bag with the soccer balls forward. To cover… my other balls.

Less than ten feet away, the group of ladies giggled. One of them mouthed something that sounded like, "I told you so." My list of people I couldn't look in the eyes grew.

"By the way, I like her dress. I'm glad she's making good use of my Christmas gift to you." June smirked. "What, you think I'm too sleep-deprived to notice she's wearing your shirt as a makeshift dress?"

"I wish."

Turning to study Pippa, June asked, "She's the one, right? Despite only knowing each other for a couple weeks, you love her."

When I didn't refute her words, she stared at me with a soft smile. "I hope she realizes her luck. Don't get a big head, but you're not awful."

I laughed and ruffled June's hair in that obnoxious way that younger brothers did. Eager to be near Pippa, I looped my arm around June and nudged her forward. "C'mon, June, let me introduce you to Pippa. Then, you can tell me you were wrong to misjudge her yesterday. I won't even rub it in."

CHAPTER TWENTY

~AUGUST~

"Ready to go home?" I asked Pippa, as the crowd started to thin out on the soccer field.

She gripped my hand tighter and nodded. I didn't remember what excuse I made to extricate ourselves. Only that Pippa's hand was in mine as we walked off the field and turned onto my street. The whole afternoon had been a blur, minus Pippa.

She was vivid. Her laughs, her body tucked beside mine, how she charmed my neighbors and friends with funny anecdotes about the show and genuine curiosity about their lives. Like my town, I was charmed all over again.

Memory by memory, pieces fell into place of the endless mystery that was Pippa. Every moment with her added another facet to my understanding and deepened my curiosity about her. Just when I thought I could almost see the whole of her, she revealed a different part.

Not *different*. Another layer. Another dimension to fall for.

Once we were out of sight of the soccer field, she asked, hesitating. "Do you think that went okay?"

Surprised, I noted the weariness in her drooped shoulders. I stopped and pulled her in for a hug. Her arms automatically went around my waist.

"I didn't realize the crowd made you tired." I rubbed her shoulders, finding the knots of stress. "It couldn't have gone better. Thank you for inviting my sister to your next boozy tea party."

Tension seeped out from her as she sagged against me. "She's fun, and I would like to make friends with the people you care about."

"They'll love you, just as I love you. You only have to be yourself. You are more than enough."

"Probably too much," she muttered.

"Exactly enough."

I leaned down to kiss her. It was meant to be a gentle kiss to reassure her. But her soft moan wreaked havoc with my plan. And her tongue… reminded me I had only one plan where she was concerned.

Pippa was the plan.

"Hi, Mr. August. Is she your girlfriend?"

The middle of nowhere with no interruptions sounded better and better.

I glanced over at the voice. A little girl, dressed in a pirate costume, stood inside a fenced yard. She pointed an accusing finger at Pippa.

"Hi, Maddy. Yes."

"Oh, dear." Maddy frowned as she put her hands on her hips. "I guess I can't marry you when I'm older. Oh dear."

Struggling not to laugh at Maddy's perfect imitation of her grandmother's favorite phrase, I held my tongue. To my left, Pippa nodded in understanding.

With full sympathy, she said, "That's a shame. I'm sure you'll find someone. You seem like a go-getter."

"I don't know what that means. I'm only six and a half."

I choked back laughter and scanned the street for inspiration. "How about Cameron down the block?"

"He picks his nose." Not impressed, Maddy shook her head. "Yuck."

"He has a treehouse in his backyard."

Perking up, Maddy considered. "That's right! A treehouse is cool. I can teach him not to pick his nose."

"His dad told me he's building Cameron a small ice rink in their backyard in the winter," I added as an extra incentive.

"Is your dad getting you a treehouse and ice rink?"

"No."

The kid nodded, decision made. With a wave, she bounded inside her house, yelling, "Nana, can I go to Cameron's house?"

Love triangle solved, I tugged at Pippa's hand. I couldn't wait to get her alone. Lock my door, disable the doorbell and phone line. Call me selfish, but I wanted her to myself before she headed back to Boston or Manhattan. A few more memories to tide me over until the next date.

When we passed Cameron's house and his infamous treehouse, Pippa stopped on the sidewalk. "I've never played in a treehouse before."

"Really?" I asked, trying to decipher the curious expression on her face.

"Yes. It feels like the epitome of childhood—impractical, imaginative, playful." Although her tone was light, she couldn't hide the wistfulness.

"Where you don't have to worry about grades or living up to your parents' expectations?" I guessed.

From the bits that she had revealed, I knew her parents and childhood were sensitive topics. Instead of the bright energy she radiated, or even her tired-but-hopeful self earlier, I could read the turmoil roiling off her in waves.

Resentful melancholy emanated from her. Her hands twisted at the belt around her waist. *My* belt.

In silence, we walked back to my house. She kept her hands to herself the entire way, her arms wrapped around her. When I stepped inside the cool foyer, Pippa stayed outside.

Had I pushed her too hard, before she was ready? For all her extraversion, Pippa's vivaciousness was limited to what she allowed others to see. For all of her adventure-lovingness, she hated risks that she couldn't control.

Staring at the welcome mat, Pippa muttered, "I hate talking about my childhood."

Okay. Okay, words were a start. She hadn't run yet, even though the slight raise of the door threshold offered a visual divide between us.

"It makes me feel… ungrateful," she bit out. "I had a great childhood. I traveled all over the world, went to the best private schools, had dedicated nannies and tutors who planned activities for me. My parents threw resources at me. Even I can't deny that they tried to give me the best. I'm an ass to grumble."

"Even if they gave you what they thought was best, their idea of best might not be what you needed," I offered.

When Pippa raised her head, her expression was thoughtful. "I never looked at it that way before."

As if just becoming aware that she still stood outside, she stepped inside the door and closed it behind her. The tight, anxious grip on my heart loosened.

"I see it all the time at school." I shrugged. "One of my star soccer players quit this week because he wanted to try out for the fall play, but hasn't told his parents, who both played college soccer. Parents call me or come to parent-teacher confer-ences with the best intentions, insisting that their kids should be one way. Doesn't mean anyone is bad or ungrateful if they want to carve their own path."

"I don't know why I'm so emotional over a stupid treehouse. It's ridiculous." Her voice husky, Pippa lifted her head.

I resisted the urge to comfort her. Pippa seemed so fragile that any movement or sound might scare her.

Staring over my shoulder, she started, "I had asked my parents for one when I was a kid. They said treehouses were impossible when we lived in Beijing. Also, impossible when we lived in London in a condo building. Then again, they said no when we lived in San Francisco. Even though the yard was tiny, there was still a large tree in the front.

"My mom said I should focus on studying and not playing. A treehouse in front of the house also didn't jive with the aesthetics of the other homes in Pacific Heights. I wished she had cared less about keeping up appearances. I wished she allowed me to do something that didn't go on a résumé."

"Now you have the chance to build your life the way you want to," I reminded her.

Because I wanted to comfort the lost girl she had been, because the woman in front of me—*my woman*—looked close to tears. Because I needed to do some-thing, I lifted her and carried her to the couch. As irrational as it might be, I missed the time before I had met her. If I had been there, I could have... what?

I hated this helplessness seeping into my thoughts. There wasn't a thing I could do about her past.

Kissing the top of her head, I wrapped an arm around her shoulders, tucking her against me. Pippa snuggled against my chest, her breathing evening out. She stayed silent for so long that I thought she had fallen asleep. I couldn't go back in time to comfort her, but if she needed somewhere to rest, I would aim to be the best damn pillow.

But I was wrong. Pippa hadn't fallen asleep. Her body shook against mine. In alarm, I twisted back, expecting tears of sadness.

I was wrong again.

"When I asked you to pet me like a cat, while on the bathroom floor at the beach, I thought that was my rock bottom." Pippa wiped away tears. Instead of weary shadows, her eyes lit up. In between laughter, she cracked out, "This—this is it. Me throwing a hissy fit over tr-treehouses!"

"Everyone needs a good cry now and then. My parents said that I cried for hours when my grandmother gave me a Batman balloon for my third birthday instead of Spiderman."

"Poor boy." Her hands traced circles around my chest.

Her laughter fading, Pippa twisted up in my lap so she was eye level with me. *Straddling me.* Not that I noticed.

"There are probably hundreds of things that I haven't done before," she said.

I'll volunteer as tribute for any experiments. For my balls' sake, I tried to push Pippa off to the side, so she didn't align *right* there. With a smirk, she wriggled back. Mischievous, sexy Pippa was in full force.

"I'm developing a knack for making a fool of myself in front of you." The tenderness in her confession paused my lustful thoughts.

Again, I was reminded of how Pippa meant so much more than her physical beauty. How she had drawn me in with her mix of confidence and worries, zest for life and need for safety, our laughter and quiet moments.

And why the combination of all of her, even her flaws, made her unique.

"You're no fool," I told her. "If something is meaningful to you, then I care, and I want to know about it. I'd rather you be yourself than hide from me."

"I will probably cry again over something silly, but I don't want you to pity me. I don't want you to think, 'poor little rich girl.'"

Before she could say more, I cut in, "I don't pity you. I see it as a privilege to be able to introduce you to new experiences, if you let me. Just as I want you to introduce me to things and people you care about."

"As long as you keep feeding me Pop-Tarts." She grinned. "They taste awful and yet, oddly addictive."

Her face flushed. Looking down at her hands, she mumbled, "I have another confession."

"Are we out of Pop-Tarts?"

"Probably. I took the whole box with me to the soccer game, and I didn't share." Her cheeks reddened. She took a deep breath in. "I don't let others see me cry. I try to be the strong one who doesn't let anything get to me. Do you know why I feel so comfortable letting you see me in weird situations or telling you embarrassing things, when I don't let others?"

My heart thumped so loud that I was surprised she didn't react. "Because you like me?"

"Because I *love* you, August," she told my chest.

I froze, trying to catch those words before they disappeared into a dream.

Sucking in a breath, Pippa glanced up. This time, her voice louder and clearer, she repeated, "I love you, August. I wanted to tell you this morning. I'm not good at talking about my feelings, and I had so many feelings for you that I got scared. Again."

Even as I wanted to run up and down the street, shouting my happiness, I loosened my hold on her. She looked ready to run—a mixture of bravery and fear. "I love you, Pippa. What made you not scared? It can't be the Pop-Tarts, right?"

Her laugh loosened up the tension in her body. "It was *you*. Watching you in your element yesterday and today. You accepting me for who I am. Your kindness, patience, your goodness, and dirtiness. You make me feel safe and as if the real me is good enough. More than anything, I want to be enough for you."

"You have always been enough," I said, taking one of her hands and placing it over my heart. "You're it for me."

"This morning, I was scared to make that leap. Except as it turns out, I had already jumped and just refused to see it. Now that I've said it, commitment doesn't feel scary, at least not with you. I love you!" she shouted.

Pippa's laughter flew up around the living room and landed on my heart. I kept the sound in my ever-growing memories of her. The words thrilled me. I couldn't imagine a future when hearing her say that she loved me would become mundane.

"I love you too," I said. "If you like treehouses, Cameron's family is going away for Labor Day. His dad is a buddy of mine. I could arrange for us to hang out in that infamous treehouse."

"Hmm." She tapped her chin. "I'd rather do something else… maybe we can think of an adult activity that you can show me instead."

My cock jumped up at her command. There were no cells or blood left in my brain to think beyond Pippa riding my cock.

"Down, August." Nudging me, she chuckled with a lightness that was the opposite of what gripped my body.

My cock didn't understand those words. Not when she loosened her hair tie, letting her waves spill around her shoulders. Not when she took off the belt, leaving her only in my button-down shirt.

"Feed me first. I heard from your sister that you're a great cook. I've never had a guy cook for me."

With a groan, I shifted Pippa off of me. When I stood up, I didn't even bother to hide the tent in my pants. What was the point?

"You up for grilling steaks?" Wincing, I remembered my poor hosting skills. "It's better than toasted Pop-Tarts."

"I'm up for *eating* steaks. No one is up for *me* cooking steaks. That's all you."

Making herself at home, Pippa rummaged around my cabinets until she found my wine stash. "I'll taste test your wine to make sure it goes with the meal. Maybe I'll try a couple glasses. For quality control and all. You have to make sure the experiment is repeatable."

Walking up behind her, I wrapped an arm around her waist. "After I feed you, how about we test if this"—I pulled her ass against my hardness, reveling in her low moan—"is repeatable? Make sure everything is up to your expectations. At different times of the day. In different rooms. To be sure."

Pippa slid her arms around my neck. The movement stretched my shirt across her breasts, arching her body and thrusting her hardened nipples in offering. "Oh yes, lots of experiments. On second thought, steak can wait. Maybe we could start the next experiment now?"

CHAPTER TWENTY-ONE

~PIPPA~

The experiments met my expectations… over and over again. I stayed that night again. And the next night.

For more experimentation.

Oh, who the hell was I kidding?

I was wild for August and craved his touch. When he dressed in his teacher khakis and button-down to head to prep meetings for the upcoming school year, I nearly jumped him.

And I did that one naughty Tuesday morning.

Who knew khakis and conversations about the New Deal were such turn-ons? *I'd like to deal his*—noooo, brain, stop it.

With no more hesitation, I rented out my New York condo and wrote in an official resignation letter to my law firm, turning my sabbatical into a decision. The only thorn became my parents' texts and calls, lamenting my recent life decisions. To say that they were shocked at my resignation was an understatement. When I finally confessed that my French language retreat was actually a stint on a reality dating show, my mom forgot how to talk for a minute.

At least, I could blame the show's NDA for not revealing to them that I had left the show with a boyfriend. As long as no one visited Beach Falls to find out that the entire town knew…

It wasn't as if I was ashamed of August. I just needed my parents to calm down before I introduced them. If I could hold off telling my parents about August until January, maybe they could watch our relationship unfold on TV and understand why I had no other choice but to leave with him.

The rest of the *month* of August passed in a delightful, uneventful rhythm. After a week of driving back and forth between my parents' house in Boston and Beach Falls, I had shown up to August's house with a car full of suitcases.

To my delight, he had already cleared one side of his closet for me, leaving me with a new set of velvet, curved hangers. To prevent my clothes from having hanger marks, he had told me.

I was in deep. In love for the first time. Saying those words out loud, even thinking them, still shocked me. But, the words had felt so right. As if they were the most natural thing. As if I were always meant to say them to this man.

Here I was, as just me, in all my flawed, unpolished, unglamorous form. Instead of feeling frightened by how vulnerable I was, my heart was filled with buoyant contentment. Love gave me an unexpected security that not only could August handle me, but he wanted everything I threw at him.

Just like that, my world became us. The two of us standing in his kitchen, barefoot, while he tried to teach me how to scramble eggs. The way he tucked blankets around me on the couch when I took a nap. The way the early morning sunlight streaked through the trees on our morning walks to The Diner for my daily muffin fix or The Flying Squirrel for my matcha latte.

To my surprise, I didn't hate small-town life. As I had found out, Beach Falls contained neither beach nor waterfalls. One of the intrepid founders of the town had misspelled "beech trees" for "beach" and mistook a tiny drop in a creek as the beginnings of a waterfall.

From that seemingly ignominious start, the town had sprouted into a real community. Half of the inhabitants could claim generational roots. The other half had adopted Beach Falls' off-the-beat, near-intrusive friendliness, close-knit characteristics with relish. After the initial grilling about the show and our relationship, the town had also opened its arms to me.

For the first time in my life, I allowed myself to live in the moment. To linger over my matcha, daydream, plot my next steps in an unhurried manner, or meander to The Diner when I got hungry. A year ago, even a couple months ago, these would have become anxiety-fueled days with wide-open calendars.

Now, they turned out to be the opposite. Not living by a precise plan was unsettling… until it became freeing. Who would have thought that I could be okay spending this much time by myself, with my thoughts?

I had changed.

Yet, I had never felt more like *me*. As if all this time, the FOMO-led chaos of my prior life had hidden my true self. The real Pippa Fleming loved a small town boy and his home, with its effusive welcome, local gossip, and hot muffins.

It was for the love of muffins that I now waited at The Diner counter at 4:30 p.m. Back in Boston or Manhattan, I would have pulled out my phone and scrolled aimlessly until I found the next place that I needed to rush off to. Here, the new me sat at one of the retro red barstools in the middle of the no-frills diner, phone firmly tucked in my Chanel bag.

Just because my preferences for entertainment had changed didn't mean that my fashion taste had. After all, how was I supposed to justify fancy bags if I kept them in August's closet?

"Hey, Pippa, how's it going?" June's husband, Ben, entered The Diner. We had met a few days ago when he and June dropped by with their twins after dinner. To Ellen, the server behind the bar, he nodded in greeting.

"Waiting for muffins and takeout," I responded. "If I hid the packaging, do you think I could pass off that I cooked?"

"Not a chance. We've been coming to The Diner since high school. It was the symbol of being an upperclassman. August will know in a heartbeat that Danny"—he pointed to the bald man dancing his way among the stove tops—"made the food."

"There goes my idea to impress him."

"You already do."

"Really?"

Scanning the tray of muffins on the counter, Ben said, "Yup. By the way, June is looking forward to the brunch you invited her to this weekend."

After pausing for a moment, Ben continued, "I've known August since we were in preschool. In high school, he was the kid who tested the depth of the ice on the lake before we rushed on to play hockey. No amount of reassurance that the ice looked thick enough could convince him not to bring his chisel and measurement stick every single time."

"You're saying he's boring? I don't think that's true at all. August is—"

"No need to defend him. I'm not insulting him." Ben shook his head with a pleased smile. "Has he mentioned his last relationship?"

I nodded. "Yeah, he told me on the first night of filming that it hadn't ended well."

"Good, I'm glad he's shared that. After that breakup, August became even more risk adverse. It means that much *more* that he's thrown himself into this relationship. We can all see it. Even June has stopped playing matchmaker."

Even though I had high hopes for the relationship, having his loved ones see that soothed my heart. "I'm glad to not fend off June's matchmaking. She's a force."

"Everyone is glad for that. None of the people she's ever set up have lasted beyond a first date, some not even that. She's the worst combination of terrible and persistent. She's lucky I tolerate her."

"No, I don't think that's true. I think you find her bossiness awesome."

Surprised, he chuckled. "Shh, don't tell her my secret."

Carrying a large bag of takeout, Ellen came back to the counter from the kitchen. "Ben, here you go. You want to throw in that muffin you're eyeing?"

"June didn't say—" He frowned. "Hm, yes, please. I'll take the blueberry muffin and a whoopie cookie. She never orders dessert. Yet, she's upset when dessert doesn't come home."

After adding the dessert into Ben's bag, Ellen grabbed a second bag from the kitchen for me. "Pippa, here's your order. Are you coming to the Harvest Festival planning meeting next Tuesday night?"

"What's that?"

"Don't say yes," Ben warned, tearing a piece off the bottom of the muffin to stuff into his mouth. "It'll take over your life for the next few weeks. You'll dream of pumpkins."

"Why don't you come for the first meeting?" she asked, ignoring him.

"Where Ellen will have already signed you up for seven committees," Ben muttered.

"Why are you only eating the muffin bottom?" I asked.

"Because June swears muffin tops are the best." Ben stuffed back the muffin top into his bag.

"Don't you have a wife and babies to take food back to?" Waving him off, Ellen grabbed her phone. "Pippa, I'll text you the information right now."

"Bye. Don't say I didn't warn you." Ben retreated. At the door, he stopped, calling out to someone on the outside, "Hey, better rescue Pippa from Ellen's committees."

In his clean khakis and a light-blue button-down, August strolled in, greeting a few customers and Ellen. Who knew teachers were so sexy? I warred with myself over kissing him in public, even as my pussy clenched at the memory of him fucking me against the wall before work.

In those same clothes.

Could he smell me on them throughout the day?

With a knowing smirk, August's wicked mouth twisted up. He sat on the stool next to me, before grabbing me to sit on his lap. "Hey, I missed you today."

Groaning inwardly at his gruff voice and the image of me on the counter, while he feasted, I shuddered. In a breathy whisper, I said, "Missed you too. What are you doing here?"

"Picking up some of those chocolate muffins you love so much. How was your day?"

"Highly unproductive. Highly enjoyable."

"Any light bulb for what you'll do next?" he asked, picking up on my first statement.

"Maybe. The paradox of having choices."

"You don't have to rush. I must admit, I enjoy coming home to you and your attempt to fool me with 'home-cooked' meals."

Leaning back, I scanned him in mock surprise. "You didn't buy that I cooked yesterday's dinner?"

He nuzzled my neck, the puffs of air from his laughter heightening the sensations. "Coming from someone who asked me what the point of preheating the oven was, it was a safe bet that you didn't braise short ribs yourself."

"I'm not very good at these things." Ignoring the family staring at me from a nearby booth, I leaned into him. If a sexy man wanted to kiss me, who was I to deny him?

"What things?"

"The whole being a girlfriend thing."

"Who says girlfriend is synonymous with chef?" Infinitely gentle, he pressed a kiss to my forehead. "You're enough, Pippa, as you are. If you're any better, I'll be out of a job as your boyfriend."

Watching him for his reaction, I said with hesitation, "I did have one thing that I'm toying with."

"Besides me?"

"Besides you." To undermine my own words, I wriggled further and relished the low growl torn from his throat. I covered that primal sound and my reaction to his need by rushing forward. "As much as my parents were pushy, I enjoyed learning from them about how they invested in companies and helped those companies grow. Plus, a few years ago, I teamed up with Tia to patent and then sell an AI tool she had built to detect fraud. It was rather exciting to 'discover' a new technology and help it grow, even if I didn't do much but file patents for her.

"It was also eye-opening to watch doors stay closed because we didn't have successful start-up experience. Did you know that less than a third of start-ups are founded by women? Did you know that investors are more likely to invest in companies where the founders are experienced? But women tend to be under-funded, so the cycle continues."

"What's your idea?" asked August.

"It's silly."

"What is it?"

The idea was risky. It had popped into my head a couple of days ago and hadn't let go. If I did this, a career path that was in the same realm as my parents', I had to bat it out of the park.

"I'd like to start an incubator focused on female-led start-ups, to provide seed money, coaching, and a place for them to learn from each other. It's a huge risk to invest in companies so early that they may still be building their product, but that's where they need the most help," I said in a rush of words.

Without a pause, August exclaimed, "That sounds amazing!"

Relieved that someone besides me thought it wasn't a shitty idea, I said, "I don't know the next steps. I'll have to do a lot of research, talk to people, figure out all the details… it feels overwhelming."

"I have confidence in you."

"Why?"

His hands squeezed mine. "Because you light up when you talk about it. I refuse to believe that when you throw yourself into something, you wouldn't succeed."

Where had this man come from? I threw my arms around his neck, yanking him down for a messy kiss.

"Shoo, this is a family establishment," interrupted Ellen, with no hint of judgment in her tone. "August, you're a teacher. I would have expected you to set a good example for the younger generation."

Putting another two smaller bags next to my other take-out bag, she winked. "Chocolate chip muffins and apple cider donuts. For, you know, afterward. Got to keep up the energy."

Takeout and post-sex snacks in hand, we strolled out of The Diner, hand in hand. A couple of blocks from our house, my purse buzzed.

Wait, when had the house become *ours* and not August's house?

"Do you want to get that?" August pointed to my still-vibrating purse.

I dug out the phone, without looking at the caller ID. "Sure, if only to tell the salesperson to stop. Hello?"

"Pippa." The voice stopped me and filled me with dread. I mentally prepared myself for more cajoling to go back to law and frustrated sighs when I said no.

"Hi, Mom." With resignation, I turned away from August and walked faster toward our house. *His* house.

"Pippa," the elegant voice came through clear, as if my mom stood next to me in one of her tailored suit dresses. "I had to hear from the housekeeper in Boston that you've decided to move in with someone from the show."

Trust my mom to get to the point.

"No, I'm not—" I stopped my instinctive rebuttal.

My feet had magically carried me up August's porch and onto the front steps. Shifting the bags of food to one hand, August pressed his other hand on the small of my back to guide me inside while his foot held the door open. Concern etched in his brows, August rubbed my back in a quick show of comfort before heading to the kitchen to deposit the food.

Giving me privacy on the call. Leaving me with the force that was Charlotte Fleming.

Help me.

Peering from the kitchen with non-matching mugs in both hands, he mouthed, "Are you okay?"

Maybe it was those ceramic mugs, with the sayings "You're grate" and "That's so cheesy!" and their associated memories of eating breakfasts together. Or the quiet reminder that he was here for me. Whatever it was, I knew I didn't want to hide him anymore.

"Yes, I have a boyfriend. His name is August Weather," I proclaimed, figuratively squaring my shoulders.

"Boyfriend. August. Weather." My mom's tone sharpened with incredulity. August's name dripped from her tongue, the derision ringing clear. "Your dad and I were curious when you decided to take a sabbatical. We were concerned when you told us that your French class was actually a reality show. Then, alarmed when you quit. Now, this… I don't know you anymore. Your dad and I are leaving Dallas and flying into Logan this Saturday. We want to meet him. Seven o'clock."

Pause.

"Please bring this… August man."

Before I could gather my scattered thoughts to form a response, my mom hung up. The click sounded just as precise as her command.

We were summoned.

CHAPTER TWENTY-TWO

~PIPPA~

"Did you know that Google used to rent hundreds of goats to munch on their grass instead of mowing the lawn at their headquarters? Can you imagine looking out your office window? Have you seen the YouTube videos of screaming goats?" My best friend, Tia, flashed a wide smile around her dining room table.

Years ago, when Tia and I were in college, we had started a tradition of drinking tea and booze while gossiping and pretending to paint. Today, the tradition continued with a few additions.

To my left, Annie laughed, her face shining with genuine curiosity. When she told me she was visiting Boston this weekend, I had invited her to the Boozy Tea Party. Next to her sat June, who had given up her paintbrush in exchange for coffee.

To my right, Tia's sister-in-law, Charlie, forced a weak grimace. She hadn't spoken more than a couple words the entire morning. While she had been shy when I had met her in the past, she had participated in conversations.

Today, her solemn blue eyes dominated her pale face. Though she wore a wrinkle-free white silk top tucked into a cornflower-blue skirt, with subtle diamonds twinkling from her ears and wrist, Charlie looked... out of sorts. Frazzled.

I couldn't put my finger on it. My mind latched on to the mysterious non-mystery of Charlie that was none of my business. Because the alternative, obsessing over the dinner to come that night with my parents… let's just say, I hadn't felt worry seize me like this since pre-St. Lucia.

When Charlie raised her left hand to brush a short, unruly piece of hair back behind her ear, I gasped. Across the table, Tia noticed me staring at Charlie's left hand, or rather, what *wasn't* on her finger anymore. Tia shook her head so slightly that only years of being best friends translated that subtle movement into a frantic warning to keep my mouth shut.

As if I needed something else as a harbinger of tonight.

This was a mistake. Attending the Boozy Tea Party had not distracted me as I'd hoped when I set out this morning, nor had Tia's enthusiastic grilling about the show. She had glowed with happiness at hearing stories about August and nearly outshone the sun when she learned that Annie got engaged on the show.

A few weeks ago, Tia and Andrew had closed on this new house. The half-unpacked moving boxes scattered around underscored the differences between us. There was no doubt that this house was another page of Tia and Andrew's fairy tale. They were moving toward their happily ever after.

No, they were *already* in their happily ever after.

Whereas, I couldn't help a looming sense of doom from creeping in, waiting to pounce on my relationship. In my head, I had run a thousand scenarios. None of them ended with my parents waving like benevolent fairy godparents, as August and I rode off into the sunset in a magical pumpkin carriage.

Stuffing a petit lemon square in her mouth, Tia waved her paintbrush like a maestro, filling in the silence. "One of my research partners, Matt Simmons, and I have been working on a new project using AI to detect falls for seniors who live by themselves. By the way, did you know virtual assistants like Siri and Alexa can be accidentally activated by random sounds like you coughing, which means they can capture data on your private conversations? It's an interesting ethics question. Don't you think?"

Rallying myself, I searched for sensible words. "Agree, there should be some regulations around that. How creepy for your conversations to be captured and heard by anyone."

"Not unlike the farmers' market at Beach Falls," quipped June. "I swear, there's more gossip exchanged than produce."

"Is Siri or Alexa listening different from software that monitors your computer behavior, though?" asked Annie, her brows furrowed in thought.

"Hello, darlings!"

The front door flung open, followed by immediate babies crying and a man cursing. "I dropped their fucking—oh fuck, I can't say fuck anymore. Babies, you didn't hear that."

My friend Kat breezed into the dining room. Last year, Tia had introduced me to Kat and her husband, Dan, a Tom Hardy look-alike with the vocabulary of someone paid by Fuck, Inc. Today, the ever-so-proper Kat looked…

"I had wine for breakfast!" Kat teetered into the dining room, making a beeline for June. "You must be June. I'm Kat. How exciting it is for your brother and Pippa to be dating. And you're Annie! Pippa said you got engaged on the show!"

Before June or Annie could respond, Dan strolled in, a car seat in each arm. Bemusement mixed with guilt crossed his face. "My fault that Kat's tipsy."

Waving her hand in her husband and babies' general direction, Kat explained, "Dan wanted to hang out with Andrew. The twins are half Dan and cannot be trusted to be by themselves without getting into trouble."

"They're also five-months-old," I remarked.

"Exactly." Kat nodded, plopping down on a chair. "They look innocent."

Across from me, Tia tracked the car seats, lingering on the babies' tiny, chubby faces. Longing radiated from her, before she masked the pain by pushing a plate of cheese at Kat.

Not wanting to draw attention to Tia, I walked over to hug Kat and Dan, before squeezing myself next to Tia on her chair. It gave me an excuse to fold her into my arms. Sagging against me, she squeezed my hand.

"I heard that you came back from the reality show with a boyfriend. When do we get to meet this guy?" Dan paced the dining room, rocking the car seats.

Kat glanced up from the cheese board, two different pieces in each hand. "Ooh, where is he today?"

"He was going to come today, but something turned up. He said he had to go run some errands."

"He's out shopping with my husband. He wanted to get new shoes," explained June, chugging more coffee. "I haven't seen him this nervous since he broke our parents' Christmas tree angel."

"August said *you* broke the angel," I teased.

"Liar!" Faux indignation on her face, June pressed a hand to her chest. "Okay, I'll tell the truth. It was Luna Broccoli, bless her cat soul. What other lies has he told you about me? If he says I'm bossy, I'm not… I just have a natural way of giving directions."

A new worry popped up. "I didn't realize August's errand was shoe shopping. I never asked him to buy shoes."

"He's probably trying to impress your parents," chimed in Annie.

"Or he needed to do something concrete while he waited." Tia's husband, Andrew, entered the room from their backdoor. "I shopped for shoes before I met Tia's parents for the first time, after we reconciled."

Beside me, Tia leaped up toward Andrew. Even months after their reconciliation, it still surprised me at their transformation. A renewed confidence in Tia. A gentleness and contentedness in Andrew, who had embodied the definition of tall, dark, and brooding before.

A slight furrow on his forehead, Andrew rubbed Tia's back in a subtle movement. The gesture of concern, of care, reminded me so much of August that my hand reached into my pocket for my phone. Unfortunately, my attempt to call him was foiled by the decidedly nonpractical nature of my jeans pockets that prevented me from carrying anything bigger than a pea.

Damn pants. Probably made by a man with usable-sized pockets.

Breaking the ensuing silence that dampened the morning, Dan announced, "Andrew, why don't you show me your backyard?"

"You want to see my backyard? It's grass and trees." Andrew frowned in question.

"Yes, the twins have never seen it before."

Eyes narrowing, Andrew pointed out, "Your twins are half asleep. Is their vision even developed—"

"Fucking come along, Andrew." Without waiting for a response, Dan marched toward the back door, using the car seats to prod Andrew outside.

In the silence that followed, I stared around the room, as everyone else stared at anywhere but each other. All except Kat, who stared at the cheese board with love.

Demolishing the last piece of cheese, she raised a glass of mimosa. "You know what I've missed the most?"

"What?" I asked.

"Cheese. Blue cheese. Brie cheese. Feta cheese. Soft cheese. Not having to check the labels to see if the cheese is pasteurized. Wine, without pumping and dumping. The loves of my life—I've missed them all." She threw back the rest of the mimosa. "I decided to stop breastfeeding this morning, and I felt all sorts of guilty. Dan gave me wine, so yeah... Tia, do you have more cheese?"

"Fed is best," chimed in June, pouring herself another cup of coffee. "My twins are a little older than yours, and I stopped after three months. My twins are better because they have a mom who is not overtired and not overstressed. Kudos to whatever method you use to get food inside your babies."

"Allergies, you know," Kat muttered, brushing a hand over her eyes.

"Why don't I get more cheese? I picked up some scones from the farmers' market this morning too." Tia picked up the empty cheese tray, glancing pointedly at me.

Picking up the delicate teapot, I stood up. "I'll come help and make some more tea."

Barely a foot into the sunny kitchen, Tia asked, "How do you feel about August meeting your parents tonight? I hate seeing you worried today, especially not after how happy you sounded on the phone last week."

"Wow, you don't waste time," I remarked. "As for tonight, I'd rather practice law again."

"That bad, huh?"

A tiny, tiny part of me stayed hopeful. This was a far cry from the last time I brought a guy home. Back in senior year of high school, I had tried to test my parents by introducing them to the twenty-one-year-old, chain-smoking guy whom I'd met at a club. His dismissive, attitude-filled answers horrified my parents.

The circumstances were different this time. I wasn't dependent on my parents, and August was miles better than my high school attempt. Still... my parents were unpredictable.

"How did you tell your parents that you broke off your engagement with Clayton and got back together with Andrew?" I asked, pouring boiling water into the teapot and adding loose leaf tea from a cannister.

Her lips tugging up, Tia answered, "I shoved Andrew into a closet to hide him from my parents."

"What?"

"Not my proudest moment. My parents had dropped by right after Andrew and I agreed to try dating again. I panicked and shoved him into a closet."

"How did you go from that to your parents throwing you a wedding reception in China in June? I was at the reception. They beamed the whole week of festivities. You can't fake that."

Arranging dessert on a platter, Tia considered her words before speaking. "Once my parents realized how happy I was with Andrew, they were happy too.

It helped that they've known him for years and have always liked him, even if he wasn't who they were expecting me to marry."

Grabbing a tiny cannoli from the platter, I bit into the crispy exterior. Not as good as The Diner's muffins, but a close runner-up. "I haven't tried to hide August. I've been canoodling with him all over Beach Falls and even joined the Harvest Festival committee. I'm on the food subcommittee."

"You're on a food subcommittee? Do they know that you can't cook?"

"I can taste test," I quipped back. "I have it bad for August. I even made out with him in a diner."

"So you're saying that I'm a genius for signing you up for *The Journey of Love*? Then what are you worried about?"

"I don't know. August and I are independent adults. I don't need others' approval…"

In Tia-fashion, she handed me another petit four. "There's a difference between needing approval and *wanting* it. Unless you're completely cut off from your parents, having their support makes it one less thing to worry about. From what you've told me, August seems like a perfect match for you. Don't worry about tonight."

"I don't want anything to drive August away." As much as I tried, I couldn't get rid of this nagging feeling that something bad would happen. The worry hung like an anvil above my head, timed to drop as soon as my parents met August.

"He's buying shoes at this moment. Plus, you said he's sampling all of your attempts at making eggs. If his stomach is strong enough for your cooking, then he can't be in a hurry to leave." Handing me a shortbread cookie, Tia raised her brow. Or tried to raise one brow.

"Eating my eggs is not a good litmus test. I'll have you know, I've mastered scrambled eggs—" Scrunching up my nose at this morning's attempt, I added, "The over hard version. I'm working on hard-boiled eggs next."

With a second shortbread cookie frozen in her hand, she gaped at me. "You don't know how to boil eggs yet?"

"Look who's talking, Mrs. Eats-Ice-Cream-for-Meals." I grabbed the cookie from her hand and stuffed it into my mouth. Shortbread cookies were vastly underrated and vastly superior to chocolate chip.

Batting my hand away from the tray, Tia reached into a cupboard and handed me the box of shortbread cookies. "My point is, you're comfortable enough to show him things you're not good at, which is huge for you. I've known you since we were kids. As much as you pretend to not care, you do.

"It speaks volumes to how safe August makes you feel. For him to see you in all your forms and still want to impress your parents, I think he has it bad too. It's hard to find the perfect intersection of—" her pointer finger wriggling "—one, someone *you* want to show your true self to."

Adding another finger, she said, "Two, for them to *want* to see you." Three fingers out, she finished, "Lastly, for them to actually *see* you. When you find that person, there's no guarantee that you'll have them forever. But at minimum, you have a foundation to start."

"Who is this romantic? What did you do with my super practical best friend?" Thoroughly impressed, I shook my head at her still-dancing fingers.

"Your super practical best friend got laid… and laid often and—"

"Ew." I waved her off, laughing. Wrapping her in a hug, I said, "Thanks, Tia."

"You bet. Should we go back before Kat starves from lack of cheese and June becomes coffee?"

CHAPTER TWENTY-THREE

~AUGUST~

Shit.

Shit. Shit. Shit.

I wouldn't consider myself a frequent swearer. But there was no other way to describe how out of place I felt when I walked into Pippa's parents' house. It was one of the few nonattached mansions on Mount Vernon Place, a side street in the Beacon Hill neighborhood of Boston.

Despite Beacon Hill and Beach Falls sounding similar, they were two worlds apart. A chandelier hung above the foyer that was worth more than my salary. For my *lifetime*. A butler took our coats. I didn't realize butlers existed as a profession nowadays.

After hanging our coats in a closet with a spinning rack, he guided us to a receiving room. *In Beach Falls*, the "receiving room" was your front porch. In *Beacon Hill*, there were enough rooms in this giant mansion to have a single room dedicated to making your guests wait before you graced them with your presence.

I knew Pippa owned fancy purses with unpronounceable names and came from privilege. The fact that this was Pippa's home when she was in Boston blew my mind. That this was one of several homes that her parents owned rocked me.

Privilege in my experience meant that you got your own birthday party instead of sharing it with your sibling. Or you got a summer trip to the Cape. My mind did not compute this level of wealth.

Instead of spending the day shoe shopping, I should have tried to win the lottery if I had any hope of impressing Pippa's parents. Maybe then I would have something to say as the four of us stared at each other in the receiving room.

Shit.

Breaking the silence, Mr. Fleming asked, "August, why don't you tell us about yourself?"

"I was born and grew up just outside of Boston—"

"Which town?" Mrs. Fleming's hands clasped in front of her, diamonds shining from her wrists and the rings on her fingers.

For a split second, I wondered if she had worn more than usual to intimate me. Because there was no way people wore that many diamonds on themselves on a regular day. Right?

"Beach Falls."

"Hm, I don't believe we know anyone from there. Are there beaches or waterfalls?" remarked Mr. Fleming. His glasses slid down an inch on his nose, giving him a professorial air. That and his gray-streaked hair and knitted vest.

He reminded me of my grandfather, who was also fond of vests. The difference was my grandfather got his at the thrift store, and I would bet twenty dollars that Mr. Fleming had never entered a thrift store.

"No." I smiled, the image of Mr. Fleming stumbling into a thrift store by accident in my mind. "It's a misnomer in part because the founder misspelled the town in a letter to his family in England."

"How charming." About as charming as rats in the sewer, judging from Mrs. Fleming's tone. "What is it you do?"

"I'm a teacher."

"At which university do you teach?"

"I teach history at Beach Falls High School and coach the boys' soccer team."

"What do your parents do?" Mrs. Fleming's rapid-fire questions continued.

"My mom was the school nurse in our elementary school, and my dad ran a local landscaping company. They're retired and live in Maine most of the year. They're in a town called Rochester Falls. There is a *real* waterfall there."

"His parents are now artists and paint charming landscapes of lighthouses," Pippa jumped in, with a nervous glance at me. "Did you know that August just bought a home in Beach Falls? His father had designed the landscape years ago.

There's a garden, a wildflower meadow to the side, a conservation area behind the house, and some peaceful areas with benches and swings."

Her lips trembled with the strain of nerves. I hated that I couldn't make this easier for her. For the first time in my life, I wished I was someone different. If only to make this moment with her parents easier on Pippa.

In front of me, Mr. and Mrs. Fleming sat, backs straight, in ornate chairs that were probably imported from some castle in France. Mr. Fleming peered at me over his glasses with calm curiosity.

In contrast, Mrs. Fleming's sharp eyes bore into me. Her dislike for me was apparent in her narrowed gaze and crisp words. Her frown deepened with every statement I made about my life.

On the bright side, I knew where I stood with her. How much worse could it get?

"What made you go on a reality TV show?" Her questions began again.

"My sister nominated me. Why not?" Okay, that didn't sound like the most responsible response. I added, "It filmed over the summer, so I could go without taking time off of work."

Yeah, teacher responsibilities, sure to impress the Flemings who could buy a school for fun. Go me.

Brows furrowed in a thoughtful expression, Mr. Fleming contemplated. "It's an interesting place to find love. Today, there are reality TV shows and dating apps. Sure different from our times. Though Charlotte and I didn't have the most traditional courtship either."

"How did you two meet?" I asked.

Dropping her facade, Mrs. Fleming's hands twisted in her lap.

Curious.

"I was at dinner with my fraternity brothers and spotted Charlotte in the restaurant. After too many shots, I got the courage to ask her for her number. We married six months later, right after graduation," Mr. Fleming explained.

"That's rather romantic. I didn't know that, Dad. Mom said you two met at a country club," said Pippa.

Her father laughed and patted his wife's clenched hands. "Far from it. The restaurant was called Cats—"

"I don't think they want to hear the boring details." Mrs. Fleming shot warning glances at her husband, whose eyes twinkled even as he stayed silent.

"Pippa, do you need a new tailor?"

"No, Mom, why?"

"Your pants have holes in them."

Next to me, Pippa glanced at her knees. "These jeans are meant to be like this—it's fashionable."

"It's fashionable to rip holes in your knees?"

"Yes."

"What will others think?" exclaimed her mother. "Why don't I book us a reservation at that boutique on Newbury that you like? Refresh your wardrobe."

At Pippa's frown, I jumped in, for the first time in my life, into a conversation about fashion. "I think she looks beautiful."

Beaming, Pippa leaned over to kiss my cheek. Surprised at the touch of affection in front of her parents, I wrapped an arm around her shoulders, pulling her closer. A stray curl from her bun escaped, dangling in front of my face. Resisting the urge to wrap it around my fingers and tug, I brushed it back.

My hand lingered on the soft, sensitive skin behind her ear. This close, I could see a mark on her delicate throat. My face flushed at the memory of the frantic, furious moment when I had bitten her neck this morning, just as my cock had entered her warmth.

Shifting on the uncomfortable chair, I pushed away the images. *And* the sounds of her cries as she came on my cock.

This was not the time.

Not the time.

I glanced up at Pippa's parents, sure my every debauched thought was tattooed on my face.

Oblivious, Mr. Fleming tapped at his watch and glanced at his wife. "It's seven thirty. Should we adjourn to the dining room?"

"Yes, let's." Mrs. Fleming stood up, not before her gaze flickered to the spot on Pippa's neck and then to me. This woman had a remarkable ability to narrow her eyes without moving her facial features.

Shit. Even knowing that there was nothing to feel guilty about, one stare from Mrs. Fleming made me feel like a kid caught eating Santa's cookies on Christmas Eve.

If the receiving room was the appetizer, dinner was... hm, moving on. The interrogation, *ahem*, interview, *ahem*, meet-the-parents continued throughout the five-course meal. There were too many utensils on my placemat, and I was one hundred percent sure that I used the wrong ones each time. At this rate, it wouldn't make a difference if I tore into the soup with my hands.

Mr. Fleming seemed content to let his wife lead the questions, chiming in every so often with his thoughts on the wine or food. I couldn't tell if he thought I wasn't complete trash or if he was better at hiding his feelings.

On the other hand, Mrs. Fleming wore her disapproval. One after another, she fired questions at me throughout dinner. Some of them were variations of each other to catch me in a lie. At one point, Pippa tried to divert the grilling with an anecdote about buying a doghouse for the groundhog who popped up every morning in our yard.

The story had the opposite effect. Her mom resumed her line of questions with more zeal. By the third course, which was followed by a tiny spoon filled with something that tasted like foamy gelato—a palate cleanser, as Mr. Fleming remarked—the only words in the cavernous room were between Mrs. Fleming and me.

Like a tennis match, she lobbed question after question over to me. I volleyed them back. If nothing else, she couldn't ding me on lying or shirking away. If I had to turn myself inside out to show them I would fight for Pippa, so be it.

After probing my family history, my career interests, one-year, five-year, ten-year goals, retirement plans, my politics, and religion, Mrs. Fleming paused. Catching my breath, I took a bite of the crème brûlée.

"How is dessert, August?"

I choked down the custard. Pippa's eyes ping-ponged between her mom and me. Was this question a clever disguise to get to… What did crème brûlée signify?

"It's delicious," I answered.

"Thank you, August, for coming to meet us on such short notice," started Mrs. Fleming. Three heads twisted to stare at her in anticipation. "Would you like some coffee or tea in the library?"

"Tea, please."

"Loose leaf okay?" Mrs. Fleming folded her napkin. "I must admit, I got used to it that way when we lived in China."

"Yes, loose leaf sounds great," I said, still confused. Across from me, Pippa shrugged. At the other end of the table, Mr. Fleming smiled around a bite of dessert.

No more questions? I didn't know what else she could ask, since she knew more about my life than the IRS, my employer, and half of my friends. Relieved, I exhaled.

"I'll ask our Chef to prepare one of the pu'er tea cakes," added Mr. Fleming.

Clapping her hands with glee, Pippa commented, "My dad doesn't offer one of his tea cakes to anyone."

"Have you ever tried tea from a compressed tea cake?" asked her dad. "One of my Chinese partners sends me a huge packet every year. You have to break them up before you can use the tea leaves. It's too much effort for an everyday tea. But then again, tonight is rather special, meeting Pippa's boyfriend."

Triumph coursed through me. I didn't know how, but I'd passed. I couldn't even fault Pippa's parents for being overprotective. In truth, I was glad that she had more people in her life to look out for her.

The four of us stood up. "I'm going to ask Chef for some more dessert," said Pippa with a cheery wave, leaving me with her parents.

The stress of winning over her parents gone, I followed the Flemings across the hallway to their library. A few minutes later, Max, the butler, brought up a tray with four teacups and a still-steaming teapot.

When Mr. Fleming asked me to call them Greg and Charlotte, I could have kissed them. When Mr. F—Greg—asked about my history lesson plans, with only mild confusion that those words spilled from his mouth, wearing these new painful loafers that Ben insisted were parents-pleasing became worth it.

Not that lesson planning equated to welcoming me into their family. But, hope bubbled up at the thought of Pippa and me as a *family*. The word contained a permanence, a promise between us. The longing was so strong that I rubbed at my chest.

At that moment, I knew without a doubt that I would forego anything to be with her. Love for Pippa coursed through me. Everything else paled in comparison to the idea of us as a family, and to be able to walk beside her through life.

As I glanced around the muted, classic library, I couldn't understand how the Flemings could sip their tea with such calm. Forget tea. I wanted to run around the streets, shouting my love for Pippa. Get a billboard, kiss her on camera at a Sox game, introduce her to my students as my…

Wife.

I was getting ahead of myself. Way too ahead.

Was I?

Just as I knew others were not the one for me, I knew Pippa was. There was no single word to describe her, for she encompassed everything important to me. My lover, my best friend, my partner.

As pleasant as this evening had turned out, I couldn't wait to go home with Pippa. *Home.*

Not home because my name was on a mortgage. *Home* because Pippa's clothes had started to fill the closets, her laptop on the kitchen table, her current book on the couch. *Home* because Pippa and I had already meshed our lives.

Our home.

Our home where I couldn't wait to tell her again how much I loved her. How I appreciated all parts of her, even the sensitive and vulnerable sides that she tried to hide from the rest of the world.

"August, you seem like a nice young man." Mrs. F—Charlotte—stood by the large desk on the other side of the library.

Nice was… good. Tepid, though.

With an envelope in hand, Charlotte headed back to us, sitting on the arm of Greg's chair. They sat as if posing for a portrait—distinguished, united.

Earlier, during the interrogation, she had acted as the sharp-eyed bulldozer, digging up secrets, evaluating my words. Now, she focused on me in that same singular way, and it took all my willpower to keep from squirming.

I looked at the envelope with confusion and seeping frustration. Charlotte tapped her long fingernails against it, the *tap-tap-tap* drawing attention to the giant diamond on her ring finger.

The hair on my forearms prickled. The Flemings had found something, an ace.

Led by loosened pu'er tea and small talk, I had walked into a trap.

CHAPTER TWENTY-FOUR

~AUGUST~

My nerves on high alert, I gripped the arms of my chair. Forget about Pippa's parents. My inner caveman needed to find Pippa, throw her over my shoulder and escape, until the threat was gone.

Only morbid curiosity kept me in my chair. With a rising sense that something bad was approaching, I tracked Greg's mild confusion and Charlotte's glee.

"When Pippa told us she was going on a reality TV show, we cautioned her," Charlotte started, her fingers still tapping. "When we heard she came back from the show with… someone, I was troubled."

Greg watched the envelope in his wife's hand. A tiny frown gathered across his forehead. "Pippa seems worldly, but she hasn't had many serious relationships. She hasn't brought anyone home since her senior year of high school."

"That was an unmitigated disaster. No matter." Charlotte opened the envelope and flashed a stapled stack of papers at me. I could only make out the words "Cipher Securities" and "August Thomas Weather" at the top. "I took the liberty of running a background check on you."

Anger rose. My jaw hurt from clamping my mouth shut. I understood grilling. I got cautiousness at meeting a new partner. What I didn't comprehend was the need to run a background check.

I had nothing to hide. But the intrusiveness of hiring a security firm rankled me. I'd bet that Charlotte wouldn't have run a background check if I had gone to

Harvard and worked in private equity. Was this the type of behavior and judgment that I would be subjected to if I wanted to be in Pippa's life?

"Very clean records," Charlotte started. "Honor student in high school, played soccer in college, undergrad and masters from UMass, good reviews from students, well-liked in your town. The private detective found nothing concerning."

Nothing concerning, my ass. My whole life was reduced to a few typed pages and this random detective's judgment. What was the point of grilling me earlier if she knew my whole life already? This was a fucking unnecessary mess.

"Good, good, glad that's all out of the way." Greg pulled the papers out of his wife's hands and stuffed them back into the envelope without reading the report.

Still watching Charlotte, he proclaimed, "Pippa has sound instincts. We all know that in high school, she brought that disaster of a fake boyfriend home as a way to test us. I trust her to find someone suitable for herself."

Charlotte glared at her husband. "Depends on your definition of 'suitable.'"

"Only *her* definition should matter," insisted Greg.

Waving aside her husband's words, Charlotte turned back to me. "Did you know that Pippa's money is held in trust until she turns forty?"

"I wasn't aware she had a trust," I answered.

Skepticism met my confession. "Has Pippa told you about her travel bucket list? It includes Antarctica, fifteen thousand dollars minimum, more if she travels the way she's accustomed to. Or how she spent her weekends before going on this show? Flying to Iceland on Friday nights for the weekend, impromptu trips to Martha's Vineyard, renting a house in the Hamptons to get away from the summer heat in Manhattan. When she's stressed, she'll fly to Paris to shop."

"You make her sound materialistic," I protested, even as my heart sank with each of her mother's words. "She's not. Pippa is more than what she buys. She's caring and warm. She has a knack for bringing people together. In fact, two of my neighbors had been fighting over the hedges that run in between their properties. I don't know how she did it, but she got them to stop pruning each other's hedges out of revenge."

Where was Pippa? Did she know her parents would act this way?

"She's thrown herself into the community at Beach Falls," I continued, determined to convince her mom that she belonged with me. "Pippa joined the book club. She's attended soccer practices. She even joined the Harvest Festival committee and is coordinating food and decorations. Everyone loves her. She—"

"Let me stop you right there," cut in Charlotte. "I don't underestimate my daughter. I couldn't be prouder of her. Despite my questions, I think your job as a teacher is admirable, and you seem like a decent human.

"But do you hear your own words? My Pippa, who has been given the best, who can have anything and anyone she wants, has been reduced to coordinating where pumpkins go and arbitrating arguments about bushes. How long do you think it'll be before she gets tired of you? How long will it be before she feels trapped? How long before she resents *you* for taking her away from what she's used to?"

Frustration and anger radiated from Charlotte. She paced the other end of the library. With his brows furrowed, Greg watched his wife before he got up. They spoke in whispers, hers at a furious cadence, his a calming murmur.

It didn't matter if Pippa's dad thought I was decent. It didn't matter if I thought I was a good man. With every click of her heels against the hardwood floor, Charlotte struck the nail further into my heart, releasing the doubts that I had tried to keep at bay.

What was I doing? Nothing Charlotte said was a lie.

How long do you think it'll be before she gets tired of you?

Like a true trap, I had overlooked the biggest skeleton of all—my hubris in trying to date their daughter. Just because I wore fancy, new shoes didn't mean that I had changed. I had wanted so much to believe that a family and a home with Pippa were possible, that I forgot how wide the gap between us was.

How long will it be before she feels trapped?

Where was Pippa?

"You're not a bad guy." Charlotte stopped in front of me. "You're just not the *right* one for our daughter."

"We should let—"

Ignoring her husband, Charlotte barged on. "You have a mortgage on your house. Your sister and brother-in-law have a mortgage on their house too."

"How do you know this?" The accusation spit out, even though I knew the answer. Money talked.

Waving a hand to dismiss the question, Charlotte reached into a hidden pocket inside her blazer. She handed me a small envelope. "It's yours. It'll cover both of your mortgages, with extra to do what you will."

Struck silent, I opened the envelope. A cashier's check lay in my hands. Six zeroes winked up at me. This single piece of paper was worth a cool million dollars.

"Charlotte, what is that?" Greg peered over my shoulder and cursed. "What are you doing?"

"It's money to buy me off." With shock wearing off, anger bubbled up inside. Pippa's parents thought I was so inappropriate for her that I could be bribed with money.

Worse, her mother had this check made *before* she even met me.

All the effort, all the questions tonight, meant nothing. Charlotte had made up her mind about me based on my lack of trust funds and fancy degrees to my name. Not because of who I was or could be to her daughter.

Tonight's dinner wasn't an opportunity for us to get to know each other. It was theatrics to show how unsuitable I was.

Message conveyed.

Resentment burned within. I wanted to yell, thump my chest. Unlike earlier, it wasn't to declare my love for Pippa. This time, my brain ranted at the unfairness of this.

To build a porch around my house, I needed to save another three to four months. With the amount on this check, I could commission porches for everyone on my street. This little piece of paper made it clear as day the imbalance of what I could offer versus her parents.

How long before she resents you?

Charlotte's words echoed like church bells in my head, loud and constant. With each second in this mansion, I could feel Pippa getting ripped away from me. I was the deviation for her, while she was the gravity toward which I would seek my whole life.

Not that it mattered.

Pippa was the only one who mattered.

I placed the envelope with the check on the side table. If Charlotte was surprised, she covered it well. Reaching inside her damn blazer again, she took out another small envelope and placed it on top of the first. "Do you want more?"

"How many of those damn envelopes do you have?" asked Greg, shaking his head. Tea forgotten, he grabbed a bottle of brandy.

"Enough, if it means giving Pippa the life she needs," Charlotte bit out. "It's yours, August. Name your price."

"I'm back!" The library door thundered open as Pippa entered, her back to us. Charlotte tucked both envelopes back in her blazer.

"Whew, that took a while, but worth it. I got some Chateau d'Yquem and begged Chef to whip up some molten chocolate lava cakes." Pippa set the large tray she carried down on the coffee table. "Oh Dad, you sly one. I see you've already gotten started on the brandy."

With a small plate of cake in hand, Pippa perched on the arm of my chair. Her other hand brushed against mine to catch my attention. *As if she needed to.* As if my body didn't stand to attention when she was near, or my eyes didn't gravitate to her every little movement as if she were my North Star.

Even with the shock that Charlotte had flung my way, Pippa still enchanted me. For a moment, I could pretend that this meeting-of-the-parents had gone smoothly, that this was another step toward forever…

Almost forget.

"What were you all chatting about? I hope my mom didn't pull out my baby albums and drive you away with embarrassing stories." Light laughter swirled around me as Pippa chuckled at her own joke.

In unison, bonded by those damn envelopes and some shared sense of protection for Pippa, the Flemings and I shook our heads. Instead, Charlotte lifted a tiny slice of cake. As expected, no crumbs fell. No crumbs would dare disobey.

Setting down his empty glass of brandy, Greg threw back a glass of whatever wine was in those tiny flutes. He hadn't challenged his wife outside of throw-away remarks, yet the deepening of the groove between his eyebrows gave me reason to think he was just as caught off guard.

Not that it made a difference.

In silence, we watched Pippa eat a lava cake. Unsatisfied by the hard arm of the chair, Pippa slid down onto my lap. I wrapped my arms around her waist. My grip was too tight, too desperate. However, instead of protesting, she leaned her head on my chest.

I should tell her. I wanted Pippa to laugh in that infectious way of hers and tell me that this was a prank gone awry, not an actual offer from her mom.

Yet, I bit my tongue to stay silent. There was a reason ostriches hid their heads in the sand. Sometimes, the world was too painful. Losing Pippa would shatter me.

So, instead, I gathered Pippa even closer to me, stroking her hair. My heart pounded against my ribs, counting down the last moments of us.

CHAPTER TWENTY-FIVE

~PIPPA~

Something awful had happened between pu'er and lava cakes.

The openly antagonistic tension from the earlier interrogation had changed into a secretive mist. Guilt and pity warred on my dad's face, while my mom stared at August in defiance.

August's heart pounded too fast against me. His grip was too tight. Even as I tried to melt into him on the sofa, he held himself stiff, coiled. Whether to fight or run, I couldn't tell.

With dessert suitably eaten, I made excuses to my parents for us to leave. They escorted us down to the foyer, where I left my parents and August to run to the restroom. Shaking off the odd undercurrent before leaving the bathroom, I headed back to the foyer.

I needed to go home with August, to recharge, to return to our normal selves. *Our home*. When had he become the source of my energy?

This evening, he had put some sort of gel in his hair. I couldn't wait to yank him into the shower. To get the gel off, of course.

Altruistic motives.

Followed by… getting us off. I wasn't *that* altruistic.

However, when I came back to the foyer, August was in a face-off against my parents. My mom pointed to envelopes in her hands, while my dad tried to grab them out of reach. With his feet in a wide stance and arms crossed, August spoke in a low, clipped voice.

Anger and defiance radiated from him. This was different from the time he'd faced off with Garrett on the beach, where August had seemed more annoyed than mad. Tonight, in my parents' foyer, with thousands of crystals from the chandelier dancing over the scene, August was fury and pride personified.

What happened the two times I left them alone? Unfreezing, I half ran toward them. "What is going on? What happened?"

No one spoke.

"Nothing. Let's go, Pippa," August said, breaking the silence.

My feet stayed rooted to the white marble floor. Was it possible that I spent the day worrying about the wrong people? Maybe it wasn't that my parents would disapprove of August and throw a wrench. Maybe—the thought stuck a pin into my heart—it would be August who realized that he didn't want to be part of my family.

Frustrated at the barrier he erected between us, I searched for an opening. "Did something happen while I was getting lava cakes or in the restroom?"

Guttural laughter wrung out of August. The coldness, the harshness of the sound grated. This wasn't the August I knew.

This August before me was brooding.

Mysterious.

Taciturn.

None of which turned out to be as exciting in real life as in books. In real life, the change prickled the inside of my skin with the conviction that August was withdrawing.

I walked closer, my hand reaching for him. He didn't step away. But he didn't take the invitation to pull me closer.

"Don't push me away. The three of you are doing something or making a decision that involves me. Don't I get a say?" I asked.

If I couldn't hear his heartbeat against my hand or feel his chest rise and fall with almost-painful exertion, I might have mistaken his face for a statue. Carved in stone, his profile was unforgiving with its strong lines and bleakness.

A wounded soul weary from the world. A warrior in the midst of deciding whether to pick up his weapons to fight again.

Fight for us… please… whatever this is.

I ran my hands up and down his arms, trying to loosen the corded muscles. To offer a sliver of comfort against whatever demons he battled. To remind him of *us*. That whatever doubts he had about meeting my parents, "us" was worth fighting for.

"Let me help. We're a team, right?"

"Are we?" The casual toss of the words hung in the night, floating between us.

In shock, I stepped back. With a growl, August grabbed those envelopes at the center of the fight. He shoved them toward me. "Open them."

"It's not what you think." My mom broke out of her silence, one diamond-covered hand reaching for the envelopes.

Yanking the envelopes out of reach, I backed into a corner. Guilt crossed my mom's face, while my dad sat down on the steps, his fingers rubbing at his temple.

Curious, I opened the unlabeled envelopes. My eyes saw, but my brain didn't understand. I held two cashier's checks. One million dollars each. Made out to August, from my mom. With a description that said, "Pippa's future."

"I don't understand." The voice sounded too far away to be my own. It belonged to a lost soul whose parents had betrayed her… it couldn't be mine.

"Your mom ran a security check on me and is trying to buy me off." That voice sounded like August's. Whiskey-deep. But those words couldn't come from the man I loved.

Because there was no way my parents, who might be demanding but pushed me for my own good, would try to take away the best part of my life. My parents *couldn't* treat my relationship in such a cruel and cold manner as with money. Right?

August spoke to my parents. "I love your daughter. I have never met anyone like her and have never loved someone as much as I do her."

His declaration should have soothed me. After all, no man had ever proclaimed his love for me in front of my parents. Yet, the anguish in his voice threw me off. This was not a willing confession. This was the precedent before a *but*.

"All the things that your detective found out about me are true. In the past, I would have agreed with you that they might be drawbacks. But you know what? I've come to realize that I like those things about me. I like being a teacher, I like living in a town where everyone knows each other, I like staying in one place and having the most exciting thing about my life be the score at the end of a soccer match."

His voice was stronger now. "There is nothing I should feel ashamed about. Shame on me that it took your bribe to help me come to this realization. I feel sorry that you think someone's worth is dependent on their wealth. It's not. I am wealthy for the friends that I have, for the fulfillment I feel in my job. I don't need to justify my life."

I wanted to cheer for him. This wonderful, thoughtful man who stood up to my parents in a way that I hadn't dared before. Who had gone from poo-pooing his life on the bathroom floor in St. Lucia to embracing himself.

It was as if I witnessed August coming into his own, his self-confidence sexy and magnetic. Looking proud of himself, August shook out his stiff arms. He took the envelopes from my hands and tossed them onto the floor.

As the envelopes floated to the ground, he stretched out his hand to me. It was an everyday gesture. However, in that moment, it was also a symbolic gesture. He was asking me to come with him.

My mom's diamonds sparkled in the chandelier light, as she brushed a perfectly tamed hair behind her ear. My dad's expression had turned thoughtful, inward. They hadn't spoken a word during August's statement.

By choosing August, was I making an implicit decision to turn away from my parents? Because, after tonight, how could they all coexist in my life?

With my mind still distracted, August's smile slammed down. "Pippa, I'm heading back. Are you staying here?"

He dropped his hand as if he had come to some conclusion. Except it was the *wrong* one.

"No!" My protest reverberated in the foyer, the tall ceilings enhancing the echo. "I'm coming with you."

Before August could say anything different or my parents found a way to pull me back, I yanked the heavy doors open and stepped out into the cool late-summer night air. Behind me, August hesitated before his ingrained politeness forced him to say good night to my parents.

His footsteps followed me, catching up as we reached his car. Without a word, he opened the passenger door for me.

Inside the car, we sat in silence as he pulled away from Mount Vernon Place. He remained quiet past the Common and the Public Garden. As we pulled onto the Mass Pike, the unspoken tension built so high that tears welled up in me.

I was too scared to ask August whether the bribery attempt had soured him on me. On us.

Relationships were hard. But witnessing the drama and demeaning way that my parents had tried to kick him out of my life? Maybe I wasn't enough to over-come that.

The more we stayed in silence, the more fear brewed within me. By the time he parked outside his house in Beach Falls, I had become irrational with doom and gloom thoughts.

"You're awfully quiet." I reached over to touch August's hair, needing a connection to him, needing anything to show that we were still okay.

Instead of turning toward my hand or pulling me into the back seat to make out like teenagers, August flinched. Without a word, he stepped out of the parked car in the driveway and out into the star-filled night.

"August, I know I hesitated earlier. It's just that… they're my parents." That excuse sounded weak even to my ears. "It's not easy for me to stand up to them."

Freezing on the porch steps, he turned to me. "Do you think it was easy for me to stand up to them? To the same parents that I wanted to impress? All the while, knowing they thought I was lower than shit?"

"I'm sorry. You're right, I should have." I nodded. "Doesn't it mean something that I came home with you?"

"Go in, Pippa. I need to… I need some time." Fumbling with the keys, he opened the door to the house.

Fear coursed through my body. My mind blanked. There were no words, no counterpoints left except for the stark terror of losing him.

Instead of rationally discussing his concerns, I reverted to my old self, the fragile, insecure old self who desperately wanted to be liked. I flashed a wide smile. The same one that I used for the paparazzi when I left an NHL star's apartment after a busted date, the same dead one that I arrived on St. Lucia with. The one that hadn't crossed my face since I decided to go all in with August, and the one I had been relieved to shed.

In this pivotal moment, all the years of hiding behind that smile rushed back. Forcing a chuckle, I joked, "Is this my dowry? Seems rather old-school. Did they give you a herd of cows too? Maybe a chest of silk?"

I held on to humor with a death grip, even as the words grated against me. "Or you could deposit the checks on behalf of the school and convince the school to name the soccer field Pippa Fleming Park."

"Pippa."

"Oh, that works too. Pippa Field. I rather like the thought of me going by a single name, like Rihanna. Think of all the cleats and uniforms this could get for the athletes."

"Pippa."

"New goal posts? Snacks that don't taste like grass, with real sugar?"

"*Pippa.* You know that's not why your mom gave me the checks."

"I'm getting used to the idea of a dowry. Though I demand a dozen chickens to lay eggs so I can practice cooking." My voice cracked. No matter how hard the protective layer around my heart told me to keep smiling, my mouth trembled from the strain.

Silence.

Splitting my heart wide open was easier than this torture. I fisted my hands by my sides to keep my arms from crossing like a shield. My nails dug into my palms, the pain a subtle reminder that this was nothing compared to losing him.

"Let's pretend tonight didn't happen. August, why can't we go back to... before? We could stay in Beach Falls and build our lives here. We could be happy together. Let's forget the money."

Longing, the same longing that poured from within me, reflected in August's eyes. That last bit of hope expanded.

"You and I both know this isn't about me taking the money," he bit out. "I wouldn't take the money."

In my heart, I believed him. Our story wouldn't end because August was exposed for his greed. Our story hinged on whether *I* suited, whether he wanted me in his life.

"All my life, I never felt as if I belonged anywhere. I've traveled the world looking for a home where I can be *me*. I thought... I thought I found it here. With you." Throwing out the last remnant of self-preservation, I pleaded, "Tell me you love me enough to overcome this... please. Tell me *I'm* enough, that *I'm* worth it."

With a growl, August smacked the front door in frustration. "Pippa, I love you."

But not enough.

That was the unspoken part. Because if he loved me enough, he wouldn't be questioning whether I was worthy enough to overcome how my parents had insulted him. If I was enough, he could overlook my momentary hesitation back at the mansion.

This was the problem of living in a small town. At ten o'clock at night, the streets were silent. Neighbors retired to their houses, tucked away behind white fences and sturdy walls. The only noise surrounding us was the deafening silence, broken up by the haggard breaths from our lungs.

"If you take out taxes, health insurance, all of that, it would take me twenty-five years on my current salary to make a million dollars. That's not even counting living expenses," he said, his voice resigned.

"So? You love your job, and you're making a difference in the next generation."

"I will always have to save for big purchases. There will be many times when I have to say no, because I don't have the money to say yes to everything. And I *want* to say yes to anything you could ever dream of."

"I don't need much. Don't you see that?"

"Maybe for now. What about later? How long before you feel disillusioned and trapped?" he asked. "I will never have the kind of money your family has. The money shows the gulf between us, never mind that your parents tried to *buy* me. They didn't even wait to meet me before they got cashier's checks drawn at a bank."

In frustration, he paced on the porch. The movements pushed him into the shadows, away from the moonlight. "I'm *reeling* right now, Pippa. I don't know what to think. Your mom doles out million-dollar checks as if they're nothing more than Pop-Tarts. These envelopes meant *nothing* to her. One million, two million, the same. Whatever is needed to get rid of me.

"I can't even comprehend the mentality where someone has infinite amounts of these envelopes. Or someone disapproving of me so much that they would resort to bribery. That's not normal. But, at the end of the day, they are your parents."

I refused to understand his words. If he wanted me to draw some supposedly foregone conclusion, I would make it as difficult as I could. "Don't judge me for their actions, and don't throw away what we have for things I can't control."

"I want nothing more than to be in your life." He leaned forward. Now, his face was bathed in moonlight, though his body was still in the shadows. Like an angelic head floating in the darkness, come to tell me my fate. "But, after tonight, how can we be together? First, unless this whole night was a joke, you'll be caught in the middle between me and your parents. I refuse to be the reason you have to choose between us.

"Second, I might be able to get a better wardrobe or learn which spoons to use at a fancy dinner, but I can't change who I am at the core. How soon will it be before you want something different? Sooner or later, you'll hate me for keeping you here. I can't let you make the wrong decision."

"Shouldn't I get to choose my mistake?" I shouted, frustration and fear coating my words.

At my last word, he shook his head. "I would still be the mistake."

"I don't mean it like that," I protested, reaching for him. "It was just a slip of the tongue. I don't mean you're a mistake. I was—"

"Here." His chest shifted up and down, his breathing hard. He handed me the house keys. "You stay here tonight. I love you enough to get past your parents' antics, if I knew for sure that you wouldn't regret choosing me. Right now, I don't know. I'd rather you hate me now than hate me later for making you stay. I'm sorry, my mind is a fucking mess. Give me time to process tonight, Pippa."

The keys clattered to the porch floor between us. A gauntlet thrown down on our relationship with us on opposite sides. Instead of fighting for us, August leaped down the three steps from the porch and walked into the night.

Staring into the shadows, I called out, "August, don't do this."

My voice broke on the last word.

There was no response. August had left me.

CHAPTER TWENTY-SIX

I couldn't go inside the house. If I walked across the threshold, there was a good chance that I'd break down in the entrance. Years later, the town of Beach Falls would gossip about the woman who melted into the floor of August Weather's house, her tears glued to the hardwood.

Right before they ate perfect eggs and cookies from August's wife.

I would be lost in memory, a blip in this town's history. Nothing in August's memory but a surreal summer.

Was I being dramatic? Sure.

But if I didn't indulge in the absurd melodrama, I might give in to the tears. If I didn't flame the rage growing within me, I might crumble with self-pity. So I let, no, *encouraged* anger, wearing it as a shield against the possibility that August and I were done.

Focusing on the image of my elegant, scheming mother gave me purpose. Listing the times when she interfered with my life grounded me as I jumped into my car and zoomed back to Beacon Hill.

By the time I parked outside the house, I was on grievance number forty-seven. In second grade, she had ignored all my protests to pull me out of soccer, which I had loved, to put me in ballet.

Dance was supposed to help me with my posture, my mom had explained. In my most inelegant way, I stomped up the driveway, my heels clicking furiously underneath me.

Number forty-eight: the porcelain dolls my mom brought back every time she and my dad left me to go on a business trip. *We have to work hard so you can have the best, Pippa.* Somewhere in this house were dozens of expensive bribes. I would have exchanged all of them for trips to the ice cream stand with my parents.

At the entrance, I pressed the sequence of numbers to open the door. The first floor was silent. Max and the other servants had left after the dinner-from-hell. Good, fewer witnesses.

Number forty-nine: how I had arrived at college without any understanding of current TV shows, because, as my mom instructed, *you can't put TV on your résumé.*

August's jacket still hung on the banister around the stairs, forgotten in our rush to leave. I grabbed it as a lifeline, before I clunked upstairs toward my parents' suite.

My mind swirled, trying to decide which offense would take the coveted number fifty. Would it be the time when my mom suggested it wasn't completely poor form to make a move on Tia's former fiancé if I waited six months, or…

Stopping, I pressed my ear against the heavy doors to my parents' suite. Muffled yelling echoed from the other side. Searching my brain, I couldn't remember another time when I had witnessed my parents fighting. They were nauseatingly in sync.

Another time, I might have given them their privacy. But with forty-nine reasons and counting, I threw the door open.

My parents sprang back. My dad's face was flushed with anger and frustration while my mom glanced away. She was the first to break the stalemate. Pulling herself up, she floated toward the en suite bathroom. "I'm going to get ready for bed."

"When you come to your senses, Charlotte, I'll be in the library." My dad marched past me and then stopped. Turning, he squinted in his familiar thinking way.

No longer visibly angry, he looked weary. I thought the white at his temples made him look distinguished. Tonight, he seemed every bit his sixty-two years.

"Pippa," he said, his voice low, "I don't agree with what your mom did. You may not believe this, but she was trying to look out for you, despite her approach. Before you yell at her too, ask her why she did it."

My dad patted my shoulder. He wasn't the most affectionate dad, which made the awkwardness of his gesture all the more touching.

Some of my anger at him faded.

Some. Not *all*. After all, he still enabled my mom.

I wiped away the threatening tears. No time for sadness. Breathing in, I gathered my mantle of fury and marched to the bathroom, ready for battle.

Inside, my mom stood in front of a large mirror. Without glancing at me, she squirted cleanser onto a washcloth. Without makeup, without jewelry, my mom looked both younger and older. I could see lines on her face that she tried so hard to hide. Her cheeks had more dark spots that I hadn't paid much attention to before.

Was it normal to have never seen your own mother without makeup before? Like my own fake smile that I had perfected in large social settings, had my mom perfected a different facade to hide behind? Despite my outrage, my heart ached to think that my mom couldn't let down her guard, not even in front of her own child.

However, when she spoke, she was back to my perfectionist mother. "It's lust, Pippa. Lust will fade. You will thank me later."

Whatever sympathy I felt dissipated. This was still the woman who had tried to pay off the man I loved. The woman who cheapened my relationship and made August question whether I wanted to be with him.

"It's not lust," I yelled, reveling in the fire flowing through me. "I love him."

Without even turning toward me, she arched one perfect eyebrow. "Where is he then?"

Her words stung, too close to the truth. Too close to my fear that even after a night to cool off, he still wouldn't believe that I was all in with him.

My hands gripped August's jacket, until I was sure my nails had dug permanent marks. Fear gnawed inside me. One hand still holding his jacket like a safety blanket, I stomped toward my mom and threw her wash towel and cleanser into the sink to get her attention. "Your plan to bribe him failed. He doesn't want money."

"Good for him, but it doesn't mean you two are compatible in the long-term," my mom retorted. She put the cleanser back in its rightful place and picked up the towel. "Relationships are the biggest investment you could ever make. If he breaks your heart... I don't want you hurt. I don't want you to make a mistake."

I would still be the mistake. The hurt in August's eyes stabbed at me. If I could take those words back... if only I had walked out with him when he first extended his hand. If only I had confronted my parents before doubt had swept August away from me… if only…

Brushing away a tear, I said, "Give me some credit. Why does everyone think I don't know myself? Why is everyone trying to make decisions, claiming they're doing it for my best interest?"

My mom shook her head. "How are you going to afford your lifestyle?"

"I have a law degree and can practice in New York and Massachusetts."

"You've quit your job."

The idea of an incubator focusing on women-founded start-ups flashed through my mind. On a different day, I might have considered asking my mom for advice, or asking her to serve as an advisor.

Tonight, I didn't want her to use it as another example of my flightiness, choosing a different career path. "I will think of something to do. In the meantime, I have savings, and August has his own job. I don't have to live my old lifestyle. By having free time to think about what I want, I've realized that so much of what I bought and did in the past was to fill a void. I don't need to do that anymore."

"So you say now." Glancing up from a five-hundred-dollar jar of La Mer eye cream, she met my gaze in the mirror. "It's not as easy as you think to adjust to a completely different lifestyle. When the newness of your situation wears off, what will you do then? Remember when you wanted to learn the piano when you were six and quit after two lessons? Or when you begged for a fish in second grade, but got tired of it after a few days? Or the dozens of other things you've changed your mind about? We're just helping you speed up your realization that this lifestyle isn't for you."

"You're equating what I did when I was a kid to picking a life partner?" Incredulity stained my voice. "I'd like to think I've grown since I asked for a fish when I was eight. Besides, by dating August and moving to Beach Falls, what if it's not adjusting to a *new* lifestyle, but realizing that I've finally found the *right* one for me?"

"What happens if one of you gets sick?" she continued, picking up a tiny jar of La Prairie nighttime oil.

"Health insurance."

"For routine things. What if something catastrophic happens? What if he loses his job? Per the background check, he hasn't worked long enough in Beach Falls to get tenure. What if there's a weather disaster? What if—"

"Mom, there are a million things that can happen. August and I will get through whatever comes our way." I grabbed the jar of oil from my mom's hand. There was something too ridiculous about arguing over money when she applied caviar oil over her face. But also… gross.

Undaunted, she picked up a jade roller. In unhurried strokes, she massaged her face.

My life was crashing, and my mom couldn't be bothered to stop her beauty routine. The fact that she calmly went through her routine infuriated me. In the oddest, most immature tug-of-war, I tried to pull the jade roller away from my mom's hands.

When she refused to let go, I threw up my hands. "Fuck, what a mess. What a fucking, shitty mess."

"Pippa, don't swear," she cautioned.

"Cursing is the tamest thing I can think of." I hurried my pacing to annoy her, resentment coursing through me. "For fuck's sake, can't you pay more attention to this conversation than your skin care? Or do I need to book an appointment on your calendar to get five minutes of your time?"

"I *am* paying attention." She turned around, her arms braced behind her on the marble counters. "Naive girl. You don't know what it's like to be hungry, to debate whether you can get away with not eating breakfast or sew your sneakers one more time without people noticing. Or how to sneak some of the school lunch food into your backpack for later, without anyone catching on."

Her voice rose, ending on a furious near-shout. I stared at my mom as she avoided my glare. "What are you talking about, Mom? How would you know any of that yourself?"

"Never mind. Forget it." Shoulders trembling, she flicked the roller onto the vanity. It skedaddled like a bowling pin into a neat line of perfume bottles, tipping them askew.

When my mom ignored the mess, I assessed her. My dad's advice echoed in my head. If I blamed my mom for not knowing what mattered to me, was I partially at fault for not trying to get to know her, beyond what she projected?

Sitting down on the closed toilet seat, I started again, sucking in a breath to keep my voice even. "Mom, I don't understand why you're so panicked. You said Grandpa was a successful businessman, and Grandma was a socialite. I get that August and I may not live the country club lifestyle that you live, but we'll make it work. I'm not naive enough to think that our life will be all rainbows and roses."

Her head bent, my mom inspected her perfect nails. I wasn't sure if she had heard me. I continued, "I know we don't see eye to eye on many things. When I'm less angry, maybe it'll be clear why you're so hell-bent on pushing August away. Right now, I don't fucking understand."

No response.

I sat on that cold toilet seat until my ass was numb. My body stayed still, my spine straight, in that way that my years of forced ballet had taught me, until my muscles ached. Until weariness took over.

Not thinking about August grew harder. Holding myself back from crying, from throwing myself on the floor sobbing because I didn't know where August was or when he would come back, sapped my energy. Even the toilet reminded me of him and our first meaningful conversation.

With a too-dramatic sigh that my mom would likely deem unladylike, I stood up and headed for the bathroom door. Maybe Tia would let me sleep over at her house tonight while I… at least, she could feed me until I went into a food coma and forgot about August.

If only he wasn't already branded on my heart.

"I didn't live that lifestyle."

My mom's voice was so low that I wasn't sure if I heard her correctly. She still hadn't looked up. Instead, she focused on polishing her jewelry, brushing each piece with one of her special cloths before placing them on a tiny tray. Fastidiousness was one of my mom's annoying traits. Staining a piece of clothing or losing anything as insignificant as a pen irritated her.

Was it simply a personality trait or something more?

Hoping that I hadn't imagined her words, I asked, "What do you mean? When we were in Florida, you took me on a tour of your childhood places: the home that you grew up in, the country club that Grandpa belonged to, the place you learned to ride horses."

"Used to." With an elongated pause, she folded up her polishing cloth and laid it in a drawer. Lost in her own memories, she seemed fragile, instead of the hurricane force of my childhood that blew me in the direction she set.

"Your grandpa made a bad investment when I was ten. He tried to make up for it by investing in another scheme but dug himself into a deeper hole. By the time he died, we were bankrupt." Shame crossed her face.

Shock froze me. I had seen with my own eyes the large white house surrounded by palm trees on Jupiter Island, Florida. I had passed by the brownstone on the Upper East Side where my grandma had grown up in, five blocks from Central Park.

Lies apparently.

"My mom's parents were well-off. They had disinherited my mom when she told them she was going to marry my dad. You see, my dad had nothing to his name when he married my mom, nothing except confidence and charisma. He could sell ice when it snowed. Until he couldn't." Her back slumped with sadness. "My mom had lived a life of luxury her entire life, and for a while, my dad was able to support her. But he took too many risks in his investments because he wanted to maintain the lifestyle he thought my mom deserved."

"Does Dad know?" I asked.

"Yes." She nodded, her face flushed with embarrassment. "I waited on him and his friends at a restaurant. It was called Cats. You can imagine by the name that it wasn't the second coming of Le Bernardin. We struck up a conversation as we tried to get ten of his drunk friends into cabs."

My mind flew to the formal, understated elegance of Le Bernardin, with its leather poufs just for purses and intricate tasting menus, and to the image of my mom serving chicken fingers and liquor to drunk college students. My brain couldn't compute my mom struggling for money. None of it made any sense.

"I still don't understand why you went so far to paint the wrong picture of your childhood. You could have said nothing. Why go through the trouble of showing me places you used to live? Why deliberately lie?" I asked.

She shook her head. "When people found out that we were bankrupt, your grandmother's so-called friends stopped calling. They told their kids—my friends—to stop associating with me. They made me feel like a second-class citizen because I had to buy clothes from thrift shops and couldn't go to the same camps as them. When I moved to New York for college, people assumed I was wealthy because I had lived on Jupiter Island as a kid. I didn't correct them. When you begged to see my childhood home, I didn't see the harm in showing you my first home rather than the tiny place your grandmother and I ended up in."

I couldn't imagine my mom in anything less than silk and diamonds. I hurt for the girl that she had been, even as pride overwhelmed me, for her ability to turn her past into the drive that propelled her and my dad to success.

Enough success to dole out million-dollar checks.

Even as understanding dawned, bitterness washed over me. "You created a false background and lied to me, because others made you feel inferior. Do you realize that you've done the same thing? By throwing checks at him, you made August feel inferior."

"It's not the same thing," my mom argued. Her eyes darted to her slippers, guilt crossing her face before vanishing just as quickly. "Your dad and I have spent the last three decades trying to make sure you don't want for anything. We want you to have the world."

A memory of August floated across my brain. Sunlight lightened his brown hair. With a spatula in hand, wearing only his gray sweatpants, he explained the different effects caused by using butter versus olive oil on the pan.

I nearly wept from missing him. I would have given anything to be back in the kitchen with him. The strength of the ache, how my heart both leaped and constricted with pain at the thought of August… Surely, my mom, who loved my dad, would understand why there was no choice for me.

"I am *not* you," I argued. "If you cared to spend time with me, you'd know that money has not made me happy in the past. What if I want something different from what you want for me? What if August is my world?"

"You would choose August over a life where everything is within your grasp?"

My mind hung on to the image of August in the sunlight. "Yes, because a lifetime with him is the only thing I want to reach for."

"You would choose him over *us*?"

August had been right. My parents, or at least my mom, would force me to choose. It was a terrible time for him to be right. I countered, "Why does it have to be a choice?"

"I don't accept."

"Don't accept what?" I pretended ignorance, knowing how much that would annoy my mom. But you know what? I was fucking annoyed at her. "You don't accept that ranch on pizza is the way to go? You don't accept that middle parts are the new style? You don't accept that the Sox should have won the game last night?"

The only reaction was the *tap-tap-tap* of her manicured nails. "Don't be obtuse, Pippa. I'm not talking about socks. I don't accept that you are choosing a life with a man you barely know. I-I'm sorry for my heavy-handedness, not for the intent behind it. Living in the middle of nowhere, struggling to make ends meet, wanting more, that's not the life I dreamed for you. Don't throw your life away."

Part of me was touched. All my life, I knew how proud my mom was and how much effort it took for her to extend an olive branch. But this was the weakest olive branch I'd ever seen. Not even a seedling.

After tonight, I also understood why she had to fight and had her defenses up. But I was her daughter. She didn't have to fight *me*. At the end of the day, none of this had to happen.

"You have to accept my decision, Mom. If you won't, then you're telling me that you can't accept me for who I am. *See* me, Mom. Love me for *me,* not some ideal of a daughter that you conjured up to live vicariously through. I'm not her. I'm simply *me*."

Before the dam of tears broke or I did something stupid like throw away all her creams, I walked away. The quietness of the door closing behind me undermined the enormity of the relationship that hung in the wind, a door that might be forever closed between my mom and me.

CHAPTER TWENTY-SEVEN

~PIPPA~

I didn't know how I drove home in one piece.

Home.

Not *my* home. *August's* house. How seamlessly his house had become my home, in a way that neither my Manhattan condo nor my parents' Boston house or the dozens of other homes were.

Deep down, I hoped August had returned and waited for me in the living room with open arms. We'd laugh about the drama of tonight, until the need for each other grew too strong. Then, he would carry me upstairs and make me forget we had ever been apart.

Those were fantasies.

The reality was a dark house, exactly as I had left it. Cold. Quiet.

Time passed while I stood frozen outside in the yard. I couldn't make myself use the keys to go inside. This house was meant for happy times. For hopeful times. Not now, not when I didn't know where August was or where his head was at.

Glancing down at my phone, I shook it. As if that action would magically cause my phone to display missed calls from August.

For future reference, it had no effect. My phone remained stubbornly silent.

Sinking into the grass, I wrapped myself up in August's jacket. It smelled like his Irish Spring soap. If this night was merely a bump in our story rather than the end, I promised myself that I would venture into Costco to buy August a lifetime supply of Irish Spring.

Wet drops fell on the dark jacket. I glanced up, but only wispy clouds covered the sky. I patted the grass around me.

Dry.

My hands reached up to touch my face. My cheeks were wet. Black mascara stains covered my fingertips. Someone out there gasped in pain, their crying muffled against their hands.

Me.

My hands. *My* tears.

The harder I tried to stem the tears, the harder I tried to swallow the anguish, the more they poured out. Tears stung my eyes. Wasn't that an oxymoron? How could something wet dry up my eyes?

The more tears welled up, the more my eyes hurt. The physical pain of pinpricks behind my lids overtook the wild mourning of my heart.

Almost.

I didn't recognize this person curled up in a forgotten blazer, sitting in the grassy yard in the suburbs, crying over a man. Old me would have booked a flight somewhere, anywhere, and thrown myself into a whirlwind of parties until I met someone new.

Old me hadn't known August. Or how content I could be in one place, with one man… the *right* man. Now that I knew… had experienced life with August, how could I go back? How could I live my life carrying that knowledge of loss?

Because, as strong as I tried to pretend to be in front of my mom, as much as I defended my choice, the possibility that August had removed himself was too real. What if taking time to think was just the first step back from me?

At the end of the day, as much as I wanted to believe that August would return, I couldn't blame him for walking away. He had been burned before by someone who wanted more than him.

After tonight, why would he risk his heart again for me? He said he loved me enough to get past what my parents had done, but what if that wasn't true? What if his love was only a reality show–created bubble?

Except… our relationship hadn't felt false.

He couldn't have faked all the times he reached for me to check that I was close by. Or, when he bought an entire matcha kit so he could make matcha lattes for me whenever I craved them.

What about all those times he introduced me as his girlfriend to his friends and neighbors in town? As if he were truly proud to be with me. And never told me to tone myself down or change to fit in. And all the times when he told me he loved me, and he lit up with surprised happiness when he heard those three little words back. None of those were for show.

Without keeping conscious track of them, I had taken August's action by action, word by word and fed them to my hungry heart. Soothed my restless, lonely soul with the growing hope that I had found a home in August.

Only to find out tonight that those moments may not be enough to keep him with me.

That my love might not be enough to conquer all.

CHAPTER TWENTY-EIGHT

~AUGUST~

"You look like shit."

I stared back at my sister's face. Her wet hair was wrapped in some sort of towel on top of her head, and she held a muffin in one hand.

"Meet the parents gone bad? Come on in." She opened the door and waved me inside.

Without a word, I followed her, almost tripping over a wooden block in the hallway.

"That's what you get for buying the twins toys." With a decided lack of sympathy, my sister threw the block into a toy chest. "Might I suggest getting them a box of tissues next? They'd be fascinated, and I could use it whenever I remember that crushing on the boy next door led to a life of cleaning baby spit-up."

My brain didn't seem to be processing her words tonight. All I could focus on was time alone. "Could I sleep in your guest room tonight?"

"That bad? What happened?" June poured herself a cup of coffee. "What were the Flemings like? Did they like your new shoes?"

Bitter laughter burst out of me, startling June. If only the issue was about my new leather loafers that I had purchased to impress the Flemings. A closet full of new shoes wouldn't have changed their minds about me.

"They're asleep." Ben popped into the kitchen, two empty baby bottles in hand. "What's up with you? They didn't like the new shoes?"

Looking at me funny, June remarked, "I'm guessing not. I told you two you should have let me come shopping with you."

"They gave me two million dollars to leave Pippa alone," I said, watching June spit out her coffee and Ben drop the bottles.

Patting her back, Ben exclaimed, "What? Who does that? Who has that kind of money?"

"The Flemings."

"Shit. This is whiskey-level shit." He pulled down a bottle of amber liquor from the cabinet.

"If you're here, does that mean you…" My sister, never at a loss for words, faltered.

"I'm not taking the money," I stated. Whatever else happened between Pippa and me, this money wasn't mine. "My brain is a mess. I needed time to think."

"What did you say when they tried to bribe you?" asked Ben.

"I gave back the checks and told them that I like my life."

"Good for you." June nodded, stealing a gulp of Ben's whiskey. "Though, couldn't you manage to tell the Flemings off and still keep the checks? I'll even split them fifty-fifty with you."

Ben chortled into his whiskey. My sister rubbed his hair with affection. "What? Your sons make a serious dent in our budget with the amount of Cheerios they eat."

Smile dropping, June frowned at me. "Wait, if you gave the checks back, where is Pippa? What does she think about this? Surely, she couldn't have known what her parents would do."

"I dropped her off at our house. I needed some time away to process everything."

"'Time away'? Oh August, you didn't push Pippa away, did you? That's—" she bit off the rest of her sentence, but I knew her well enough to know she thought I was acting like an idiot.

"After seeing where she comes from, maybe she's too different from me," I protested, even as part of me wondered if June was right.

June scoffed. "Everybody is different. She seems at ease here."

"For now." I rubbed at the ache in my chest. This was not the time for my brain to flash up images of Pippa on the sidelines of my soccer practices or how at home she looked, curled up in a blanket on my couch. "Her parents must know her best. If they think she'll become tired of me, shouldn't I listen to them?

I would do *anything* for her. But what if *my everything* is not enough? How long until she gets tired of the novelty? How long would it be before she regrets foregoing her life for me? I'm just saving us future pain."

"Or you're being an ass by not trusting her. Think about her words and actions. What has she done to make you distrust her?" June asked.

My mind blanked. I couldn't think of anything but eggs. Ridiculous, overcooked eggs I forced myself to eat. Eggs that Pippa cooked every morning, because she knew I liked them for breakfast.

Faint alarm, bells rang. I clamped down on the doubts creeping in. I was doing the right thing. I was protecting both of us from an ugly breakup in the future. I was sure of it. So why did doing the right thing hurt so fucking much?

Interrupting my thoughts, Ben said, "Hey, June. No need to chew into him tonight. It's clear he's been through enough. Let's give August some time."

"He's my brother—"

"Time," insisted Ben. He ushered me up the stairs to the guest bedroom, which had been my bedroom as a kid.

The room hadn't changed much since June and Ben bought the house from my parents. My twin-size bed with the blue checkered quilt stood flush against a wall. The sturdy desk was stuffed in a corner. My soccer trophies were hidden behind history books on a small bookshelf.

"You know where everything is. There are unused toothbrushes in the bathroom," offered Ben.

"Thanks," I said. We both knew it was for more than toothbrushes.

"Anytime. When you're ready to talk, I'll be here. We can grab the poles and go out to the pond, just the two of us, like old times."

I nodded, though I couldn't imagine the old times. Without Pippa.

Sinking into my bed, I stared up at the ceiling with the glow-in-the-dark planet stickers. My mind replayed the scenes of tonight. Of Pippa hesitating, calling me a mistake. Of Pippa near tears asking me not to go. Of her mom showing me the checks, the background check, the opulence of the Flemings' home…

The last time I had bought a brand-new pair of loafers was for a two-year anniversary dinner with Zara. It was at that same dinner where she dumped me, saying that she wasn't interested in building a life with me anymore. Zara had turned off her feelings with the same ease as turning off the faucet.

Fear that Pippa would turn off her feelings for me one day, just like Zara, had played in the back of my mind. When would Pippa wake up and realize that she wanted something else? It was bound to happen. Tonight just sped up the process.

However, June's question earlier intruded into my dark thoughts: *Think about her words and actions. What has she done to make you distrust her?*

Even through the unexpected mess of tonight, the answer was clear: nothing.

When I woke up the next morning, my brain was still swimming through a fog of regret. The only clear thought was that I was an absolute idiot. With that knowledge rumbling around my brain, I went down to the kitchen to the smell of coffee.

Bless June and her coffee addiction. One day, I would tell her that coffee was not the same thing as water. But not today.

"Good morning," called out Ben, sliding a plate of eggs over easy on toast to me. "You get thirty more minutes of peace before June comes back from her stroller fitness class with the twins."

"Good morning." I stared at my plate. The eggs were runny, the bread was crispy. I missed Pippa's awful rubbery cooking.

By the sink, Ben cleaned baby bottles and bowls of what looked like banana mush. This Ben was a far cry from the Ben who would kick soccer balls with me and go to McDonald's at midnight. Ever since the twins were born, we had spent less time together. The time that we did spend together was filled with babies or stories of what the twins did.

Yet Ben was my closest friend. With his quiet, nonjudgmental support, he had been with me at every major moment of my life.

"I feel like an ass for leaving Pippa last night," I started.

"Yup," he nodded in agreement, as if me being an ass was a foregone conclusion.

"Last night, I felt ambushed by those checks. Her parents were a wake-up call to how different our lives are. It made me question how sustainable our relationship could be. It was like a bubble had shattered, and we were thrown back to reality. Except, I didn't know what the reality was anymore. I needed time to think and figure out what to do."

"Understandable. Have you figured it out yet?"

I ran my hands through my hair. "I know that I love her and can't live without her. Pippa was not who I expected to fall in love with. One moment, she was the most interesting person I had ever met. The next, she was everything. She *is* everything to me."

"People think June's and my relationship was easy, because we grew up as neighbors," Ben said. "You know this better than anyone else. June and I are opposites in personality. She can't even workout without having a dozen other people around, and I like to fish by myself. Our relationship wasn't easy. No, we decided to go to the same college, find jobs near each other, move back here. *Decisions*, not coincidences. Good relationships are based on making decisions to be with each other every day."

I stared at Ben as if seeing him for the first time. Maybe, because Ben and June had seemed inevitable, I had assumed their relationship was smooth sailing.

Also, with painful clarity, I was confronted with how wrong I had been last night. Since I'd known her, Pippa had never lied about where she stood with me. Once she committed, she had never wavered. All of Pippa's actions since coming to Beach Falls reinforced that. She had moved clothes to my house. She had made friends with people in town and got involved in town events.

I was the one who hadn't chosen her last night. *I* hadn't chosen to believe her or in our relationship.

Last night, I hadn't questioned *my* love for her. However, by doubting *her* love for me, I had failed her. By walking away, I had ended up hurting her even more. My actions and words made her believe that my love wasn't strong. I had handled everything so very wrong.

Pain stabbed at me. The possibility that she had packed up her things from our house wrecked me. In a few short weeks, she had become both home and an adventure for me.

Until Pippa blasted her way in, I hadn't noticed that I was going through the motions. Life wasn't about playing it safe, guarding my heart, while watching others live. That was no life at all.

No, life was about waking up with my world curled up against me and going to sleep knowing that I had brought smiles to her face. It was about rushing home because I couldn't wait to see her and missing her so damn much when she wasn't around. It was about sharing our past to forge a future.

And I might have thrown all that away.

I might have had *everything* and thrown it in Pippa's face. After waiting all that time for Pippa's walls to come down, it turned out that it was me who needed to let go of the last layers of self-protection and leap.

Ben patted my back. "Since I have nine months on you and infinite relationship wisdom, young man, let me share something else I've learned. You can't be half in the relationship, half out, afraid that she'll leave. You have to trust her enough to stick around. It's not a healthy relationship if either of you have to walk on eggshells, afraid that something you do or say or simply *are* will push the other away. Do you trust Pippa to know her own mind?"

"Yes." This morning, I had no hesitation.

"Thank goodness you came to your senses. June left me with strict instructions to smack you over the head if you were still acting like a fool. You shouldn't have walked away, but that's the past. What are you planning to do now?"

"I need to do something to prove to her that I love her, if she's still around," I said, voicing my fear out loud. Ideas spun around in my head, from lavish trips that would kill my bank account to throwing myself at her feet. If there was even a hint that she could forgive me, I would spend the rest of my life showing her how much I loved her.

Ben put down his fork. In his deliberate, think-before-speaking way, he finished chewing his eggs. "Want to hear what I think? One, you were a buffoon, which we've already cleared up. Two, do you know how I know she's the right one for you?"

"No."

"Because she's still at your house."

"How do you know?" My heart rate picked up. The image of Pippa in our bed, or reading on the couch in her pajamas, squeezed at my heart. Or she could be screaming my name while throwing my dishes out the window and trashing my place.

Ben rolled his eyes. "June drove by your house out of curiosity before her stroller class. She texted me that Pippa's car was still there."

"Did she see Pippa? How is she?" I asked. I put my hands on my knees to stop them from tapping.

"Don't know." Shrugging, Ben picked up his fork again. "June promised me she didn't barge in. However, I'll take a wild guess and say Pippa is probably feeling like shit. You did leave her."

"I'm an idiot." Pausing, I added, "Not saying you give good advice, but I'm glad we talked."

"What did you say? You think I'm a genius? It's about time someone recognized that."

"You said Pippa's still at the house?"

"June's a reliable gossip." He smirked. "What are you going to do about it?"

"Grovel."

CHAPTER TWENTY-NINE

~PIPPA~

After the cry fest that watered half of the lawn, I pulled myself together to go inside the house. Without August's presence, the house felt off. Foreign. Lonely.

A year ago, I would never have stayed in this house by myself, never mind with a huge unknown hanging over me. My skin would have crawled at being cooped up with only my thoughts for companionship. Ironically, that same restlessness had partly driven me to the beach.

Where I had met August.

Maybe without the drunken cat behavior of the first night on the beach, I wouldn't have felt comfortable enough with August to be myself from the get-go.

At some point in the night, I fell into a heavy sleep. Or comatose state. Hard to tell the difference between the two when I woke up groggy.

One shower later, the doorbell rang with its familiar chorus. I opened the front door and promptly shut it again.

"Pippa? Open the door, please."

I ignored my mom, my mind not computing that my parents had left their uppity world to come to Beach Falls.

"Pippa, we already saw you."

With an overly dramatic sigh, I opened the door. The sky was filled with low clouds, a dark omen. My dad was in his usual long-sleeve button-down with a vest, and my mom wore a crisp white blouse and tan slacks. They wore twin expressions of confusion, as if they had taken a wrong turn at Beach Falls on their way to Bloomingdale's.

I wasn't ready for another round of disappointment and arguing. Closing the door behind me, I stepped out, barefoot, onto the porch. In a ridiculous attempt to defend August, I couldn't let people who had tried to bribe him into his home.

Arms crossed, I glared at them. "Why are you here? How did you find the address? Oh, the investigator, right?"

They looked different… more frayed. Either my mom had been crying, or rubbing caviar over her face didn't have the intended effect.

"I-I like your outfit," she said.

I frowned. In contrast to my parents' ever-present business casual wear, I had thrown on a plain white T-shirt and jean shorts.

Whatever game they were playing, I would not participate. No more lulling me into a false sense of security before ambushing me. I had learned my lesson last night.

"Are you doing anything different with your makeup? You look lovely."

Frowning at my mom again, I bit my tongue to stop the snarkiness from escaping. It had taken twenty minutes to scrub mascara off my face this morning. The waterproof part of the mascara didn't hold up under tears last night but did hold up surprisingly well when I tried to wash the evidence of my tears this morning. On the plus side, I had found a circuitous route for rosy cheeks from all that scrubbing.

My dad threw up his hands. "Pippa, what your mom meant is, we're here because we're sorry."

"Yes, that."

"Charlotte." He glared at my mom.

Her mouth in a firm line, she glared back at him. After serious, secret eye talk, she turned back to me. Her shoulders drooped. "Pippa, I'm sorry. But I meant—"

"Charlotte."

"I was trying to—"

"Charlotte."

Huffing and looking not unlike someone caught with candy in their mouth at the dentist's chair, she sighed. "I'm sorry. I was an ass. No 'buts.' Your dad and I discussed it, and we *both* support you in whatever you decide."

Her gaze not quite meeting mine, she whispered, "Don't choose between August and us. We want to be in your life… in whatever way you want. What do you want us to do with those checks? I can give them to you and August as a present. You could use it to buy pants with no holes—"

"Charlotte."

"Mom!"

"Fine, fine. No conditions." Her mouth twisted up in a self-deprecating smile. "Despite our—*my*—clumsiness, we do trust you and lo-love you. As you are."

If I thought I had cried my lifetime supply of tears into the grass last night, I was mistaken. Straggler tears sprinted forward.

However, if this moment was a tiny step toward rebuilding my relationship with my parents, then I needed to start with how I truly felt. After the disastrous turn of last night, I couldn't slide back into hiding my feelings to avoid disappointing my parents.

"I don't forgive you completely for what you did. It was shitty, and it may have ruined the best relationship I've ever had," I said, in between gulps of breath.

"I'm sorry." My mom blinked rapidly, and her shoulders slumped further. "I'm so sorry. I shouldn't have tried to superimpose my own fears on you. I've tried to escape my past and build a new life that I forget that not everyone wants my life. I don't know what else to do except say I'm sorry."

It would have been so easy to hold on to anger. To allow fury to patch over the holes in my heart caused by August leaving. In the end, it wouldn't have accomplished anything except delay the grief momentarily.

Reaching out, I grabbed her hand and squeezed. "I've tried my whole life to have your approval, but I've realized that I don't need it. In the past few weeks, I've found myself, for maybe the first time ever. I'll accept your apology, but you have to show me through actions that you accept me before I can trust you again. By action, I don't mean writing me a check. I mean, continuous support of me, giving me space to choose, standing behind my decisions even if you don't fully agree, listening to me. Truly listen to me."

With an emphatic nod, she said, "I'll try. I promise to try."

Turning to my dad, I continued, "I know you thought last night was wrong. You should have stood up for me and August."

"I know." He nodded so furiously his glasses slid halfway down his nose. "I'm sorry. I regret it more than you can know."

In a scene that I couldn't have imagined when I was younger, my parents and I stood awkwardly in a circle, more ourselves than ever. I squeezed my mom's hand while she patted my back in erratic patterns, as if still trying to figure out the best way to do this. My dad held my other hand.

We were a long way from healing. There were almost three decades of learned behavior and interaction patterns that we had to unlearn. But, today was a start. Even if our relationship was shaky, my parents had committed to trying.

Which was more than I could say for August.

Sadness took over again. Different from the overwhelming panic that caused my tears to water August's lawn last night. This morning, I was caught in a numb limbo.

"I want to call August and get closure," I told my parents. "If he let last night convince him that I'm making the wrong choice by choosing him, then maybe this is for the best. I don't want to walk on eggshells with my partner. At the end of the day, I deserve someone who will fight for the possibility of happiness with me."

My mom grasped my hand tighter. "I wish I could solve this for you."

"But we will stay out of this," said my dad, his voice gruff. "Because we do trust and respect you, even if our actions haven't always shown that."

"Unless you tell us to jump in."

Laughing, I lifted my head from my mom's bony shoulder. "No more checks in tiny envelopes or private investigators, okay?"

With reluctance, she stuck out her hand. "Deal."

CHAPTER THIRTY

~PIPPA~

Closing the door of August's house behind me after my parents left, I slid down to the floor. With my head in my hands, I stared at the uneven wooden floors. In front of my parents, who had shocked me by taking the first baby steps to show support, I could hardly fall down crying and ask for help.

But now that I was alone… memories upon happy memories of August flooded my brain, until my breathing grew ragged. Watching August attempt to make matcha lattes for me, sitting on the couch at night with my feet propped up on his knees as we talked about our day, snuggling close to him before drifting off to sleep. Even ridiculous actions that he probably didn't remember, like his hand grazing my waist when he tried to get by me in the kitchen, or kisses on my neck while he looked over my shoulder.

An unescapable ache rooted in my heart, spreading with free rein until my whole body become a tight coil of hurt. For the first time in my life, I had entered a relationship as one hundred percent myself. I wasn't just showing August who I was. I was also discovering new parts of myself, with August by my side.

Yet, the entirety of me hadn't been enough for him to stay.

I wanted to fight for him, for *us*. But I couldn't be the only one fighting. Our relationship was doomed unless he trusted what we have together.

No more crying on the grass or on the floor. No more self-pity or trying to argue with people who thought they knew best. No more running away from myself. Determined, I picked up my cell and typed my thoughts into a note on my phone.

Footsteps sounded in the distance. With barely enough time to recognize that the steps were right outside, the door smacked against my back, sending me sprawling on the floor.

"Pippa?"

My heart leaped at August's familiar voice, even as the rest of me froze. Did he sound just a little relieved to find me here? Or was that my overactive imagination wishing, when in reality, he was simply happy that I was no longer sprawled on his lawn?

"Pippa, can you move from the door?"

The topic of my hurt for the past day, the source of so much joy for the past few weeks, and the man I had fallen in love with, stood beyond a wooden frame. I wanted nothing more than to throw myself into his arms and demand that we forget the past day.

Yet, I didn't move.

If I opened the door, I might fall at his feet and take anything August would give me. For the sake of my future, for *our* potential future, I had to stand up for myself. I owed that to myself.

With a hand pressed against the door to keep it from opening farther, I got up on my feet. Even through the inch of open door, I could smell the faint Irish Spring of August's soap. I breathed in the scent, stirring up a mixture of comfort and nerves.

"Could I come in and see you?" he asked.

I imagined him running a hand through his brown hair, a perplexed frown crossing his face. My fingers twisted, fisting to keep from yanking the door open and smoothing his frown away.

Sucking in a big breath, I whispered, my cheek pressed against the door, "No. It would be too hard face-to-face."

"Pippa, please."

The plea in his voice caught my breath, holding it hostage. *Breathe.* His voice was nearer, as if he leaned against the outside of the door.

Just inches separating us.

My fingers gripped the doorknob, to anchor me in place, to steady me. Ignoring the cries of my heart, I opened the note on my phone. "It would be too hard to see you and not want to… I need to do this before you come in. I wrote down what I wanted to say to you. Well, I wrote—I wrote bullets. I was too worked up to write a full-fledged speech."

My weak attempt at humor and laughter sounded thin to my ears. *Breathe.* Blinking until the letters came into focus, I sucked in a deep breath. "You suck."

"I know. I'm sorry." Bitterness and resignation coated his words. "Leaving you last night was the worst decision I've ever made. I should have stayed and talked it through with you. I owed you that respect. Instead, I was a self-absorbed ass for thinking I knew what was best for you."

"Yes, I agree you were an ass," I repeated, surprised. His apology threw me for a loop. He said he should have stayed last night, but *not* that he had changed his mind about our future.

I scrolled down to the next line on my phone and tried to see the words beyond my impending tears. "I didn't expect to meet someone like you. I didn't even realize I wanted someone like you. Being with you has been the biggest learning curve for me. I've learned that I don't need materialistic things to make me happy. I've learned that I can be at peace with myself, that I can love myself. In turn, I've realized how much I can love someone else. So much that I hurt when I'm not with him. So much that even when we fight, all I want is to run to him."

On the other side of the door, August shuffled. The door pressed against my hand.

"No, August, don't open the door yet. I'm not done. I've learned that I deserve to be loved. I deserve to be with someone who appreciates me, who *believes* in me, who believes me when I tell them what I need. If you're not—if you're not willing to be that person..."

It was too late to hold my heart together. Tears were already falling down my cheeks. "If you can't be what I need, I'll be o-okay. Not today. Not tomorrow. Maybe not for a long, long time. But I'm strong, and I-I believe I can pick myself up. Against everything I've been taught, I've laid out all my figurative cards. You know that *I* want to be with you. But I don't want to be with you... no, that's not true.

"I *can't* be with you if you doubt my decision or doubt our relationship. I can't live with the constant fear that one day, you'll push me away with the mistaken belief that it's for my own good. I need to know that you're all in, and that you believe that I'm all in too."

I paused before adding, "You're wrong that I'll get bored or we're too different. We're the same on the things that count, and different in ways where we can add to each other's lives. Despite my worldly travels, I have lived half of a life. You've shown me a better world. August, let me go if you can't be in this relationship without doubts. Let me go."

"I can't."

"Can't what? Can't be without doubts or can't let me go?" Frowning, I puzzled over those two little words.

"Can't let you go." An echo of my heart still beat for this man. Even as the pained rawness of his promise soothed the ache inside, even as hope lifted its head, I didn't dare believe. Wanting to stay wasn't the same as believing in me, in us.

Better stay grieving than grieve anew.

I dropped my hand. The door opened. As the hay house fell with one huff of the big, bad wolf, my protection flew away at the sight of August in the doorway. Except unlike the pigs, I had no backup places to flee to.

Tall and familiar, his eyes shined with uncertainty. An unshaven start of a beard covered the bottom of his face. Instead of a crisp button-down or a clean shirt, he wore a wrinkly old T-shirt with a frayed hem.

He looked like shit.

He was the most beautiful sight I had ever seen.

"Hi." He tapped his hands against his pants. After a moment of silence, punctuated by the tapping, he started again, "I don't have notes. I'm not good with words, and I think you deserve more than words after I left you last night. Instead, can I show you something?"

"Okay."

Walking a step behind him, I followed him outside to the driveway. Even as my impatience railed to know which direction he had settled on, I bit my tongue to keep the questions in.

"I borrowed this from a buddy." August pointed to an unfamiliar truck in the driveway.

Squinting up at him, into the sun, I said, "You seem to have a buddy for everything."

"That's the benefit of knowing everyone in town." Walking around to the back, he lifted the tarp to show me what was underneath. "I, um, got these wooden planks."

"I see." That was a lie. I didn't see the point. Shaking my head in confusion, I let out a frustrated puff of air.

"Do you see the cedar tree up front?"

Bitterness welled up as I turned away from August to stare at the row of tall trees at the front of the property. Turns out, while I was fighting to keep my heart from breaking, the object of my obsession had spent last night and this morning hanging out with his buddy and admiring trees.

Glaring at him, I bit out, "No. All of these trees with green, spiky, pine stuff look the same."

"Come, let me show you." Without waiting, he grabbed my hand and tugged me toward the third stop of the yard tour, after the riveting displays of truck and lumber.

I stomped along, even as my hand gripped his. Despite this tour-guide-foolery, my heart skipped at the feel of his hand around mine. My heart was not a rational organ.

In front of a particularly tall and wide tree halfway between the house and the front edge of the yard, August stopped us. "This is the cedar tree. It's the oldest tree in the neighborhood. Or at least, according to the eighth grade science class from a couple years ago. It's lasted through rain, storms, earthquakes, generations of families moving in and out of this neighborhood. It's sturdy."

"Okay, it's the Giving Tree. Cool. So what?" I retorted, yanking back my hand.

"I'm sorry." Jittery, he shifted from one leg to another, as both of his hands tapped against his legs again. "I'm sorry for getting in my head last night and sorry for hurting you. I was an ass... fuck, I screwed up when you're the last person I want to hurt."

Startled, my heart sped up. At the tiniest sign of hope, my heart catapulted toward him, even as my mind tried to rein it back. But it was too late.

Or maybe just the right move.

"I'm sorry for how I handled things with your parents. I knew how different our backgrounds were from the first time we met. Even though I had no chance, I couldn't stay away. When we came back here, you fit in so well that I thought a future with you was possible."

My heart careened to a stop on its race to him. *A future with you was possible. Was*, not *is* or *will be*.

"Then the dinner with my parents came," I said, resigned.

"Yes that. Those checks threw me off. They solidified my fears of how wide the gap between us is."

Is. He still thought the gap was too wide. I protested, "I told you I don't care about the money. Or if I did, I could get my old job back."

"But *I* cared. I want you to have *everything*. I want to give you everything you want." His voice had risen with passion. Looking away from me, August glanced at the cedar tree next to us. "You were right."

"Which time?"

"When you said that I was making decisions for you. I made a mistake. I heard you but didn't believe you when you said you didn't need fancy things. I projected my fears onto you when you've given me nothing to doubt you. Instead of leaving you, I should have trusted you. I'm sorry. After I realized what an utter ass I'd been, I borrowed the truck and went to the lumber store." He stopped, waiting.

This was it? He thought about it, apologized, and moved on… with wood? The burgeoning hope crashed down, harder than one of his beloved wooden planks at the sight of an axe.

I couldn't live in this limbo anymore. Because I couldn't take the proximity to him any longer without throwing myself at him, my earlier resolutions be damned, I backed up. "August, stop. I don't understand what the fucking point of this tree and lumber is. Ugh, you infuriating man… I… ugh…"

I wished that I had never learned to cry. Anguish battled my anger while I ricocheted between the two emotions until I was dizzy. My eyes clouded with tears so much that my last sight of August was blurred.

Leaving my heart at his feet, I marched away. Twenty feet to my car. Only a few more minutes before this torture was all over, and I could wade my way out of the broken pieces of my heart. I only had to hold it in for a few more minutes.

"Hold on, Pippa. Sorry, I suck at this. Wait, let me try again." August ran up beside me, his arm reaching out to touch me before withdrawing.

I should keep going. For my own protection, I had to leave before I fell apart and embarrassed myself even further. August was sorry but that didn't change the future. Except… my feet betrayed me. I stayed rooted, waiting in anguish, waiting for further confirmation that I had been a fool.

August's mouth moved but no words came out. His hands tapped a wild beat against his legs. He sucked in ragged breath after breath as if the world rested on his chest. In some ways, it did.

My world.

"What I can offer is a new list of adventures we can conquer together." His voice broke the tension. Low, halting at first.

Clearing his throat, he continued in a steady voice, his eyes locked on mine, "Sleepovers under the stars, Pop-Tarts until our stomachs hurt, leaf peeping in the fall, potlucks with friends, drive-in movies in the summer, kissing you in the rain. I want to wake up next to you every morning and go to sleep holding you in my arms. I want to grow old with you and still make out in The Diner with our walking canes. I want to take strolls after dinner, and have our neighbors gossip, 'Look at them go. After all these years, he's still in love with her.' What I can offer you is me. All of me. For the rest of our lives."

"You still love me?" I couldn't process his words. My world had been turned upside down, sideways, shaken in the past twenty-four hours.

"Me loving you has never been a doubt in my mind," he said, shaking his head. "I'm sorry I made you question whether I love you enough. Because, the truth is, Pippa, I love you more than anything. In a terrible, long-winded way, I'm trying to tell you that I should have trusted that our love was enough to conquer any difference. I should have trusted you to know your mind. Let me prove to you that I'm all in. Let me make it up to you. That's why I have all of this wood. I'm building you a treehouse. It is first on the list of adventures."

Stuffing his hands in his pockets, he walked toward me, his steps slow and uncertain. He was so close now that I had to tilt up to watch him. His chest brushed against mine.

"What?" Pressing a hand to my spinning head, I stared at him. My breath rushed out, pitter-pattering to the frenzied beat of my heart.

"If-if you want. It'll take a few months… four, five… in between class and soccer. Maybe longer if I need to trim some branches."

He loved me and was building a treehouse.

For me.

Maybe I had imagined it. Maybe it didn't mean what I thought it meant. Because why would he… "Stop talking about trimming branches. You're building me a house in a tree because you love me?"

The daft man took in my question and answered slowly, "I do love you, though I'm not sure this will be a house in the trees. I'll have to test how strong the tree is. It might be a house *around* a tree. With sturdy stairs, instead of a ladder, so you can still wear heels."

He wasn't smooth, or quick to the point. In fact, he was terrible with words. The absolute worst.

August might be clueless, but this man wanted to build me stairs for my heels. The earlier anger had dissipated, leaving a hollow space inside for hope, for love to fill in. My shoulders shook with overwhelming emotion, bursting, expanding. I burst out crying.

"I love you," he said, turning me into his chest, as his arms wrapped around my shoulders. In a fierce whisper, he repeated, "I love you, Pippa. As much as I want to, I can't change how I reacted yesterday. I didn't choose you yesterday, but I promise to choose you every day from here on out. I promise to trust your words and actions, and not let my own insecurities get in the way. Let me make it up to you for the rest of my life. I want you to feel secure in our love, because I'm *all* in on us. Tell me you'll give us another chance, please."

The words slowly sank in. The sincerity of his words finally reached my shell-shocked heart. "You realize the tree is in the middle of your front yard, in full view of your neighbors?"

"Yeah. I don't want you to doubt that I'm proud of you. You deserve to be *you*, in the open." His hands lifted to frame my face, tilting me up so we were only a breath away. His familiar brown eyes shone with love, with unwavering conviction.

"I love you for *you*, Pippa. Let me be your home, your safety, your cheerleader, as you conquer the world. I can be your sounding board when you create your incubator, I can be your pillow when things go wrong, I can feed you when you're hungry. When someone tells you that you need to hide your true self, I can tell them to go to hell. Because your true self should never be hidden. Your true self should be loved. If you let me, I'll love you for the rest of our lives. I don't want you to sacrifice to be in my world, and I don't want to give up my life to be in yours. I want us to carve our own world. Together."

His profession induced fresh tears to cascade down my cheeks, a mixture of effervescent joy and staggering relief.

"I love you. I love us now and what we could grow into," I cried, between sobs.

"I've fallen in love with all of you. The sassy, sexy, thoughtful, funny parts. Every part of you. For as long as you want, I choose you, without doubt, without reserve." His hands on my face, August sucked in a ragged breath. He leaned down to kiss my tears away.

As if sealing that promise, the sky thundered in agreement. The earlier clouds opened up, crying tears of joy. Drenched from the rain, we stared at each other, our smiles mirrors of the exhilaration inside. We laughed, the sound light and full, happiness tinting every note.

August brushed his lips against mine. He explored me with soft, lingering kisses, as if we had all the time in the world. There was no more finesse or pretenses, just us in this moment, reveling in this newfound happiness.

Angling my head closer, he deepened the kiss, his hands running along my body. I lifted his soaked shirt to touch his wet skin. I needed to feel his warmth, to make sure this was real.

"Looks like we can check kissing in the rain off the adventure list. I see your list and raise you a new bucket list," I whispered, breathing hard.

August drew back to watch me with a smile. "What's on it? Where are we going?"

"Here. The list is *us*."

His jaw clenched with emotion. With his hands around my face, he pulled me close to him, close enough that I could see myself reflected in his eyes. He scanned my face, seeming to memorize every freckle, every dip and curve. He growled, his voice husky with emotion, "I love you."

"I love you, August," I said, staring, unflinching, into his eyes. Why did I ever consider him ordinary when nothing about this man was short of extraordinary? "I didn't realize until I met you that I had been chasing other people's dreams my whole life. I don't want to do that anymore. I want to hold fast to my dream, which is you and whatever life we create together."

"Then, let's not wait any longer, for you are my world and my future," he promised. Glancing over his shoulder, he frowned. "Should we rescue the wood planks from the rain?"

"They're under a tarp. I have another idea—a better use of wood." I pulled him closer by his shirt, our wet bodies pressed against each other. "Come inside your house, and I'll show you."

Sucking on my bottom lip, he growled, "*Our* house."

"Ours."

Not waiting any longer to start *our* life in *our* house, I dashed off toward the front door, slipping and sliding on the wet grass. On my heels, August chased me, picking me up in his arms. With laughter circling around us, we ran home.

Our home.

EPILOGUE
~PIPPA~

Los Angeles, early January

"Are. You. Ready. For the most *dramatic* reunion show *ever*?"

One eyebrow raised like a Disney villain, Mark turned away from the audience to face the three rows of contestants. "Let's catch up with our contestants. Why don't we start with one of our first love matches, Pietr and Hailey!"

The four engaged couples, Pietr and Hailey, Drew and Amelie, Kaiden and Vidhya, and Beckett and Annie, were seated in the front row before a small studio audience. August and I, along with a few of the single contestants, sat in the second row, with another group of single contestants behind us.

"Hailey, Pietr, you two got engaged on the show," started Mark, with a beaming smile at the scowling couple. "But it seems that it hasn't been roses—"

"He cheated on me!" screamed Hailey on cue, as she yanked off her engagement ring to throw it at Pietr's face.

Pietr swatted away the ring. "We were on a *break*!"

As Hailey and Pietr shouted accusations back and forth on stage, with Mark prodding along the drama, I remarked to August, "They unfollowed each other on Instagram, but I didn't expect this."

"You didn't expect two people who got together for the sole purpose of gaining social media followers to break up?"

"Call me an optimist. I seem to have developed a soft spot for couples who find love in unusual places." My heart beat stronger at the word *love*. Needing to touch him, I rested my hand on August's thigh. Without pause, he picked my hand up to kiss the back of it.

"Must be something in the water, for I suffer from the same hopeless romantic syndrome. Except, I don't have a soft spot. Quite the opposite, especially for a certain redhead who likes—"

"August!" I poked him.

Ignoring the cameras around us, August laughed and pulled me closer until he kissed my protest away. In the midst of Pietr and Hailey hurling accusations at each other, an audience member dancing with joy at finding the thrown engagement ring, and the subsequent tussle with the security guard who attempted to take the ring away, August and I made out under the stage lights.

My brain barely clocked in the prosaic interview with Drew and Amelie, or the awkward update with Annie and Beckett. Through the surprising on-the-stage wedding of Kaiden and Vidhya, officiated by Mark, August held me in his arms. When Mark pronounced Kaiden and Vidhya married, August brushed away my tear of happiness. When the DJ played the latest sappy love song, we swayed on stage.

Never mind the cameras, the mics under our clothes, or the audience. Nothing mattered as much as being together, my head resting on August's shoulder, our hearts beating to the same melody.

The five months after filming had been the happiest ones in my life. I had low expectations going on a reality TV show, never guessing that I could walk away with a real relationship at the end. After the disastrous meet-the-parents, August had made it his mission to prove to me how committed he was until every single last one of my reserves fell away.

For the first time in my life, I felt like *me*. No pretenses, no mindless drive to be someone else or to meet someone else's expectations. When I faltered, August was there to prop me up, to remind me that I didn't have to walk on eggshells for anyone.

Finding myself, finding August, had turned out to be the best adventure.

~AUGUST~

Beach Falls, two days later

. . .

"What are you doing?"

Startled, I turned around. Caught. My fingers were stained with the evidence.

"Why are you digging up the flowers that I planted?" Sleepy, Pippa pointed to the pile of Christmas roses at my feet and the dirt on my hands. The winter wind above us blew, opening her fleece jacket to show the lace of her nightgown underneath.

The third nightgown that I had bought this month, after ripping the other two.

Months since she moved in with me at our house in Beach Falls, the sight of her bare skin still excited me. The curve of her lips, still swollen from an early morning *greeting* still commanded blood to rush down to my cock, despite the wintry chill.

Ever perceptive, Pippa walked over to stare at the circle of wilted Christmas roses around the base of the cedar tree. The same tree where a finished treehouse stood above our heads. "They look dreadful. What are you doing to my flowers?"

"Nothing." I shifted to stand in front of the pots of white roses and pink paint.

She frowned. "You told me that these were special Beach Falls roses that wilt at night and re-bloom in the morning."

"Hm, did I?"

"I thought I had a green thumb."

"You have wonderful hands."

Bending down, Pippa pushed me away from the white roses, still in their pots, and examined her wilted pink ones. She picked up a paintbrush and the pot of pink paint. "How long have you been replanting my roses?"

I sighed. "Since the beginning. You looked so happy decorating the treehouse and this tree. Your original ones only lasted one day before the groundhog ate them."

"Fonzie ate my flowers?" she exclaimed. "What a betrayal."

"They didn't have pink ones at the store this morning. I thought I could paint these pink."

"Do you think I'm so naive that I wouldn't know you painted them?"

I grinned.

"Fine. Next time you tell me about magical flowers, I'll call your bluff." Disgruntled, she rolled her eyes. "Since we're in the midst of confessions, I have a confession too. When I volunteer to cook, I actually buy takeout. I made a deal with Vijay at The Chateau. He keeps some of our plates there for the food. I drop the clean plates with him in the mornings."

"I know." I smirked. "He asked me the other day if I like the combination of feta and mint. Imagine my surprise when you 'cooked' lamb with whipped feta and mint the next day."

Stepping toward my open arms, she burrowed her nose against my coat. I couldn't be sure, but I thought I heard her sniff me. I caught a hint of the Irish Spring that she kept buying from Costco.

Meshing our lives together hadn't been glamorous. Much of Pippa's time had been occupied with her incubator. She had cried frustrated tears at the sheer amount of work needed and then happy ones when applications poured in. I spent afternoons and weekends on the soccer field, and most evenings grading homework.

Over the past few months, we both had moments as fish out of water. The first time Pippa realized that stores in Beach Falls closed at six. Or for me, accompanying her and her parents to a fundraiser for athletic programs and donating the two million former-bribe dollars.

But through it all, our love had only strengthened. Each day, we had chosen each other to share our lives, to compromise, to believe in each other, and to accept each other for ourselves. She had expanded my world, and I hoped I had shown her that sometimes, the best adventure is the life you build with someone you love.

She wasn't just my girlfriend. Pippa was so embedded in my life that I couldn't imagine a world without her. My heart beat to her command. My lungs sucked in her warmth with every breath I took.

I was completely head over heels in love with her. No doubts, no holds.

Raising her head, Pippa asked, "You're sweet to plant flowers to avoid hurting my feelings. Do you mind that you're with someone who can't keep plants alive or cook?"

"No." I shook my head.

Looking down at the frown that marred her forehead, I cupped Pippa's face, my thumb brushing against the soft line of her jaw. "I told you before that I don't need you to be a chef or gardener. You are enough. I fell in love with you, every piece of you. The more memories we create, the deeper I fall in love with you."

"I love you," she whispered, with that secret smile she reserved just for me— soft, tender, lighting up her entire face.

I bent to kiss her. "Come inside with me. I have some ideas to warm you up, and every one of them would scandalize our neighbors."

Echoing my earlier words to her in St. Lucia, Pippa whispered, "You would be worth it."

Though I hadn't known at the time, love was indeed worth it. The past pain, fears of rejection, and the risk of opening my heart to be hurt—I would go through that a hundred times, just to be here in the cold, with the love of my life in my arms. For love was the biggest gamble, and if you were lucky, you were rewarded with the adventure of a lifetime.

ACKNOWLEDGMENTS

This book took almost two years. Ten months of writing. Another eleven months of on/off editing. There were so many moments when I wasn't sure if I wanted to continue writing and when I felt such imposter syndrome. I would have stopped without the support of these people (I like bulleted lists):

- Author friends who shared their own struggles, gave encouragement, answered my random questions. Special call outs to Cathy Yardley for helping me work through plot issues and Piper Sheldon who let me be her assistant at Book Bonanza. They are both such inspirations!
- My editors and beta readers who saved this manuscript! To Angela Houle, Jennifer Levine, Nicole McCurdy, Lexie Eldridge, Elyssa Patrick, Lorraine Heath, Reina Robinson, Marla Esposito – THANK YOU for reading and providing invaluable feedback! You gave me confidence to send this story into the world
- My husband who encouraged my coffee shop visits to write and listened so patiently to me explain plot bunnies. In many ways, August embodies his patience, kindness, goodness, and willingness to accept me for exactly who I am. He is the person whom I tell my weird secrets to. His love for me is strong enough for me to be completely myself around him, and not worry that he'll run away
- My kids who are no longer babies *cry*. You give the best hugs
- My parents who are not effusive with their words but have always shown their love for me through actions. I am proud of everything they have been able to accomplish, and I hope they are proud of me
- Brooke, Penny, and Fiona for their support and guidance of this baby author's journey. I am forever grateful that you took a chance on me!

- AND, readers, reviewers, bloggers!!! You seem to magically know when I need a boost. When you tag me, message me, or write a review, it always surprises and humbles me. THANK YOU!!!

Now, August and Pippa are out of my head and in the world! I've loved them individually, and I love them together. I hope their story resonates with you. You are loved, and you deserve to be loved for exactly who you are.

Love,
Nanxi

ABOUT THE AUTHOR

Nanxi Wen thought she was going to write the greatest historical novel. Turns out, her characters decided that they want to be in the 21st century with modern plumbing, online shopping, and reality TV shows.

She lives in New England with her husband and two young kids. When she is not despairing over word count, she enjoys reading, snacking, drinking coffee, sitting by the fireplace, hanging out with friends, and daydreaming.

Sign up for Nanxi Wen's <u>newsletter</u>!

Find Nanxi Wen online:
Website: https://nanxiwen.com/
Facebook: http://bit.ly/3jdMerD
Goodreads: http://bit.ly/3o9oDKs
TikTok: @nanxiwenauthor
Instagram: @nanxiwenauthor

Find Smartypants Romance online:
Website: www.smartypantsromance.com
Facebook: www.facebook.com/smartypantsromance/
Goodreads: www.goodreads.com/smartypantsromance
Twitter: @smartypantsrom
Instagram: @smartypantsromance
Newsletter: https://smartypantsromance.com/newsletter/

ALSO BY NANXI WEN

Give Love a Chai

Meet Your Matcha

Code of Honor by April White (#2)

Code of Matrimony by April White (#2.5)

Code of Ethics by April White (#3)

Cipher Office Series

Weight Expectations by M.E. Carter (#1)

Sticking to the Script by Stella Weaver (#2)

Cutie and the Beast by M.E. Carter (#3)

Weights of Wrath by M.E. Carter (#4)

Common Threads Series

Mad About Ewe by Susannah Nix (#1)

Give Love a Chai by Nanxi Wen (#2)

Key Change by Heidi Hutchinson (#3)

Not Since Ewe by Susannah Nix (#4)

Lost Track by Heidi Hutchinson (#5)

Ewe Complete Me by Susannah Nix (#6)

Meet Your Matcha by Nanxi Wen (#7)

All Mixed Up by Heidi Hutchinson (#8)

Educated Romance

Work For It Series

Street Smart by Aly Stiles (#1)

Heart Smart by Emma Lee Jayne (#2)

Book Smart by Amanda Pennington (#3)

Smart Mouth by Emma Lee Jayne (#4)

Play Smart by Aly Stiles (#5)

Look Smart by Aly Stiles (#6)

Smart Move by Amanda Pennington (#7)

Lessons Learned Series

Under Pressure by Allie Winters (#1)

9 781959 097358